PRAIRIE

PRAIRIE OF THE DOGS

A NOVEL

LG BRANDSEN

LUMINARE PRESS

WWW.LUMINAREPRESS.COM

Printed in the United States of America

Cover design by Gareth Southwell

Luminare Press
442 Charnelton St.
Eugene, OR 97401
www.luminarepress.com

LCCN: 2023909634
ISBN: 979-8-88679-238-6

For C. and H. … and K.

Part I

SCOOTER

Chapter 1

SEPTEMBER 13, 1985

Prairie du Chien, Wisconsin

I t is late summer. The cicadas vibrating in their ecstasy or doom almost overcome the murmurs from the stands. The earth's tilt has changed the light since midsummer. The obtuse angle gives the stands, the Mississippi, and the nearby fields a golden patina. Despite the autumn light, the heat and humidity linger such that the lights above the field bleed into the thick air as the sun sets.

A train sounds its horn as it pulls along the river, just blocks from the field. As if the whistle and clatter have woken them, the cheerleaders stand and fuss with their uniforms. They look to their captain, resplendent in her two minuscule pieces of brightly colored Spandex that match their own. She dashes off a winning, crooked smile and cocks her hips as a signal to start their synchronized movements. They push their pom-poms and dial their arms. They shimmy and they chant. They are correct and on time.

"Scooter Larioux, he knows what to do." They say it several times in succession as if it is some kind of incantation. And, in a way, it is.

"First and ten, Frenchmen!" The PA bellows.

Scooter has somehow wound up on top of a Cheese-maker linebacker who barely managed to drag him down after a gain of fifteen yards. As Scooter rises to his feet, he presses his facemask into the linebacker's.

"All day." Scooter spits as he says it. He hops onto his feet and trots back to the huddle. He bends down on one knee, turns from side to side, looking into the eyes of his teammates, and barks out a play in a hoarse, legato growl.

It is the second game of the season, and Scooter does indeed know what to do. The Frenchmen batter the Chee-semakers on a steady dose of their senior quarterback's option runs and occasional rainbow passes to streaking wide receivers. There are scouts in the stands watching this man, a solidly built six feet four inches with hands like baseball mitts, impose his will over the farm boys who try to tackle him.

In the second half, the Cheesemakers manage a plodding touchdown drive consisting mostly of three-yard runs. On the Frenchmen's next possession, Scooter responds with two twenty-yard runs, each culminated by stiff arms that send string-bean cornerbacks out of bounds, their limbs flailing. Scooter finishes the drive with a twenty-five-yard touchdown pass to Dickie Snopes, the fastest Frenchmen receiver.

Because the opposing team scored, as a sort of punish-ment both to them and his own defense, Coach Larsen puts Scooter in at middle linebacker. On the first play of the drive, the Cheesemakers gain six yards when their right tackle pancakes the Frenchmen's left end, Walter Hill. After the play, Scooter walks up to Walter and slaps his midsection.

"Walter, hit the kid!" Scooter's open hand sends a wave across Walter's considerable girth. Walter gasps and a slight whimper escapes his puffy face.

Scooter mutters, "C'mon Walter, it's football for fuck's sake." He backpedals to his position behind the line.

The Cheesemakers never make another first down.

THE LOCKER ROOM DOOR OPENS TO A SMALL BACK PARK-ing lot bordering a park with scattered oak trees and the occasional willow broken up by paths all leading to the Villa Louis, a mansion built more than a century ago as a monument to a personal fortune gained trading furs caught by Native Americans and French Voyageurs. The mansion sits next to the Mississippi on a slight rise that, unlike the land all around it, never floods. It is generally accepted as true that the rise is an ancient burial mound.

Scooter steps out of the locker room wearing a tank top, long khaki shorts, flip-flops, and a Brewers cap. He has a huge dip in his cheek. Three men with college logos emblazoned on their breast pockets are there to shake his hand and pat him on the back.

"Nice game, son."

They all say the same thing. They hand him cards and offer dinners and propose visiting his family's farmstead. Sam Martin, the sportswriter from *The Voyageur* asks a few questions, and Scooter nods and grunts one-word answers.

Scooter turns to see Diana, the head cheerleader with the crooked smile. She has changed too—into jean shorts and a worn Henley shirt offering a hint of cleavage. Her green eyes sparkle reflecting the lights still peeking over the stands. She tilts her head and pulls her chin in the direction of a white Trans Am T-top she was gifted by her daddy on her sixteenth birthday.

Scooter nods at the scouts and promises to be available for a call over the weekend, says goodbye to Sam, takes Diana's hand, and walks toward the car that radiates speed, purity, and the ultimate in high school celebrity.

It is Friday night in Prairie du Chien, Wisconsin. Scooter slouches into the passenger seat and puts on the radio. Springsteen's straining vocals on "Hungry Heart" stab into the night air. Diana jams the key into the ignition. She pushes a strand of straight black hair behind her ear. She wipes a smudge off her rearview mirror and takes a moment to look over her face, ensuring perfection. She kisses Scooter on the cheek.

"Nice game, babe," she states the obvious with a little laugh. "How did I look out there?"

Scooter smiles and says, "Diana Dillinger, the pride of Famechon Ridge," as if he is introducing a professional wrestler.

Diana pulls out into the night, heading north out of Prairie toward the Crystal Spring House and the right turn onto Famechon Ridge, one of the many ridges stretching like so many fingers west to east from the great river, with coulees and jagged ravines separating the digits of land. A memory of a bigger water and an ice-age past.

The Dillingers live on a gentleman farm at the west end of Famechon Ridge. Their oversized log cabin has sweeping views of the Mississippi below. Outbuildings and maybe the only private pool in Crawford County scatter the property, as does a menagerie of goats, ducks, geese, and a wild turkey that found living with the domestic flock easier than scratching for seeds at the edge of cornfields and listening for coyotes stalking through the corn rows.

Scooter lives about four miles east of Diana, over a

rollercoaster of hills and dales that can make the stomach drop and the tires momentarily leave the road if sufficient speed is attained (and the Trans Am is built to attain it). The Larioux Dairy Farm sits between two of those hills, bisected by the ridge road. On the north side of the road, there is a whitewashed house and an old brick and wood-sided milk barn as well as a variety of sheds and silos. In the yard in front of the house is a white sign with a drawing of a Holstein cow in the middle. There is a fleur-de-lis at the top of the sign, and under the cow it reads Larioux Dairy Farm.

Across the road are fields with alternating rows of corn, soybeans, and alfalfa planted in a classical contour farming style to prevent what precious topsoil there is from flowing down the coulees and into the Mississippi. The fields are broken up, the tillable land stolen, by ravines thick with trees, too steep for tractors.

Scooter's grandfather, Louis, paid five hundred dollars for the farm at a Sheriff's sale in 1915, having won such sum in a bare-knuckle contest in front of the Villa Saloon the night before the sale. Louis's family, and now descendants, have lived there ever since.

No one knows where Louis actually came from. He was raised by the Lariouxs, a half-feral family of Cajun "river people," who lived in the shanty town that everyone ironically called Little Paris. But Louis was not born of the Lariouxs. The legend is that he just showed up in Little Paris one day as a toddler, the Mississippi lapping at his baby toes. All that was missing was a mat of reeds. Mrs. Larioux couldn't help but take in the boy. He was raised as one of them, but everyone could see the difference. Louis was bigger than any Larioux who had ever lived. And Louis had jet-black hair, while the Lariouxs' skewed red.

Diana pulls off the ridge road onto the Dillingers' dirt driveway and through the opening of a split-rail fence. She yells at Little Tommy to get out of the way, the bird's wattle bouncing in the headlights, his uneven trot escorting the car. Scooter and Diana see the flickering light cast by a bonfire beyond the house. They park and walk around the house.

Lynyrd Skynyrd's "Gimme Three Steps" is playing on a boom box. There are about twenty people, mostly cheerleaders and football players, sitting around the fire on camp chairs and stumps.

Dickie Snopes and three of his relatives—either cousins or brothers, hard to tell with that group—are shotgunning beers in a semicircle around the fire. There are twelve Snopes kids that live on a small farm across the road from the Dillingers'. More Snopes cousins populate small farms scattered along Famechon Ridge. Everyone jokes that the Snopes are the best breeding stock in the county, are an invasive weed, spread faster than the clap, or some phrase with a similar meaning. No one really thinks it's funny anymore, but it is mandatory small talk, second only to the weather. Scooter's dad leases land to plant corn and hay on two farms on the ridge, each one owned by a different Snopes.

Walter Hill arrived at the Davis compound on the rickety motorcycle he and Dickie built from discarded bike and motorcycle frames in shop class. He is still wearing his football helmet on account of his not being able to afford a motorcycle helmet. He has taped beer cans to the sides and threaded a double straw through his facemask. Walter, Dickie, and everyone else turn as Scooter and Diana walk up to the fire; the guests hold plastic cups into the air and whoop into the night, saluting their king and queen.

Past midnight, one by one the revelers slip into the house to find a place to curl up. They have the huge house on the ridge to themselves. Diana's parents are watching summer slip away and enjoying the racing scene at their vacation home in Elkhart Lake. Her older brothers are already back at their east-coast, not-quite-Ivy league schools planning keggers, ironing their madras shirts, and suppressing their Wisconsin accents. Diana sits on Scooter's lap next to the fire.

"You have to take me home, babe," he says.

She shakes her head and nuzzles his ear.

Chapter 2

SEPTEMBER 14, 1985

"Up." It's all Scooter's father, Pierre, says; well, barks really, passing Scooter's room coming out of the bathroom on his way downstairs.

It is four thirty in the morning. Scooter rubs his eyes and stares at the ceiling. He would die for more sleep. *Every second of every day someone tells me where to go and what to do,* he thinks. He can taste beer, and Diana's scent lingers on last night's clothes piled at the foot of his bed. He smiles, *Well, maybe not every second.* But between Pierre ordering him around and football coaches doing the same, it occurs to him that he is always doing someone else's bidding. No one ever asked him about any of it. He shakes off his wallowing. If he doesn't get up now Pierre will kill him.

He hoists himself off his single bed and pulls overalls over a Bucky Badger T-shirt. He walks as quietly as he can, so as to not wake his mother, down the narrow, creaky, wooden stairs past the framed pictures of his ancestors and through the dark house to the back porch, where he bends and slips on his rubber milking boots. The driveway passes a clapboard granary that holds trash, empty feed pails, and the accumulation of fifty years of farming detritus.

Donny Jones's beat-up Chevy is parked next to the granary. As Scooter walks past, Donny rolls off a stack of hay bales, winks at Scooter, takes out a tin of Copenhagen, and puts three fingers' worth between his lower lip and gum. It is a toss-up as to who is more hungover this morning.

Donny is rail thin, with long, ratty reddish hair and a beard that looks as though it has never been cut. The crows' feet around his eyes belie the age of a man who has only recently seen thirty. Donny is a biker. And he lives hard. He is wearing tight jeans and a faded black Harley-Davidson shirt that billows at the sides because Donny has cut off the sleeves, with a dull knife or his teeth by the looks of it. His torso, and maybe more, although Scooter certainly would never know because he has never seen Donny out of his tight Levi's and work boots, is enhanced by a variety of tattoos ranging from the Harley-Davidson bar and shield, to naked women, to skulls. You could call the artwork better than prison quality, but it may depend on what prison you're talking about and, in any case, it's not much better. On rough nights, Donny drives up to the farm after the bar or some lady friend kicks him out and sleeps in the haymow or the bed of his pickup or on burlap sacks in the granary so that he doesn't oversleep for the morning milking shift. Last night was one of those nights.

Irene, Scooter's mom, doesn't let Donny in the house. He is regarded by her as slightly more than a dog. He is allowed on the back porch for lunch, which she hands out to him on a plate without any acknowledgment. Despite his lack of social polish, Donny is about the hardest worker and strongest man for his size that anyone in those parts has ever met. And for this, Scooter's father loves him.

Donny offers Scooter the tin of chew as they walk down from the granary to the milk barn that sits just off the ridge road. Scooter takes a healthy pinch and inserts it into the side of his mouth next to his molars. They step into the tank room and hose off their milk boots before entering the barn. Pierre turns as the two enter and lets go his first-of-the-morning Harvey Kuenn-style, slow-motion performance spit, sloshing tobacco-blackened saliva in a graceful arc into the manure gutter that encircles the stalls in the milk barn.

"You guys look like shit," he says quietly. He has already ushered the cows from the pasture across the street into the barnyard. The cows are lined up at the door, their udders heavy with milk, wanting the relief of the morning milking. The cows shuffle single file down a center aisle, selecting from the twenty stalls, ten on each side, constructed from round metal bars next to which hang milking machines attached to hoses that run across the roof of the barn to the tank room. Once twenty cows have come into the barn, Pierre closes the lower half of the barn door, and the cows waiting outside—the next shift—poke their heads into the barn. Pierre, as he always does, turns on a little portable radio tuned to a station playing big-band music and giving hourly farm reports.

The barn walls are chalky white. There is a palpable calm in the room, accentuated by the heat and the rich smell of the cows, punctuated by lime and antiseptic.

The men move slowly and deliberately and keep their voices down so as not to spook the cows. They move on the outside of the stalls and open metal yokes for the cows to push their heads through. Then one of the men squats down alongside the stall, submerges the teats in iodine, and deftly places a vacuum tube over each of the teats. Once all twenty cows are hooked up, the men step back and lean against the wall with one leg bent pressing the soles of their milk boots against the wall. They chew and spit and talk quietly, mostly about football, for a few minutes, until they reverse the process, disconnecting the equipment and preparing for the next shift of cows.

After the last shift has been milked, they sweep down the barn, pushing all the manure, stray feed, and straw into the gutter. Someone, whoever is closest, turns on a motor that moves a metal track at the bottom of the gutter pushing the manure out of the barn into a pit that contains an auger that drives the manure through a pipe that exits the barn like a raised downspout. The manure spreader parked below the pipe collects the droppings of the day as they rain down. As the barn empties itself, the men sprinkle and sweep lime over the floor.

Pierre takes an empty sheet pan from the windowsill and walks into the tank room. He bends down and opens the spigot at the bottom of the stainless-steel milk tank, filling the sheet pan with creamy, not yet cool, milk. He places it in front of the door to the tank room, and from nowhere emerge a dozen or so cats meowing, batting, and jockeying for position around the pan.

The men walk slowly up the gravel driveway and onto the cement walk that bisects the front lawn, which ascends to the house. The house sits on a rise that allows for a view across the road and into the pastures and fields. The walk circles the house and the men take the left fork to the back porch, which faces a row of tall pines, planted as a windbreak during the depression, that shelter the house from a small back field that slopes from the house into a ravine.

They sit on a bench on the back porch and take off their milk boots and hang their hats displaying John Deere or Pioneer logos. Donny steps out onto the back stoop in his stocking feet and sits with his back against the house. He rests his eyes. Irene passes a plate of leftover chicken and biscuits out to him.

Pierre and Scooter step into the kitchen and start gathering their breakfasts. Scooter pours two cups of coffee and takes one cup out to Donny. Scooter then pours himself a glass of milk from a pitcher. The top two inches of the milk are whiter and less dense, pure cream. He grabs an entire pie tin that still contains half of last night's dessert and sits down at the kitchen counter.

He watches his father pour himself a cup of coffee and fill a bowl with Raisin Bran. Irene has foot-square drawers below the long back counter of the kitchen. The drawers contain baking staples like sugar, flour, and brown sugar. Pierre opens the center drawer containing sugar and takes an entire scoop. He distributes it into the coffee and on top of his Raisin Bran. The cereal is almost completely covered by a crystalline mountain with rivers of milk flowing down to the bran-flake earth.

"For heaven's sake Pierre, just watching you eat is going to give me diabetes," Irene says. "Say, can you two get the spare picnic table from out back of the garage and put it with the other? Also, please straighten up the back porch before you go milk tonight."

Pierre looks up slowly. "Moving furniture is like a religion with you, woman."

Irene rolls her eyes. "This could be the last good night, at least on a weekend. I want to sit outside. I am putting a roast in the smoker."

Scooter asks, "Okay if I invite Diana?"

"Yes, dear," she says. "As long as you are not up too late. I know there is a lot your father needs done this weekend."

Pierre raises an eyebrow. "How about I check and see if Donny has any dinner plans? Maybe he could bring a date too…"

Irene clucks. "Don't push your luck."

Between the morning and evening milking shifts is the time to feed the cows, spread manure, and do any odd job that needs doing, like mending fence, fixing a drive shaft, mowing the lawn, or tending to sick cows. They are perpetually behind on these projects.

For farm kids, there is no football practice on weekends. Scooter, and Coach Larsen for that matter, know that Scooter's father will get more work out of Scooter's body than Coach Larsen ever would anyway.

"What's the plan for the afternoon?" Scooter asks.

"Back pasture, you and me mending fence. Donny will feed and spread."

Scooter nods.

The garage smells of oil. Irene's powder-blue Buick Regal is crowded by dusty toolboxes, broken generators, random gears, saws, and chains. The single window that looks up to the house is browned with grime. The amber light coming through barely illuminates the contents of an old red tool chest. Scooter opens it and, more by feel than sight, locates a pair of pliers and a wire cutter. He already has a .22-gauge rifle in a canvas bag slung over his shoulder, and he digs around the top drawer of another toolbox for shells. He pockets a handful and steps out into the day that is growing hot and muggy.

His dad maneuvers an old, rattling Bobcat skid-steer loader to the above-ground tank of diesel fuel next to the garage. Pierre isn't as big as Scooter, but he is not a small man; just north of six feet with broad shoulders and thick legs. He looks like a circus clown folded into the small cab of the Bobcat. He turns it off and starts filling it up.

"Are we taking that?" Scooter asks.

"Yep," says Pierre.

"Why?"

"You'll see. You follow in the truck."

Scooter puts the tools and gun in the passenger seat of the truck and waits for his father to finish. The truck starts with a spinning whine. He follows his father down the drive. They turn left onto the ridge road and drive east for about a thousand yards, then turn right onto a dirt road that runs between the cow pasture fence and a cornfield. Pierre gets out, ducks under the raised bucket of the Bobcat, and swings open a red metal gate made of round bar.

It's a good three miles on the winding, rutted road to the end of their land. The road is bordered by rows of corn that are nearly ten feet high. The corn stalks are still green in mid-September. The dirt road reaches the crest of the ridge as they crawl along at just above a walking pace—the fastest the Bobcat can go. When they reach the crest, they can see corn rows give way to deciduous trees, the tops of which drop away steeply into the coulee below.

They come to another gate, beyond which is a fenced pasture with room for about fifty beef cows. The cows shuffle their hooves to get off the road and out of the way of the Bobcat as Pierre navigates it through the open gate, continuing on the dirt road through the pasture. These cows don't see people every day and are more skittish than their Holstein cousins.

Abruptly, Pierre stops the Bobcat, and Scooter is obliged to do the same in the truck. The cows scamper away from the path. Pierre grabs the handhold, leans out of the operator's compartment, and looks back at Scooter.

"Snakes!" he yells.

Scooter, without rushing, takes the .22 out of the canvas bag and loads the gun with the shells jangling in his pocket. He gets out of the truck and walks past the Bobcat. In the middle of the road are three timber rattlesnakes sunning themselves in the morning sun. Scooter shoulders the gun and fires, hitting the middle one in the head. His second shot also finds the mark, hitting the snake on the left in the head. The third snake, apparently sensing mortal danger, slides off the road and into the alfalfa on the side. Scooter cracks the gun, inserts two more shells, closes, and fires all in one action, hitting the snake's body just above the rattle, which starts shaking like a buzzer. Scooter walks up the road, stands next to the two dead snakes, and shoots almost directly down at the third, which is still writhing on the side of the road. Pierre gets out of the Bobcat and picks up the two snakes on the road by the tails. Both are a little over six feet long.

He throws them in the bed of the pickup and says, "Nice weekend stew for Betty," with a laugh, referring to their crazy neighbor who favors rattlers. He grabs a chainsaw out of the pickup bed and drives the Bobcat to a section of fence where the trees have branched out enough to hang down and touch the fence, bowing the top strands of wire. Scooter walks up with the wire cutter and pliers.

"Set those down," Pierre says. "Take this and get in the bucket." Pierre hands Scooter the chainsaw.

"What's your plan here, old man?"

"You're going to stand in the bucket, I'll raise it and drive along the fence line, and you can cut down the overhanging branches."

"Fuck if I am," says Scooter.

Pierre's eyes narrow and bore into Scooter's. Scooter thinks he could probably take him if he has to. But he isn't sure. After a few seconds, Pierre looks down and spits.

"Ah, I get it. Precious ballplayer with the pretty girlfriend, wouldn't want to fall and get a booboo. Fine, I'll do it!"

Pierre gets out of the Bobcat, grabs the chainsaw from Scooter, and points it toward the operator's compartment. Scooter scrunches his body into the operator's compartment, and takes the controls.

"You are a fucking lunatic," Scooter says under his breath. At the same time, he can't help but admire his old man, who sometimes seems more wild beast than man and answers to no one.

Pierre winks at his son while opening the throttle of the chainsaw and spreading his legs so that his feet touch the sides of the bucket to brace himself. As Scooter raises the bucket, Pierre lifts the running chainsaw high above his head, like some horror-movie antihero.

Chapter 3

SEPTEMBER 14, 1985

The barn is left to the cats as Scooter steps out of the tank room and onto the gravel drive to see the cars of the Larioux clan parked three deep in double file. The orange from the setting sun reflects in the kitchen windows swung outward from above the kitchen sink. Scooter can hear voices and laughter. The smell of smoking meat reminds Scooter how hungry he is.

Uncle Jim is on the stoop behind the back porch having a smoke. Scooter and Pierre say hi and go inside to change. Donny stays back and bums a cigarette. Scooter and Pierre take off their boots and hats and spend an extra amount of time at the deep porch sink using coarse soap to scrub off the grease, manure, hay, and the dirt of the day.

In the living room, the TV is on, and the news from LaCrosse is just ending with the weather guy and the sports guy making predictions about the Badger game coming up next. Diana is sitting on the wooden, bench-style sofa with her tanned legs crossed. She lifts her chin as a sort of greeting to Scooter as he walks into the living room. She is sitting with Aunt Mary, Scooter's mom's sister. Diana is parroting Aunt Mary's heavy Wisconsin accent. Diana starts sentences with "now say," and ends them with "don't you know," all in a singsong style. Despite the age difference and Aunt Mary's loose grip on reality, the two sound like two best friends gossiping.

The rest of the family is in the kitchen drinking old-fashioneds. Aunt Mary favors dry martinis. The one in her hand likely isn't her first of the day.

"Look at this handsome young man," she says as Scooter walks up.

"It looks like I have found the two loveliest ladies at this party. How did I get to be so lucky?" Scooter responds.

As he sits, Diana touches his forearm and slides her hand down his arm until her hand is in his. She uses her other hand to pick a few stray pieces of straw out of Scooter's hair. The news coverage cuts to Camp Randall and the beginning of the Wisconsin game.

Aunt Mary looks at Diana and Scooter as they both look at the TV. "Just think, Scooter, next year this could be you about to play and Diana on the sideline."

Scooter and Diana look at each other and wince. The pressure and finality of that prediction and the reality of the coming of the next chapter of their lives is not quite something either is prepared to confront.

Aunt Mary toddles outside for a Virginia Slim in the moist night air.

Outside the front door are two picnic tables set with paper tablecloths, a big bowl of potato salad, watermelon, cucumber salad with dill, fresh crescent rolls (which is what everyone really cares about), and glass jars of fresh milk. The roast has already come off the smoker and is competing for space with the old-fashioned station on a giant cutting board. Uncle Jim is taking his time cutting the meat with an electric carving knife and effusively praising its perfection. It is pink inside with a line of darker red just before the deep brown sear of the crust. The juices slide across the board and fill the groove that follows the board's perimeter just for that purpose. Jim loads up two serving trays with sliced meat, and everyone files out to find spots at the picnic tables.

Irene looks at Pierre, and he stands and folds his hands.

"Come Lord Jesus, be our guest and let these gifts to us be blessed. Amen."

He sits and everyone starts dishing up and passing bowls. Scooter's first go-round is an entire plate of meat with three crescent rolls thrown on top. There will be seconds.

After the pie and ice cream and the last curse at the pathetic Badger defense, the car doors slam and red taillights flash, then turn and disappear down the ridge road heading back down into the floodplain and south to Prairie.

Irene closes the door to the dishwasher on the last load of dishes. Pierre is already in his blue silk pajamas that he got for Christmas. He smells like lavender on account of the lotion that was part of the same gift. He says his goodnights and climbs the steep, narrow staircase to snore more loudly than anyone imagined was possible.

Diana and Scooter slink out to the middle of the huge sloped lawn. They lean back, resting on their elbows, between an elm tree and a weeping willow, looking up at the Milky Way, and find Orion. Diana rolls onto her hip and traces the length of Scooter's torso from his neck to the top of his Levi's with her fingertip. Scooter turns to meet her and kisses her lips. She rolls on top of him. Scooter puts his lips to her ear.

"I can't imagine anything feeling better than this," he says.

THE NEXT MORNING AFTER BREAKFAST, DONNY AND Pierre exchange smiles on the back porch. As they pass the granary, Donny takes off his shirt, revealing a tattoo of a skull with wings spreading from its ear holes across the expanse of his muscle-rippled and sun-browned back. He does side bends, raising one arm and then the other above his head, with the alternate hand on his hip.

A few days before, Donny baled about five acres of hay that was mown earlier in the week. This afternoon's task is to load the bales onto a wagon, drive it back to the barn, and put it up in the haymow.

Donny and Scooter sit with their legs dangling off the back of the hay wagon, which is hooked up to the old truck. Pierre drives as Donny and Scooter bump and bounce in the back of the wagon over the rutted dirt road.

Pierre turns off the dusty road into the dry field with stiff spikes of freshly mown hay sticking up from the ground. Every fifteen or twenty feet sits a green rectangular bale of hay in rows parallel to the dirt road. There are twelve rows of hay that stretch about the distance of three football fields. Scooter takes off his shirt, throws it into the open window of the truck, and stretches yellow calf-skin gloves over his hands. He walks out behind the trailer. Donny stands inside the trailer looking out the back. Donny puts in a golf ball-sized dip and rolls his shoulders a few times while clearing his sinuses.

Donny looks at Scooter and winks. "Don't slow us down, young pup!" Donny bangs on the railing on the side of the wagon. In response, the truck fires up and the trailer starts slowly moving.

Scooter walks up to the first bale, which weighs about forty pounds, and picks it up with his left hand jammed under the baling twine and his right hand on the back end of the bale. He hurls it up into the wagon. Donny grabs it and slides it along the wood-plank floor to the front of the wagon, toward the pickup, pushing it until it is flush with metal front gate.

The truck and the wagon never stop moving, gradually increasing speed until the end of the row. By then, Scooter is at a full run from one bale to the next. Donny holds the rail of the wagon with one hand, cackling like a madman as he grabs the last bale in the row and stacks it halfway deep into the wagon. Scooter is breathing hard now and knows that his dad will go even faster on the second row because Donny has less distance to move stacking each bale.

The second row done, Scooter jumps onto the wagon. He and Donny sit on a narrow strip, the last part of the wagon not occupied by hay, their bare skin pricked as they rest against the stack. Scooter's face is red, and pieces of hay stick to his chest and back. Pierre drives them back to the milk barn. There, Donny loads the bales onto a conveyor that reaches up to a third-story window that opens into the haymow. As the bales fall to the floor and bounce, Scooter scrambles to grab the bales and neatly stack them as far away from their landing point as there is room to, all while avoiding the trap doors and open holes that allow the men to efficiently drop the bales into the milking parlor.

Scooter fills a metal bucket with water from a spigot outside of the tank room and dumps it over his head. He sits on the end of the now empty wagon. His black bangs are plastered to his red face. His stare stays straight ahead as his dad whips the wagon around the gravel drive to head back out to the bumpy road. "Round two," he yells as Donny chuckles and hands Scooter the tin of Copenhagen.

Chapter 4

NOVEMBER 21, 1985

They make the trip to Madison for the semi-finals of the Division II state tournament and double up in hotel rooms. They watch *Rocky* on VHS in a conference room. It is the first trip the Frenchmen have made to state in ten years. Scooter ended the regular season as all-conference and led the team in rushing, passing, and touchdowns. This is the first weekend Scooter hasn't had to do chores in over a year. Looking around the room, he can see the guys getting hyped up during the last fight scene in *Rocky*. Even he feels a little tingling down his arms as Rocky guts through the final beating.

The Frenchmen's opponents are the Two Rivers Raiders. If they win against Two Rivers, the Frenchman return in a week to play for the state title.

The Frenchmen are not favored to win. Two Rivers is known for being big and hitting hard. In particular, they have a highly recruited safety who roams the middle and is known to be a headhunter named Cecil McGraw. Scooter can tell Cecil is already in Dickie's head.

"I'm not scared of Cecil," Dickie says as soon as the lights go out. The two lie in their queen-size beds under scratchy sheets and stiff bedspreads, staring at a stucco ceiling. "You've probably hit me harder in practice than anything he can do."

"Don't worry. I won't throw you into him," says Scooter. "Just focus on the ball and you'll be fine."

Their game is scheduled for three o'clock. They arrive at Camp Randall, the giant football stadium where the Badgers play, at eleven thirty. They change in the storied, musty locker rooms and walk down the tunnel under the mammoth stands and out onto the field without pads around noon to throw the ball around and get loose. There is a lot of nervous energy.

Scooter paws at the thin AstroTurf with his cleats, getting a feel for his footing. He practices taking snaps from the center, Marc Cooke. As soon as Marc snaps the ball into Scooter's big right hand, Scooter drops back quickly, stabbing his feet at the ground. He practices taking three-step and five-step drops. As he backpedals, he is deliberate and careful to bring his knees up to his waist so as to avoid snagging his cleats on the glorified carpet below.

After about five minutes of snaps, the team lines up in a formation like a marching band and starts stretching. They are serious and mostly quiet. Then Scooter throws some passes to Dickie and the other receivers, with Coach Larsen watching and throwing balls back to him.

"Step into it, son," he says. "Watch where the sun and the shadows are."

The lower stands are almost full. The school has sent buses of students along with the band and the cheerleading squad, whose only concession to the fall air is flesh-colored nylons. The Sawmill Saloon has also sent two old school buses complete with kegs in the back for parents to make the trip. There are plenty of rowdy locals along for the ride too. Scooter recognizes many faces in the crowd.

The first play of the game for the Frenchmen offense is a simple "run right," with Marc pulling to take out the guard and even Dickie blocking the cornerback as Scooter sprints along the line. He gets to the edge, almost at the sideline, and plants his foot. It sticks in the turf. He falls awkwardly, and some bulky Raider crashes down on his sternum, forcing the wind out of Scooter's body. He lies on his back for a beat as the Raiders side cheers the loss of yards. The Frenchmen side goes discernibly quiet.

Dickie runs back and kneels down next to Scooter. "You all right, Scoot?"

Scooter gets to his knee and slaps Dickie's hand away. "What does it look like? Get back in the huddle and fucking focus."

They run the same play again. This time Scooter is more careful with his plant foot. He rounds the corner gingerly but in time to square up and break the tackle of the outside linebacker. He lowers his head and paws at a cornerback, sending him to the ground too. Scooter steps on the cornerback's shoulder and cuts upfield for a ten-yard gain before Cecil dives at his legs, forcing Scooter out of bounds.

The game goes back and forth throughout the first three quarters. The Raiders offense operates with balanced precision. When the Frenchmen think they are going to run, the Raiders pass; when the Frenchmen set the defense for run, the Raiders are ready to throw. The Raiders quarterback's jersey is clean. Yet Coach Larsen refuses to put Scooter in on defense. Scooter is their only chance on offense.

Scooter carries the ball on almost every down. His jersey is stained with an artificial green and his knees and elbows are bleeding from rug burns that ooze with a fluorescent-pink mixture of blood and pus.

The Raiders go up seven with just over two minutes remaining. On defense, the Raiders do everything they can to stop Scooter. On the first two plays of the drive, the Raiders have seven men in the box, with man coverage on the receivers and only Cecil floating back in space. On the first play of the drive, Scooter runs to a three-yard gain. On the next play, he can only find two yards before he is dragged down by a pair of linebackers.

Back in the huddle, Scooter turns to Dickie. "Be ready," he says, brooking no argument.

Scooter fakes as if he is going to run left and the cornerback covering Dickie bites, blitzing up to the line. Dickie's bowlegs churn up the sideline. He is uncovered as Scooter lets the ball go. But just after the ball leaves Scooter's hand, he sees Cecil charging to his right. As the ball is about to drop into Dickie's arms, Cecil launches himself headfirst with legs trailing in the air behind him. Cecil hits Dickie in the ear hole just as the ball floats into his hands. The impact makes a crack like a thunderclap and Dickie flies out of bounds. He comes to rest with his face down and his arms awkwardly behind him.

Cecil is performing some ridiculous gravedigger celebration next to the sideline. Scooter runs downfield. He stops and looks down at Dickie as the trainers get there. Dickie is moaning and starts to stir. The trainers stabilize Dickie's neck, backboard him, and lift him onto a golf cart. By now Dickie is awake and moving his hands and feet. Scooter can see the tears in his eyes. Scooter takes off his helmet and leans down.

"I'm sorry, Dickie," is all he can think to say.

Coach Larsen calls a jet sweep on the next play. Scooter is supposed to hand the ball to the wide receiver and just step back and watch the play unfold. He has other ideas. He fakes the handoff to the wide receiver and somehow squeezes and then bursts through the line.

Scooter is looking only at Cecil. He runs at him, deliberately targeting him at full speed. Cecil, also running toward Scooter, squares his shoulders and prepares to take aim with his patented launch and spear. Scooter makes no move to evade him. In fact, Scooter leaves his feet first, launching all of his 240 pounds at the safety. They collide midair, facemask to facemask. Cecil is propelled onto his back, with Scooter coming down on top of him. Cecil is out cold. Scooter's body buzzes as he sees the trickle of blood from the bridge of Cecil's nose. Scooter can't help himself. As he gets up, he steps on Cecil's stomach. The ref throws a flag and ejects Scooter from the game. Without him, the Frenchmen drive stalls and they lose the game by seven. Scooter doesn't care.

Rocky Peregrine is waiting for Scooter outside the locker room. A former marine and current head coach of the UW football team, Coach Peregrine's hair is in a perpetual flattop and he wears tight Dickies shorts year-round. The shorts ride high and stretch over his Buddha belly. Scooter starts to back away as Coach Peregrine comes in for a hug, pulling the senior in tight.

"Sorry things turned out the way they did, son. You played a hell of a game. But that was boneheaded bullshit at the end. You have to cut that shit out at the next level."

Scooter, still reeling from the hug, says, "Uh, yeah... Oh, by the way, coach, I was planning on accepting on this trip whatever happened, so if it still stands, I am accepting."

Coach Peregrine smiles and nods. "Let's head to my office to sign the papers."

Coach Peregrine notices Scooter's parents walking up and puts his hand out for a shake. Irene accepts and is given the bonus of an awkward hug. "It looks like I will have the pleasure of getting to know the two of you much better," says the coach.

Pierre merely glances at Coach Peregrine and walks over to Scooter. "That was stupid enough to shock me, and that is saying a lot."

Scooter suppresses a smile and looks down and nods, trying to be solemn.

The three walk up to Coach Peregrine's office to sign some papers.

Pierre looks at Coach Peregrine and says, "I expect him back every weekend for chores, other than game weekends, and on game weekends he needs to be back on Sundays."

Coach Peregrine starts to laugh and then catches Pierre's dead-serious look and somewhat menacing stare. "I am sure we can find some arrangement that works for everyone."

The Lariouxs drive west down University Avenue and out of town. Pierre's eyes are locked straight ahead. "I meant what I said to Coach Peregrine. A scholarship is not a way out of your responsibilities."

"Got it," is all Scooter says. But he knows he is done with that life. He is above it. No one can stop him. Sometime past Middleton, Scooter falls asleep and doesn't wake until the tires touch gravel.

Chapter 5

AUGUST 8, 1986

S cooter hugs Irene, picks up his olive drab duffle bag, gets into the passenger seat of the Trans Am, and jams the duffle between his legs. The rest of the car is full of Diana's clothes all perfectly folded and packed into an organized system of bags and bins known only to her. The sun makes them squint as they speed over the hill to the east of the farm at speeds that make their stomachs drop and the suspension lose compression as the car floats above the ridge for a moment. Scooter looks to his right and sees Pierre chugging and bouncing along the dirt road to the back pasture in the old open-cab John Deere tractor that pulls the manure spreader.

A couple of hours later, they turn off University Avenue north toward the lakefront dorms. Football practice starts three weeks before classes. Diana is also there early to start tryouts and (hopefully) practice for the cheerleading squad. Scooter, along with all of the other freshman football players, is staying in Birch Hall, a thirty-room dorm with its own cafeteria in the basement and a back door that opens to a gravel path that describes the arc of University Bay.

Stepping out of the car, Scooter can smell the lake and feel the thick stillness of the summer air. Scooter grabs his bag, and Diana follows him into the limestone building to find his room. They pass a guy wearing faded jeans and a black Rolling Stones T-shirt with the sleeves cut off smoking a cigarette. He nods and pushes his blond hair back over his forehead as Scooter and Diana walk into the lobby.

Scooter's room is on the second floor, just above the entrance. There are two twin beds, with matching dressers and two metal desks on either side of the room. He is not the first one to arrive. There is a black stereo on a desk. Above the corresponding bed is a Europe '72 Grateful Dead poster. Scooter throws his duffle on the bed with the bare wall above it. He opens a closet near the door and finds clean sheets and a pillow. Diana helps him make the bed. Scooter looks around, taking in his small surroundings. It seems way too small a space to contain him.

Diana snuggles up next to him and puts her arm around his waist. "I can't believe this is finally beginning," she says, "but now I am off to see my digs. Elizabeth Waters Women's Dormitory. It has the ring of a mental institution. Wanna come?"

"Nah, I think I'll stick around and meet some of the guys, maybe my roommate."

Just then, the blond-haired smoker from the entrance steps into the room and holds out his hand. "I'm Ferris. Salutations." The way he says the word "salutations" draws out the letter "a," adding syllables to the word.

"I'm Scooter. This is Diana."

Diana smiles and holds out her hand, and Ferris actually kisses it like some movie duke or something. "Well, I'll leave you boys to get acquainted." Diana says. "I'll be back later Scooter."

Both watch, involuntarily, as she exits the room. Scooter sizes up Ferris. He's not very big, but the muscles in his arms are defined to the point that Scooter can see veins in his biceps. Scooter thinks Ferris can't be much over six feet tall.

"You must be the great Scooter Larioux," Ferris says. "We have heard a lot about this man-child who is going to lead us to Pasadena. I must say, you are a big dog." He pronounces dog, dawg.

"Uh, yeah, I guess."

"I'm the kicker. I'm from San Diego. I suppose you don't know where we can get weed around here?"

Scooter chuckles a little and shakes his head. He starts unpacking his clothes. Ferris turns on the stereo, deposits a cassette, and cranks up The Who.

Throughout the day more cars, trucks, and vans pull up with unusually large freshmen who lumber up the stairs carrying suitcases, duffle bags, and random pieces of furniture. Around five, Coach Peregrine shows up. He struts down the hall of each floor, yelling, "Meeting in the mess… meeting in the mess!"

Scooter has been sitting on his bed listening to Ferris wax nostalgic about his summers lifeguarding at Del Mar beach and the California girls that frequent said beach. It's not not entertaining. They walk out into the hall and join the flow of corn-fed teenagers down the stairs into the basement, where they will be getting much-needed nourishment for the next year. There are long wooden tables with benches, and the boys (they still are boys after all, even if very few of them are under two hundred pounds) find seats and look up at their leader.

"Men, my job is to turn you dewy-eyed momma's boys into champions. It's not going to happen with a lot of cuddling and soft kisses."

Scooter fights the urge to crack a smile, or worse, laugh.

Peregrine continues. "Practice starts tomorrow morning promptly at six—or zero six hundred for you military types. We meet at the tents on the east side of the fields. It is a five-minute walk from here, if that. If you are not there by five fifty-five, start looking for a ride back to whatever shitty Podunk town I dragged you out of. Got it?"

"Yes, sir," the boys respond in a firm but less than enthusiastic way.

"What!?"

"YES SIR!"

"Good! You are football players! Not schoolgirls. Not mice. If you have something to say, fucking say it! Now, this is where you will eat all your meals. Mrs. Winchester back there…"

They all look simultaneously and see for the first time a woman with curly gray hair and a white apron over a blue dress who looks out behind the counter of an institutional kitchen. Her cheeks flush a little and she gives a small wave before placing her hand back at her side. She returns to the stainless-steel workbench where she works a rolling pin while clouds of flour billow around her.

"Mrs. Winchester will take care of you. You take care of her! If I hear anything different, first I will kick your ass and second, I will ship you back to your sad Podunk town."

Ferris elbows Scooter in the ribs and leans into him. "I guess coach has never been to San Diego," he whispers.

Peregrine's eyes dart toward them and Ferris looks down at his lap. Coach continues, "On the table in front of you is your playbook and practice schedule. You should start reading it tonight. I realize some of you are half morons, but at least try to get through it this week, and if you don't understand something, ask one of your coaches. They will be bright-eyed and bushy-tailed to meet you tomorrow morning. It's going to be hot. Drink water and plan on puking. Nighty night, gentlemen." With that, Coach Peregrine salutes, spins on his heel, and waddles up the stairs and out into the late afternoon sun.

Scooter and Ferris take their playbooks up to their room and sprawl out on their respective beds.

Ferris laughs. "There are really only two plays I need to know, and I'm pretty sure everyone does 'em the same. I'm going to go find some weed and beer. You, on the other hand, better study the shit out of that thang."

Scooter grunts and lies back on his bed. He tries to concentrate and remember the terminology for different formations and the name of plays and out of what formation each play is run. It is a dizzying amount of information. His eyelids start sliding down his eyeballs in a way that is comforting and warm. He is woken up by the weight of Diana's body pressing down on top of him, her lips touching the skin between his chin and neck.

Chapter 6

AUGUST 11, 1986

Scooter checks the clock radio. It says five o'clock. The sky outside is just starting to lighten from pure black to navy blue. He puts cleats and a water bottle in a backpack and quietly closes the door. Ferris is rock still in his bed. Scooter goes down to the basement and smiles at Mrs. Winchester as he pours himself some coffee. She stacks pancakes on his plate. He douses them in maple syrup, then finds a table and eats his food.

It is already hot outside. He passes the Natatorium, the last building before the expanse of what must be twenty football fields known as University Bay Fields, or U-Bay Fields for short. He can see tents and tables set up at the east end of the fields and a gaggle of coaches shooting the shit in red Dickies and white polos, arranging clipboards and pens on folding tables, filling cups, and setting up cones all while drinking coffee out of white foam cups.

It is only a little after five thirty, and Scooter is one of the first players to appear. He walks up to a table inside the tent. An assistant coach is sitting behind the table with a stack of red nylon duffle bags behind him. The practice schedule is taped to the table.

"You must be Scooter. Here are some practice clothes, cleats, and water bottles." He hands Scooter a duffle bag. "Quarterbacks and wide receivers are together this morning. You are to meet on Field One, which is the field closest to the road there. Coach Harrelson will be along shortly."

Scooter nods and starts walking toward Field One with his duffle bag. Coach Peregrine meets Scooter as he steps out from the shade of the tent and into the first sunrays of the day.

"Good to see you early," says Coach Peregrine.

Scooter nods.

"Don't expect that to give you a leg up on anything. I need to see effort today."

Scooter looks at Peregrine and waits a beat. "Sure thing, coach."

Scooter continues over to Field One and sets his bag down on the sideline. He opens the bag and tries on the cleats. There is a red mesh shirt with the number 4 on it. He takes off his cotton T-shirt and replaces it with the mesh one. Then he starts stretching his shoulders and bending over to touch his toes. A tall, gangly coach with wild curly hair, a clipboard, and a cigarette between his lips joins him on the sideline.

"Coach Harrelson, call me Harley." He shakes Scooter's hand excitedly. "I've heard a lot about you. Looking forward to getting this going today."

The other players start arriving. There are skinny, tall wideouts and shorter, stockier guys that look like track stars ready to explode out of the blocks. In all, there are fifteen in the group. Scooter is by far the biggest. There are three other quarterbacks. Luke Davis, the returning starter, walks over to Scooter.

"Are you Scooter? I'm Luke. I guess I'll be showing you how all this is done. For starters, make sure you keep track of my bag today."

That's never going to happen, Scooter thinks.

Luke is maybe two inches shorter than Scooter, but probably fifty pounds lighter. He has long arms and geometric features, including a chin with a diamond-shaped dimple. His eyes are a light blue, the irises circled by a much darker color. His hair is sandy blond and styled to be pushed to the side. Scooter thinks he would look more at home at a country club than football practice.

Coach Harrelson flicks his cigarette and walks onto the field and faces the sideline and his charges. "Men…ya gotta wanna! That's really all I can say to you today. No one else can do for you what you can. Let's have a good practice." He pops the whistle into his mouth, blows it, and says, "Line up on the goal line." Everyone trots to the goal line and finds a spot. Scooter is toward the middle of the pack. Near Luke, but not right next to him. "Down and back, jog!" Harrelson blows his whistle. Then it is high knees, then butt kicks, then side-shuffles, then carioca, then running 60 percent, each drill done one hundred yards at a time. Some of the players are already huffing and puffing, and this is only warm-up. Harrelson blows his whistle again.

"Today, we start with the hour of power. We have a need for speed in the fourth quarter. Speed begets speed. The drill is sixty 100-yard sprints starting every minute on the minute. No pain, no gain! On the line."

Harrelson blows his whistle and the players burst off the line. The receivers churn their legs and quickly get up into their track-runner form, sailing down the track with only the balls of their feet ever touching the ground. The quarterbacks run hard, but not with the same form or aggression. Another assistant coach stands at the opposite goal line with a watch in his hand reading off times, "eleven seconds, twelve seconds." On the first sprint, Scooter watches Luke and does the bare minimum to stay roughly even with the junior quarterback. They both cross the goal line somewhere in the fourteen-second range with Luke straining at the end to finish just ahead of Scooter.

After each sprint, the players stretch a bit and shake out their legs, knowing that they have some time to rest before the minute is up. Gradually, they all again find their places on the line and look downfield at Coach Harrelson. He puts up his hand then drops it with a little kung fu flair as he yells "Go!" They all fly off the line again. This repeats every minute on the minute.

Scooter settles into a rhythm. His times are in the fourteens and fifteens. He never presses. He stretches his legs and stride in the middle of the field. Scooter keeps his eye on Luke, letting him win most of the time…until the last five sprints. As they near the end of the hour, everyone is bending over, putting their hands on their knees, searching for air that is not there, and feeling the acid burn in their overused muscles. Scooter stands with his hands on his hips and looks at Luke. Coach Peregrine has come from the tent to watch the end of the first round of torture. Scooter decides it is time to show them what he can do. On each of the last five sprints he is seconds ahead of the nearest quarterback and beats many of the wideouts. His times are in the twelve-second range.

After the hour of power, Coach Harrelson gives them a break to use the port-o-lets and get some water. The players queue up at tables covered with already-filled cups of Gatorade and water. They chug liquids and grab wet towels to put around their necks. The vibrating chatter of the cicadas has picked up to an electric hum that matches the intensity of the rising sun and seems to rattle the thick air.

Scooter runs his hand over his short black hair slicked against his scalp, which is warm to the touch. A sheet of sweat runs down his back. He soaks a towel with ice-cold water, and drapes it over his head, closing his eyes as he relishes the coolness. With his eyes closed, he can see the rhythm of his heartbeat in the blood vessels in his eyelids illuminated by the bright sun.

He feels something hit his shoulder and he pulls the towel off his head. Luke's stupid diamond chin dimple is jutting up toward Scooter's face.

"Nice work, fucking brownnoser." Luke tries to step through Scooter and push him to the side, but Scooter holds his ground, and the best Luke can do is sort of grind his shoulder into Scooter's arm and awkwardly spin around him.

Harrelson blows his whistle. "On the line. Quarterbacks line up, two in front, two in back. Receivers, two lines of five, split out five yards from each line of quarterbacks. We are going to start with ten-yard ins and outs. Three-step drops. Receivers in the right-side line, run the in; left-side line, run the out. After you catch the ball, finish to the sideline and jog back to the opposite line. Quarterbacks, switch lines after each throw. Each play starts on my whistle. This first round is four minutes."

Scooter lines up next to Luke. The whistle blows, and they both prance back three steps each holding the football up to their chins as the receivers sprint, then cut. Luke lets his ball go first, a straight-line spiral that spikes the rookie receiver, Sterling, in the chest, just as he steps into his break toward the sideline. Sterling looks surprised that the ball is on him that quickly. It bounces off his chest, but Sterling gets his hands on it, juggles, and then squeezes the ball to his chest as he sprints to the sideline and jogs back down to get in line, tossing the ball to one of the observing coaches.

"Hands!" Harrelson yells.

Scooter lets his throw go moments after Luke's, but it does not have the same speed and describes a slight arc as it lands in the outstretched hands of the Badger's star receiver, Ed Song, who powers to the sideline and gracefully jogs to the back of the line.

Scooter and Luke switch lines, and the drill continues. On each throw it seems that Luke is just ahead of Scooter, and the balls Luke throws are violent projectiles compared to Scooter's rainbows. Scooter cringes as he hears the smack of the ball hitting the receivers' hands from Luke's passes, sometimes seconds before Scooter's receiver gathers the ball. Scooter even starts to cheat with his eyes, glancing at Luke, to see what the gangly prick is doing differently than him.

For a full hour, they continue with essentially the same drill, but with the receivers running different routes. Slants, screens, comebacks, hitches, they finish the drill moving down to the ten-yard line and throwing fades to the corners of the end zone. Coach Peregrine walks between the fields but lingers longer at Field One, watching his quarterbacks make their throws and whistling from time to time when Luke throws a dart that is particularly accurate or fast.

After the hour, Harrelson blows his whistle three times and yells, "Huddle! Look at your schedules. It's eight thirty. You have two hours, then we meet at the Nat for weights. Go take care of yourselves. Eat, drink, rest, stretch. These weeks are long, and I don't want any excuses. You want to make this team, you need to be at your best. You want to win this season, you need to be able to finish the race."

The players gather their things and go off in different directions to ingest calories and prepare for what's next. The upperclassmen ride off on mopeds, the linemen's backsides spilling over the sides of the seats as they bounce off to their apartments or the training table. The freshmen walk in rows of two back to Birch.

Ferris trots up and walks next to Scooter. "How was it?"

"Pretty tough," says Scooter, "you?"

"Money," says Ferris. "Just kicking. I don't remember missing even one."

"I hope Mrs. Winchester has something for us," says Scooter.

Ferris laughs. "Yeah, I bet. I could murder some nachos right now."

As expected, Mrs. Winchester does have something whipped up for the players. On the counter between the kitchen and the seating area is pan after pan of egg-bake: hash-brown potatoes topped with eggs, topped with melted cheese, all interlaced with sausage and bacon. Another row of pans is full of sticky buns with caramelized brown sugar on top. The side table has pitchers of milk and various types of juice. The tired players thank her and take huge helpings, silently hunching over their plates and shoveling spoons and forkfuls into their mouths. They are so tired it takes effort to chew.

Mrs. Winchester smiles and says, "Eat up, boys."

Chapter 7

AUGUST 11, 1986

The Natatorium is divided into two sections. There is the cavernous pool area connected by locker rooms to a six-floor building that includes basketball courts, gymnastics gyms, and weight rooms. The sixth floor is a honeycomb of weight rooms, each room housing different equipment for different purposes. There is a squat room, with rack after rack encasing raised wooden platforms like stages covered with stains from various human fluids and chalk, a machine room with a circuit of various Nautilus machines, and an upper-body room with benches and barbells in the middle and dumbbells on racks against the wall. There are other rooms too with a variety of equipment to stress and contort the human body.

The leather or Naugahyde or neutrino, or whatever the benches are upholstered with, is stained from generations of sweat, rubbed to a shine, and cracked from friction and pressure applied day after day by kids struggling to become stronger. The smell is musty, with a hint of sour and a sprinkle of leather, always accented with a backdrop of chlorine from the attached pool complex below.

The trainers and coaches are waiting on the sixth floor. They divide the players even more than they were divided that morning. Each position, be it quarterback, wide receiver, or offensive lineman, is taken by a trainer to a different room. Scooter and the other quarterbacks follow a kid who looks to be no older than Scooter but has the bearing of a baby rhino. He struts them back to a room with various stretch cords, boxes, medicine balls, and mats. He points to a stack of mats against the back wall and motions for the quarterbacks to sit down.

He starts talking in rapid staccato bursts. "Okay guys, I'm Josh and I'll be your trainer or, as I like to say, strength coach for this season. Our goal is to put together a program that helps with strength, speed, and flexibility. But we are not lineman. We are not trying to get as big as possible. So, a lot of this stuff will be higher reps or bodyweight exercises. Plyometrics, anyone know what that means? Never mind. That's part of it too. Anyway, I don't like to waste a lot of time, so the first thing we need to do is to get your basic weightlifting maxes. So, let's start with you on the end, what's your name?"

"Scooter Larioux."

"Ah, Scooter, I figured that was you. You actually do look like a lineman," Josh chuckles, "but you are not going to lift like one. So, what is your bench-press max?"

Scooter looks at Luke to his left and back up at Josh, who has a pencil pressed to a clipboard. Scooter says, "Well, I actually don't know. I have lifted before, obviously, but honestly not that much. I'm a farm kid, so in high school, we didn't have to do weights with the team. I guess they figured we got worked out enough at home, and they probably figured right."

"Well, we'll figure it out," Josh says with a grin, showing a missing canine tooth.

They start by alternating from squat presses with medicine balls, upright rows with stretch bands, box jumps, pull-ups, and some jackknifes with medicine balls. Then they go to the upper-body room. The linemen have just left. Their scent lingers. On the rack of one of the benches is a barbell with two 45-pound plates on each side.

Josh looks at Scooter and says, "Do you think you can bench that?"

Scooter says, "I'm really not sure, I mean I assume, but I just don't do this that often."

"Let's see," says Josh.

With the other three watching, Scooter straddles the bench and then lies back. Josh stands behind him with both hands on the bar. Scooter feels the knurling in the bar and tries to line his hands up an equal distance apart.

"Your hands should be right at your shoulders when the bar meets your chest," says Josh.

Scooter presses the bar off the rack. He slowly draws the bar down and then fires upward.

Josh starts counting out the reps. "Ten, eleven, twelve, thirteen…twenty, twenty-one…" At twenty-five reps, Scooter's arms give the faintest hint of a quiver, and Josh grabs the bar and says, "That's it! I don't want to be the guy that breaks you. But holy shit, that would have been one of the best in the combine last year and maybe the best quarterback ever! You serious that you don't do this?"

"I mean, I have," says Scooter, "just not much and not for a while."

The other quarterbacks are looking on in disbelief. Luke shakes his head and mutters something about bestiality under his breath.

"Well, we're not trying to max out in this group today, so everyone find a bench and settle in. We are doing four sets of fifteen reps on two minutes rest, so find a weight that you can do fifteen reps no problem. It will get hard, trust me."

Scooter sticks with 225.

After the workout, they descend back down to the first floor and file into the locker rooms to shower. The football players enter the large open shower room as the swim team files out. It is like two distinct populations of hominids passing each other on some sun-beaten savanna millions of years ago. In stark contrast to the football players and their almost geometric bulk, the swimmers are tall and lanky, their limbs like supple eels cured in chlorine. They have red circles around their eyes from their goggles. They have the distant gaze of someone who has just been through some sort of trauma.

On the walk home, Scooter's body feels heavy. The heat only adds to his exhaustion. The only thing keeping him conscious is a ravenous hunger. He shuffles down to the basement, downs as many calories as he can, and uses the railing to pull his mass back up the stairs. He opens the door, takes a step, and flops on his bed.

Chapter 8

AUGUST 15, 1986

What is known as the Football Frat House, or "Double F," is a four-story, stone mansion on Langdon Street. The backyard slopes steeply to a pier extending into Lake Mendota.

The lake is just starting to reflect orange. Scooter sees people walking around the back, and he and Diana follow, holding hands. There is a driveway along the side of the house and a connected garage with two raised doors. The garage opens to a large windowless basement with a concrete floor. The room is devoid of any decoration, except for speakers hung at each corner and a rough wooden bar at the back of the room. There is no furniture. The place smells of stale beer and stale beer. Luke is standing at the bar with a group of linemen handing out cans of Old Milwaukee from cardboard pallets stored in a walk-in cool room directly behind the bar. The cool room is stacked to the ceiling with cases. The linemen wear shorts and polo shirts that strain to cover the expanse of what lies beneath them.

"Hey Frosh, who is this lovely lady?" says Luke, who looks like an alien among the linemen. He is wearing dock-siders and white shorts with a blue Nautica polo. Sunglasses are perched on top of his flowing sandy hair. He looks like he just stepped off a sailboat or finished a round of golf.

Diana looks up at Luke, holds out her hand, and says, "Diana Dillinger, I'm with Scooter," in a way that is a little teasing and accompanies that crooked smile of hers.

"Too bad. Anyway, listen, Diana, if you need any help with your English classes, I have pretty good relationships with all the profs. I wrote a short story that was published last year and am thinking about going to the Ivies after all of this," he swirls his hand around the concrete party room, "is over."

Diana's smile hardens. "I've never even gotten a B on a test, much less in a class, but if it looks like that is going to change, I will be sure to give you a call." Diana winks in a way that shrugs off the interaction.

Scooter just glares at Luke. *What a fucking preppy nerd*, he thinks.

"Survived your first week…or at least most of it," Luke says to Scooter and hits him on the shoulder a little too hard to be natural. Scooter takes his beer and wanders off toward the center of the room. Some of the cheerleaders have arrived. They all wear tight shorts and half shirts. Their hair is in ponytails off the sides of their heads. Diana turns to talk to her friends, and they look at Scooter and smile. He nods back.

A giant, pea green 1975 Grand Marquis rumbles up to the first garage door. Remarkably, it has only two doors, each with seemingly enough metal to make an airplane wing. The door on the driver's side creaks under the weight of its own metal as it gradually opens. Ferris stretches his leg out of the door and slides off the maroon seat in a white Adidas tracksuit. He has an enormous joint stuck into a white headband. Two girls negotiate the airplane wing of the passenger door. Ferris beelines to Scooter.

"Champ, this is Linda and Sharon." The girls smile at Scooter and snap their gum. "They are lifeguards at the Nat. Fellow travelers." Ferris winks. "Girls, you are meeting the future king of this city." Ferris lights the joint and offers it to Scooter, who shakes his head. The girls puff and pass the joint in an impromptu circle with Ferris.

As the darkness envelopes them, the music gets louder. Scooter steps out back and looks down at the lake. It is a black mirror. He can hear the party echoing out over the water. He takes a deep breath.

He wades back into the madness to look for Diana. She has gone exploring the house with the cheerleaders. The basement is crowded now. Cigarette smoke, perfume, and cologne compete with the stale beer smell. The linemen are yelling and bumping each other's chests at the bar.

There is a pitcher of beer between them and they take turns bouncing a quarter off the table and into the pitcher. One of them whoops, and the four huge humans on one side of the bar all point at their counterparts on the other side. Big Butch Bukowski wraps his giant hand around the pitcher and starts chugging. All the lineman start pounding their meaty hands on the table in rhythm.

Diana smacks Scooter's behind and he turns to see her, three cheer girls, Ferris, Linda, and Sharon grinning at him like idiots.

"Little ganja safari for you kids, huh?"

They all giggle.

"C'mon babe, we want to go down to State Street," Diana says.

Ferris leads the parade past the frat houses. The fireflies have come out, and as they wade through the thick velvet of the night air, they can hear occasional whoops and yells carrying over the lake from the house they just left.

They descend the five steps down into the Kollege Klub. They order a round of Lites, and Ferris puts "Don't Stop Believing" on the jukebox. One of the cheer girls asks Scooter how he and Diana met.

"We grew up together," is his response.

The cheer girl smiles. "That is so sweet."

The truth, Scooter thinks, *is that she is Diana Dillinger, the queen of Famechon Ridge, and I am Scooter Larioux; how could we not wind up together?* Yet he remembers being nervous, maybe for the only time in his life, when he asked her to homecoming sophomore year. He will never forget the hint of mischief in her eyes when she teasingly answered him, "Oh, I guess so, Scooter."

They march up the gradual hill that is State Street as it ascends to the limestone Capitol building that glows as a beacon to the students stumbling about. They duck into State Street Brats with its multiple levels and dozens of televisions and a giant screen to project the Badgers on Saturdays, then The Irish, then The Plaza. At two thirty, the line to get into Parthenon Gyros stretches half a block, hugging the wall of the restaurant and its ionic plaster columns framing a mural of the Greek Isles.

One by one, Scooter, Diana, Ferris, the cheer girls, Linda, and Sharon, step up to the counter and ask for the same gyro, fries, and Coke, and shuffle down the line, paying at the cash register and receiving a plastic basket lined with paper with Pita bread on the bottom, a generous mound of shaved meat covered with cucumber sauce, tomatoes, and onions, all topped with perfectly crisped, golden french fries.

"Holy shit," says Scooter, "these are the best fucking french fries I have ever had."

The room is loud, filled with college kids shooed out of the bars eating ravenously. Ferris's eyes are at half-mast and a deep pink. He eats fry after fry and then the entire gyro without ever setting it down. He sucks down a mouthful of icy Coke and lets out a huge belch as he leans back into the plastic chair.

"All right! That. Was. Epic!"

Scooter shakes his head. "It's been a pleasure ladies and Ferris, but I need to get to bed; no rest for the wicked, I still have practice tomorrow." He looks at Diana and tilts his head. They walk out holding hands.

Chapter 9

AUGUST 23, 1986

The band is on the field and Scooter can hear the occasional strain of a trumpet or oompah from a tuba find its way through the tunnel and into the locker room. He sits on a padded folding chair in front of an empty locker in the visiting locker room. He laces his pads, and one of the equipment assistants helps him stretch the white number 4 jersey over his shoulder pads. He stands up and tucks the jersey into his pants, he stretches his socks up over his calves, and tightens his shoes. Coach Harrelson comes into the middle of the locker room.

"Ya gotta wanna!" he slurs. "For many of you this is the first time you've played on this field. It's just like any other field. It's the same dimensions.

"Today, you are wearing white. That should piss you off! You are the B team. For those of you that are freshmen, you were stars in high school. You proved yourself worthy of being recruited and us coaches said we wanted you to come play for us, and now here you are. On the White team! There is a real chance you won't play at all this year. You certainly aren't starters. THIS is your chance. THIS is your chance to show us coaches that we are wrong: that you aren't too young, that you aren't too small, that you are the BEST. But you gotta wanna! Upperclassmen in this room, you should be really pissed. You have been disrespected. You have had your rightful place taken from you. THIS is your chance to get it back. I want you all to go out there and show me that you deserve to be on this field against Michigan in two weeks. I want you to show that the White team isn't some B team shit squad. That it's a mistake and an insult that you are wearing white today. THIS is your chance. Win on three; one-two-three."

The whole room erupts in a yell of "WIN!" The circle of players that has formed around Harrelson closes into a tight mass in the middle of the room, jumping and yelling in unison. Harrelson starts down the tunnel and the players follow. Harrelson is walking as fast as he can. The players are behind him trying not to trample their coach, but they cannot contain their energy. Eventually the players break free, running around Harrelson on either side. Harrelson ducks and puts his hands up as if protecting his head. He is caught in an eddy of a rushing river of testosterone and exuberance. The players sprint when their cleats touch the plastic green turf.

SCOOTER STANDS BEHIND THE CENTER AND SURVEYS THE defense. Even before they get down into their stances, he can see that the Red defensive line is bigger than the White offensive line. Big Butch is lined up on Scooter's left and is practically frothing at the mouth. The safeties are up. The more experienced, bigger, faster Red team is going to come out and try to attack early, putting Scooter and his band of freshmen and overlooked upperclassmen on their heels.

From the sideline, Harrelson signals a bootleg right. The concept is that as Scooter rolls to his right, the receivers cross over the middle, hopefully shaking off their defenders in the mass of converging bodies. Scooter calls the play, and they break the huddle. The running back stands just to Scooter's left as another layer of protection against Butch. Scooter can see his center nervously looking left and right. Scooter slaps the center's posterior hard and snuggles his hand up underneath him as he barks out the snap count. The center snaps the ball, and Scooter takes three steps back and begins rolling to his right. The right side of the line holds up reasonably well, but the receivers are well covered. Scooter can sense Big Butch surging toward him from the left, like a wildebeest. With rabies. Scooter hears Butch snorting. Scooter shoots a quick look to his left over his shoulder. The left tackle and running back are on the ground and Butch is running freely at Scooter. Butch emits a kind or shrieking sound like a train turning rusty wheels, or a banshee on the attack.

Scooter continues rolling to his right. The linebackers are sagging back, expecting a throw over the middle. Scooter is now past the right side of the line, outside the right tackle. No receiver has come open. Scooter plants his right foot in the turf and changes his trajectory from lateral to vertical just as Butch lowers his shoulder. Scooter instinctively shoots out his left hand, hitting Butch in the facemask with the heel of his hand. Hard. Butch's head snaps back, but his legs still churn. Scooter pushes down on Butch's helmet, driving him into the ground and providing Scooter leverage to accelerate upfield. A linebacker dives at Scooter's legs. Scooter runs through the linebacker's outstretched arms. Scooter continues in a straight line up the sideline and jumps over a safety, and now all that is between Scooter and the end zone is a cornerback trying to square his shoulders and find an angle to take Scooter down, or at least knock him out of bounds. Scooter lowers his head and crashes into the cornerback's facemask with the crack of plastic striking plastic. The cornerback loses his footing and falls onto his back with his head bouncing on the turf. Scooter runs into the end zone.

The crowd that has gathered at Camp Randall to witness the prowess of the starting team and its ascendency to a top-ten preseason ranking is all but silent, stunned, not really knowing who this freshman is. The other players on the White team high-five Scooter and smack his butt as he runs back to the sideline.

He runs past Coach Harrelson and straight to his receivers. "Make some cuts, I'm not running this thing all day." He sits down next to the assistant quarterback coach. He hears a single yell from Ferris on the Red team's sideline.

"FUCK YEAH!"

ON OFFENSE, LUKE DISSECTS THE WHITE TEAM'S SECondary, who look confused and often have no idea the ball has been thrown. But the Red team falters in the red zone. With the defensive players concentrated in the shortened field, Luke's receivers are no longer open. The Red team comes away with field goal after field goal.

Ferris is perfect. He struts onto the field, prances back a few steps behind the line and then to the left of the holder. Ferris then shakes out his legs and shoulders and jumps on the balls of his feet. He settles himself and waits for the center to snap the ball. As soon as the ball leaves the center's hands, Ferris rhythmically paces toward the ball, timing the whole show perfectly every time. He holds his follow-through—his right leg held high pointing to the sideline—after each kick, like a golfer holding his club aloft to savor a perfectly shaped shot. Every time, the ball strikes the net behind the uprights before starting its descent.

The Red team has no answer for Scooter. He physically dominates everyone on the field and makes his teammates look better than they are. In the storied history of the Red and White Game, it is the first time the White team has ever defeated the Red. The Badgers play the national champions, Michigan, in two weeks.

AFTER THE GAME, BOTH SIDES REASSEMBLE IN THE HOME locker room for a post-game debriefing. Luke throws his helmet against his locker as he enters. The freshmen are giddy but try to hide their giddiness behind the busy tasks of taking off and hanging pads and jerseys. They exchange knowing looks and stifle laughs. Butch and the upper-class D-linemen act like silverback gorillas staking out their territory. Everything they do is loud and with big movements: banging helmets, knocking against lockers, stomping around. It's as if they need everyone to know they are mad and won't stand for this kind of loss. The coaches march into the center of the room with their bellies protruding, barely held in by their Dickies shorts, which always seem stretched to capacity. They form a semicircle around Coach Peregrine, who stands for about three seconds tapping his foot, awaiting the rapt attention of his squad. It doesn't come. He looks around in disbelief, the tension building in his face, his carotid artery pulsing out the beat of his increasing heart rate.

"HEY!" he yells.

Players turn and the huddles of players break apart slightly, if lackadaisically, to face him. Luke barely turns from his locker. His head stays down.

"Quit fucking moping!" Peregrine screams. "No one lost to an opponent. We were playing ourselves. This is a team. Goddammit! This is a team. I appreciate that you guys are competitive, and you want to win. Great. But the important thing is that the team wins. If there is anyone here who thinks his starting position is owed to him, raise your fucking hand." No one raises their hand. "If there is anyone here who thinks his personal success is more important than the success of this team, raise your hand." Peregrine waits a beat on this one and looks around the room. He locks eyes with various players. His eyes linger over the seniors and Luke. He looks straight at Butch. No one raises their hand.

"Well, I'm glad we got that out of the way, because what I saw out there today is nothing to mope about. I saw some pretty fucking good football out there today. I also saw a few pretty bad plays. We play Michigan two weeks from today. Two weeks. The goal of scrimmage is to get better. The goal of everything is to get better. Everyone needs to study the film of this game and find out what he needs to do to get better. Not better for himself or to help him start. But to make this team better. To push us further toward our goal, which is to win every fucking game this year starting with the one in two weeks. Is there anyone in here that cannot get enthusiastically behind that? Is there anyone in here that cannot put the interests of the team in front of their own? If there is, then get the fuck out right now!"

Again, Peregrine scans the room, his chin jutting forward, challenging his players to assert their individual identities against this thing that they have bound themselves to body and soul, this pulsating mammalian smelly organism known as "team," which they all had pledged and vowed to serve at any cost to their own individualism or personal comfort and interest. But everyone knows it is more complicated than that. In any event, no one challenges the coach.

"This is a good football team. If you get your heads out of your asses and start supporting each other, this will be a great football team. As Coach Harrelson says, PMA! If I see or sense or even catch a fart-scented whiff of anyone not pulling for this team, wishing ill for their teammate, or generally harshing my mellow, I will send you back to whatever padukaville I dragged you out of. Capiche? Now bring it in. Team on three. One-two-three TEAM! You have the day off tomorrow. Get yourselves right. I will see you Monday morning and I expect to see you all with the focus to come together and work to kick the shit out of those stinking Wolverines."

With that and a snort, Peregrine storms out of the room.

There is an awkward quiet as the players dress. The Red team has stopped their juvenile tantruming and go about the business of generally getting their shit together, getting themselves cleaned up, and getting out into the last Saturday night before school starts. As he exits the team room, Ed, now dressed to the nines in tight white jeans, boat shoes, and a black mesh top, yells across to Scooter, "Hey freshman! You are a mean motherfucker." A group of younger players follow Ed out of the locker room, absorbing the charisma he casts off, hoping to soak it in. Ed is the only untouchable on the team. He is the only one who will no doubt play on Sunday someday. And he has just crowned the next quarterback.

Chapter 10

AUGUST 25, 1986

The atmosphere at practice on Monday morning is different. Coach Peregrine comes up to Scooter after warm-ups and puts his arm around his shoulder.

"How are you feeling this fine morning, son?"

"Pretty good," says Scooter.

"Good, that's good," says the coach.

Harrelson has an agility circuit set up for them for the conditioning hour of practice. It involves suicides on half of the field with ten push-ups at each line. After each suicide, they run three laps around the field. Scooter sleepwalks through that portion of practice, barely breaking a sweat. Harrelson blows his whistle, and they line up on the end zone.

"We are going to do five sprints from varying positions. You will assume the position I call out and then when I blow the whistle, you sprint to the other side. Got it? First… push-up position."

They all line up on the end zone line with their hands shoulder-width apart, holding their bodies off the ground as if they have just completed a push-up. After about twenty seconds, Harrelson blows the whistle. Scooter explodes up and out, his body in a diagonal position, like a missile at launch. At fifteen yards he is standing straight up, his legs and arms churning. He can only see one player out of the corner of his eye, Ed Song. They have left the others behind. Scooter churns as hard as he can, pressing his feet into the ground and throwing his arms forward with each stride. His lungs burn, and he can feel his hamstrings stretch and then contract, in rapid succession. He stops accelerating and lets his body coast through the goal line. Scooter sees Ed finish first, by just a step.

"Elite Speed!" yells Harrelson.

In the throwing drills, the balls leave Scooter's and Luke's hands almost simultaneously. The slap of leather on the receiver's hands is bang-bang staccato, like a base runner's foot hitting the bag just after the ball smacks the first baseman's mitt.

After the drills, Luke avoids Scooter. As soon as they are dismissed, Luke gets on his moped and heads off, presumably to his apartment and some combination of protein shake, Gatorade, and self-loathing.

AFTER STRENGTH TRAINING, ON THE SIXTH FLOOR OF the Nat, Harrelson gathers the receivers and quarterbacks in a back room. There are thick mats arranged in rows on the floor. There is a chair with a boom box on it in the front of the room.

"Everyone grab a towel and find a place on a mat." Harrelson dims the lights, and he tells the players, "Lie back on your mats with your arms at your sides." He turns on the boom box and the sound of the ocean starts playing.

The ocean sounds fade to the background as a calm British voice says, "Welcome to this physical meditation session. I trust you are comfortably positioned, either on your back or in a chair. Close your eyes and start breathing in through the nose…out through the mouth." The rhythm of the ocean is joined by the sound of players' breathing. "Now return your breathing to normal. Feel the weight of your body," says the British man. "Feel yourself sinking into the floor on each exhale."

The sound of the water and the British man's instructions grow more distant. Scooter feels himself sinking. He sees Pierre driving the Bobcat into the back pasture, bouncing in the operator's compartment, cursing the heat of the day and the slow machine. Scooter feels a smile creep across his lips. The next thing he knows he is opening his eyes. The lights are on, and Harrelson is standing over him.

"Goddammit, Larioux. This is for you too. This is how we get the PMA. Positive Mental Attitude. We need to sync our bodies with our brains, man!"

"Sorry, coach." Scooter props himself up on his elbows and rubs the sleep out of his eyes.

Chapter 11

AUGUST 31, 1986

The yellow road base on the driveway is still crunching as Scooter hears the slam of the screen door and sees Irene powerwalk around the corner of the house, wiping the flour from her hands on her apron. She hugs Diana and holds her out at arm's length to get a good look at her as Scooter hoists his duffle bag full of dirty laundry out of the back seat and skips up three steps into his mom's embrace.

"You look bigger, if that is even possible!" Irene says with delight.

Diana says her goodbyes, and Scooter and Irene walk up to the house. They open the door. Pierre is sitting in his leather recliner reading *The Wisconsin Dairyman*.

"Well, if it isn't the prodigal son," he says looking up from his glasses at half-mast. Scooter can detect a hint of a smile and places his hand on Pierre's wide shoulder.

"It's also your only son. Hi, Dad."

It is between the morning milking and afternoon chores, and Scooter has a feeling his dad is going to do everything he can to get the most out of Scooter's brief visit. Scooter finds himself looking forward to it; wanting to do some work not just for work's sake, but to actually accomplish something.

"Are you hungry, honey? I have some tea ring," says Irene.

"Don't mind if I do." Scooter sits at the kitchen counter.

Irene pulls the braided round pastry with cinnamon and pecan filling out of the oven. She cuts a mammoth wedge for Scooter. He pours himself a glass of ice-cold milk, the top third pure cream.

"Don't get too comfortable out there. We have fence to mend in the back back and need to take the horses," Pierre practically shouts into the kitchen from the living room.

The back back is the furthest fenced pasture from the house. It drops precipitously into the coulee. Too steep for the pickup and dicey on a tractor or Bobcat.

Pierre has already stashed two lead ropes on the back porch. Scooter and Pierre gather the leads and open the door to Donny, sleeping soundly, slouched on the stoop, his back against the wall.

"Let's go," Pierre says. Donny shakes off the sleep like it is nothing. "Donny, you're spreading, we'll go see about those fences and any adventurous cattle."

The Lariouxs cross the road to a small fenced-in pasture eaten clean by the intermixed horses and cows. Donny walks to the machine shed to get the tractor and pull the manure spreader, which is full from cleaning the barn last night and this morning, out to the fields, dripping contents along the road that will dry into defacto speed bumps in the afternoon sun. Pierre has two carrots in his back pocket. He opens the gate and starts clicking his tongue. Two dun-colored horses with black manes trot up and stick their snouts into the men's shirts, knowing what is coming. Pierre gives them both a carrot and clips the leads onto their halters. Just like that, Pierre and Scooter are leading the horses through the gate, looking at Donny's skinny ass and following him to the machine shed.

The horse tackle is in the cavernous machine shed on the opposite side of the cow yard from the milk barn. Hay bales that don't fit in the hay loft are stacked on one side of the shed. The tractor and combine are parked on the other side. Parked in the yard in front of the machine shed is an old haybine—its rusty tines like the teeth of a prehistoric shark yanked from the depths. The ends of the tines reflect the sunlight where Pierre has found time to file them to razor sharpness.

At the front of the machine shed, stacked hay bales form the walls of a three-sided room where a horse can bed down if it gets sick or is foaling. The makeshift room smells strongly of hay, leather, and horse sweat. They lead the horses in and tie them up to a repurposed wood fence nailed to the wall, then grab brushes and start brushing the horses. The horses stand and chew, snickering and chasing flies with their tails. Scooter and Pierre put on saddle blankets and saddles. They tighten the straps around the horses' girths, look away, then tighten them again. The crafty horses inhale and expand their chests to preserve slack in the girth straps as a sort of precursor to a bid for freedom. Their idea is that once they get on the trail, they'll exhale and slip the girth strap and run free as god intended (At least, that is the horse's perspective.)

Scooter and Pierre ride the horses out of the shed, following Donny's manure drippings along the shoulder of the ridge road. Scooter and Pierre neck rein the horses off the road and onto the sunbaked path. The horses walk side by side on the path that they know as well as the men do. Everything is quiet but for the crickets and the swishing of the horses' tails. It is hot and a little dusty, and Scooter feels every muscle in his body relax.

"They say up at the college that you may start." Pierre looks over at his son.

(The college is actually the old feed mill in Eastman, where oftentimes in the afternoon the old farmers go to buy feed, drink glass bottles of Coke out of an antique vending machine, chew tobacco, and just sit around and shoot the shit.)

"I'm not counting on it, but if I were coach I would start me." Scooter chuckles a little at his immodesty. "I've been working hard. I like Coach Harrelson. There are some good players, Ed obviously. Luke Davis doesn't care for me much, and I suppose it's his team until I take it. We'll see. How come you old men at the college seem to know so much about everything? By the way, how are you?"

Pierre gives his son a sideways glance. This isn't the kind of thing they usually ask each other. Nevertheless, he obliges as best as he can, "Oh, just dandy. Mom's on me to stop chewing, though." Pierre leans over his horse and lets a long brown drool plot its own trail in the dust. "Not sure that's really even healthy at this point. She told me to at least try Bandits, but I told her that's like taking a bath with my socks on. When will you know who starts?"

"Find out tomorrow."

"Well, I'd like to know before hearing one way or another in the paper. Give me something to tell the boys up at the college."

"Right, I'll let you know."

They round the bend in the dirt road as the hillside falls off into the coulee. Scooter can see a pile of tools and a roll of wire where his dad left off the day before.

"You know what's missing out here?" Pierre asks, standing up in his saddle.

"Sixpack of beer and some hula dancers," says Scooter.

"Well, I see you're still a moron. No cows. Fuck."

The road continues past the pile of wire and tools and traces the fence line along the escarpment between field and forest. One of the fence posts is down and the barbed wire, which was already old and sagging, is now trampled into the dirt. There are little prongs of wire sticking up as if some ancient insect were emerging from the earth. They ride the horses through the break and see the black shapes of the cows moving among the shadows cast by the golden latticework of sunlight filtering onto the hillside.

"How many cows are back here?" Scooter follows his dad as the horses pick their way between trees. Exposed limestone is interspersed with soft soil. Scooter can hear water running over stone somewhere below him. The horses move slowly, shifting their passenger's weight right and left with each step.

"I think there are thirty-five, but that's only a bit better than a guess," says Pierre.

They continue down to a little trickle of a stream that flows over some limestone and forms a natural pool with a rock wall sheltering one side of it. About ten cows are loitering around it looking guilty, like they are out for a smoke or something. They twitch a little when they see the men on horses. Pierre kicks his horse and it jumps over the stream onto the cows' side of it. Pierre gets downhill of the cows, turns the horse, and starts riding up toward the cows, whooping every now and then. The cows groan more than moo as if submitting to the inevitable. They stutter step and hesitate, stamping their hooves, as they are forced back across the stream.

Scooter rides his horse across the slope, fanning out from his father. Scooter sees three cows just below him. He circles wide and gets below them. He turns the horse and starts chasing the cows up the hill. Scooter and Pierre push the cows through the downed fence and then dismount, keeping their horses on the forest side of the fence. They stand up the fallen fence post, stretch one strand of wire, and loop the end over the post to make a temporary fence. They then guide the horses back down the hill to find more cows out wandering.

They are tired riding back and frustrated at not accomplishing what they set out to do that day—they didn't plan on spending the whole afternoon wrangling stupid cows hellbent on being where they shouldn't be when there is a whole big alfalfa field just sitting there for them to live their happy little lives in. It is getting near milking time too, and they still have to brush the horses, turn them out, and get to milking to keep the milk cows happy.

"Putting out fires, that's all this fucking job is," says Pierre. "Did you hear the one about the farmer who won the lottery?"

Scooter is pretty sure he has, but it probably doesn't matter.

"They asked him what he was going to do with the winnings, and he said, 'Keep farming 'til it runs out.'" Pierre spits again, leaving another brown line in the dirt, his Hansel and Gretel reminder of the path taken.

Scooter laughs a little. He thinks about saying something about how maybe one day he, Scooter, could support his mom and dad. Then he thinks better of it and puts in a pinch of chew instead.

Chapter 12

SEPTEMBER 1, 1986

The paper announcing the names and positions is posted in the dining room Monday morning. Scooter will start against the number-one team in the country, the Michigan Wolverines, displacing a very good junior quarterback named Luke. Mrs. Winchester can barely contain her excitement. It literally bubbles out of her with little saliva bubbles as she coos and finds any reason possible to pass near Scooter. She asks about six times if there is anything special he wants for breakfast.

He says, "Maybe a waffle."

Ferris's face betrays mild amusement as this all goes on. Mrs. Winchester is like a starstruck teenager. The other freshman give Scooter long looks and smiles. He nods back. He looks at Ferris.

"The bitch of this whole thing is that we have to fucking go to class this week too."

Ferris laughs.

They walk out together, into the September morning that is starting to carry the promise of winter, and turn toward the fields.

Coach Harrelson hands out little binders to the quarterbacks and receivers. "This is the plan for Saturday," he says. "We'll go through it this afternoon before film. Get on the goal line; time to warm up."

Practice has radically changed. There is a clear division between starters, second team, and the rest. The entire morning practice is dedicated to running actual plays that will potentially be called on Saturday and in going through various game-day scenarios. Coach Harrelson pulls Scooter aside before they go into their first five-play sequence.

"Okay, champ, I know you can get out there and flatten people whenever you feel like it, and we will talk about where that fits in on Saturday, but for today and tomorrow, you stay in the pocket no matter what. Run the play as written up."

"Okay, coach."

He does. Repetition after repetition. In the huddle, Scooter calls the play that has already been decreed and explained, if necessary, by the coaches. This is just offense, no defenders. They run five plays and if there is any mistake—dropped ball, lineman out of position, incorrect motion, sloppy snap count, etc.—they start over.

After the first hour, Harrelson gives them a water break and Ferris takes a break from displaying perfection at forty yards.

"How is it going, roomie?"

"It's boring as fuck," Scooter says, looking down at his red jersey.

Harrelson blows the whistle and calls out the next five plays. "Any questions?"

They run through each play. Scooter is precise and gruff with the snap count. His voice like that of a large dog with a penchant for enunciation. The receivers run hard, planting their cleats in the ground and pushing off at ninety-degree angles into their cuts. The linemen explode forward with their hands up, ready to do combat with an invisible defender, moving their arms in fluid kung fu-like moves to throw an opponent off balance—change his energy.

There is not much time to even shower after practice. Scooter is in sweatpants pulled up to his upper calves, flip-flops, and a Badger football T-shirt. He finds his way to the Humanities building halfway up the steep ascent of Bascom Hill and finds a seat in a semicircle of twenty or so desks as students are introducing themselves.

She is three seats away from Scooter in the semicircle. She has crimped blond hair, chopped at her shoulder. Her blue eyes pop behind dark eyeliner. She is wearing a Sex Pistols T-shirt with enough holes in it to display the bright pink bra underneath. If you're looking, that is, which Scooter guiltily feels he shouldn't be.

"I'm Misty, from Santa Monica. My biggest interests are punk rock and raising chickens." She snaps her gum and looks to the student to her left as if what she said is completely normal.

Scooter can't take his eyes off her.

The class is a survey of twentieth century American literature. The professor ends his introduction with, "I am grateful and excited to share this journey with you." That hadn't occurred to Scooter before, the journey part. But he thinks it is right.

The students smile and nod. Scooter steals a glance at Misty. Her red backpack is at her feet. On it are sewn Black Flag and Descendents patches. And some patches of cats. She is wearing red low-top Chuck Taylors with no socks.

She bounces her heel up and down, resting the palms of her hands on her knee. Her nails are painted black. At the end of class, she looks over her shoulder at Scooter.

After class, Scooter humps his way back down the hill to Dairy Sciences 101. The Dairy Sciences building is attached to what is essentially a working farm—although there are only about thirty milking cows—and a working dairy that produces its own ice cream. Scooter smells the familiar scents of hay and manure as he hustles to class; his legs feeling the strain of practice. The classroom is modern white with stadium seating backing up from a long white countertop with a stainless-steel gas fitting at one end and behind that a multipanel white board. Sitting in the stadium seats are about forty students straight out of 4H. Scooter feels like he knows them all. The boys wear Packers and Badgers T-shirts and pressed Wrangler or Lee jeans. The girls are in pleated jeans or long skirts with floral print tops. None of the hair in the room is styled. They have crisp, stiff-looking backpacks with new binders, pens, and notebooks. The professor has on a stiff button-down shirt with a Cargill Seed logo and brand-new jeans.

"This class is going to examine new methods of herd management," he announces as Scooter sits down. "I know you all, or at least most of you, think you know how farming works and the right way to do it," he snickers. "Prepare to have your minds blown. And please keep an open mind."

Scooter looks at the dork and has serious doubts that there is anything this man could say that would blow his mind. But he settles back and buckles up for the ride.

After a riveting explanation of goat dietary preferences that fell short of blowing Scooter's mind, class mercifully ends. The Dairy Science building is close to Birch. Time to shovel in some more calories before afternoon strength and conditioning.

Mrs. Winchester is still atwitter. She has roasted several hams and scalloped pan after pan of potatoes. There are also pans of steamed green beans, and baked fresh bread that liquefies butter upon contact. Scooter takes the back corner table and enough bread and ham for three sandwiches with two glasses of milk to wash it all down. He cracks *The Great Gatsby* and turns pages between chews, ignoring the players coming in, all looking a little shell-shocked from managing the first day of classes and practice before a game that is undoubtedly the most important one of any of their lives.

At the Nat, Harrelson has the room prepared for mediation, and Scooter thinks that a nap would feel just about great right now. He arranges towels for padding and neatly rolls two for a makeshift pillow.

Harrelson bends down and says, "You, more than anyone, need to stay awake for this. More than you know, son, this is a key to playing well." He ends with, "PMA, ya gotta wanna!" in a rushed, slurred mumble. He stands in front of the group and presses play on the boom box as he stoops and slinks out of the room, theatrically bobbing his head. He is, undoubtedly, off to smoke a heater in the afternoon sun among the oak trees next to the lake path behind the Nat.

Scooter gives it a shot. He flexes, then relaxes his muscles in descending order from his forehead down to his feet, ultimately pointing his toes and then relaxing them. He listens to the half-whispered, slow tones of the narrator or yogi or whatever the name is of the spiritual guide taking him through the exercise. As it ends, Harrelson reemerges to turn on the lights. The players sit up, rub their eyes, and stretch. Scooter actually feels good. More awake and relaxed than he was before.

The last class of the day is Biology. It is mercifully on the west side of campus in the science quadrangle. It is a requirement for Scooter and taught in a huge lecture hall. There are easily over one hundred freshmen finding seats and looking around the room. Scooter looks up the slope of the amphitheater of desks and sees Diana in the second to last row sitting next to another cheerleader. She is perfectly put together in a black skirt, white blouse and gray sweater. Scooter beelines up the stairs and turns sidewise to negotiate the narrow gap between rows of seats. He takes the seat next to Diana, cramming his huge legs under the white counter that runs the arcing length of each row of seats.

"Well, Diana Dillinger, the pride of Famechon Ridge! To what do I owe this honor?"

Diana rolls her eyes. "I see you didn't bother dressing up for class."

He laughs. He reaches into his bag and takes out a notepad. TAs are walking up the aisles handing out syllabi. Then Misty appears. She slides into the aisle on the side opposite the one Scooter entered. She shimmies past Diana and turns as she passes Scooter. Her breasts are lifting her shirt a little bit above the waist of her pants to reveal a taut stomach and a bellybutton piercing.

"Hey," she says, "mind if I sit here?"

"No, be my guest." Scooter finds himself sitting between

Diana and Misty. He tries to act nonchalant. *This is college. We are all just people.* He focuses on his breathing, like the yogi says.

Diana looks at him, narrows her eyes, leans into him and whispers. "Do you know her?"

"Not really, she's in my English class."

Diana smiles a rictus grin; Scooter can see the muscles in her jaw twist and build pressure between her molars. He nods, sighs, and takes out his pen.

THAT EVENING, AFTER SPENDING ALMOST TWO HOURS looking at the Michigan defense on film with Harrelson, he goes straight to Liz Waters. Diana is in sweatpants and a half shirt, sitting cross-legged on her bed. She has books spread out in front of her, but she is on the phone. She waves him in. The bedsprings creak as he lowers his mass on the end of the bed. She is describing classes and her professors and the number of students and the bell tower and what she had for lunch and cheer practice and will she stay on the squad and how she needs to go shopping. Scooter realizes he forgot to call Pierre and tell him he has been named the starter. But after Diana's body language in Biology, he knew he needed to come over here and show that she is the most important thing in his life. He leans back on the bed and tunes out the call. *This could take a while.* He closes his eyes and starts going through his play calls, the different offensive sets and defensive reads, and tells of the Michigan cornerbacks and safeties. He wakes to Diana slamming dresser doors. He props himself up on his elbows.

"I'm going out! Apparently, I can't even hold your attention when we are in the same room."

Scooter drops his chin to his chest. "I'm sorry. I guess I dozed off. I am here because I want to spend time with you. I came straight here after film study."

"Well, it looked like today you might want to spend some time with that punk slut. Scooter, I could have gone to Princeton. I am here to be with you. You better not make me regret it!"

"Babe, I'm yours. Trust me, you will never regret it. Look at you, you're Diana Dillinger, the pride of Famechon Ridge! The cream of the…"

Diana slows down and sits back on the bed. She leans into him and puts her head on his chest. "Everyone wants a piece of you."

Scooter shakes his head. "I don't give a shit about any of that. I am here to do one thing. Well, two. Kick ass and take your panties off."

Diana groans and pulls his head down to hers to kiss him on the lips.

He wakes to blue moonlight. From the window, he can see the moon's pale path across the lake. He rolls onto his feet, slowly, so as to not wake Diana, pulls on his sweatpants, T-shirt, and flip-flops, and slowly opens the door. The quiet of the early morning is haunting. Squirrels are scampering here and there, their claws skittering and clattering on the trunks of oak trees. He can hear, even from the high bluff on which the dorm is perched, the light lapping of waves put into motion somewhere in the middle of the lake, or even on the other side, eventually journeying across to slap the shore. The sun has not yet stirred. He is cold in just a T-shirt, and he can see his breath. He picks up the pace, wishing he had tennis shoes on. He gets to Birch in time to see Mrs. Winchester entering the front door. He hangs back to avoid an awkward conversation, but she hears the slapping of his flip-flops and turns to see him plodding across the small parking lot.

"Scooter! You frightened me, you naughty boy. Why are you up so early?"

"Oh, just couldn't sleep, thought a walk might help."

"Are you worried about the big game?" He can tell his pending answer concerns her; she is a little flushed and holds the door open as he starts up the steps.

"No, Mrs. Winchester, I'm used to getting up early to milk cows. My body just doesn't let me sleep late." He can tell this answer absolutely thrills her.

"Well, what do you want for breakfast sweetie? I can make anything you want."

"Oh, thanks. Maybe eggs and toast…"

"That sounds lovely," she says as she glides down the steps, ready for her mission.

Scooter ascends to his room and delicately inserts his key. He slowly opens the door. Ferris is sound asleep and snoring. The stereo is on and emits a sort of electronic hiss across the room, the tape having spun out its length hours ago. Scooter notices the volume is turned up to about eight. It is four in the morning. Scooter sets his alarm and settles in to try to get an hour and a half of sleep.

Chapter 13

SEPTEMBER 6, 1986

There is a crispness to the light as Scooter and Ferris walk from Birch to Camp Randall. The parking lots are filling up and the fans are opening their tailgates, spreading out whiskey, cherries, bitters, Squirt soda, and of course, beer. The smell of just-lit charcoal swirls through the air, spicing the morning air. On Breese Terrace, bordering the stadium, students have stereos out on their porches. Kegs have been tapped. Girls with red and white overalls and nothing but a bra underneath are dancing to "Thunder-struck." It is eight thirty in the morning. Ferris smiles and shakes his head.

"This is what we're here for, man!" Ferris says.

Scooter, for the first time he can remember before a game, feels a little tightness in his chest. He also feels a lightness in his stomach, like when it drops out driving too fast over the hills on the ridge road. It is going to be a long two and a half hours before kickoff.

They make their way past security and get into the locker room. The position coaches are gathering their charges to go out onto the field for warm-ups.

Harrelson asks Scooter, "Well Scoot, how'd you sleep?"

Scooter nods. He really just wants to hit something. Hard.

The receivers and quarterbacks jog onto the field and Harrelson leads them through their usual stretches, high knees, butt kicks, toe touches. They run some half-speed forty-yard shuttles, and then Scooter throws passes in the end zone with an assistant coach next to him feeding him balls. He alternates throws to his right and left as the wide-outs half-jog, half-run their routes.

They go back into the locker room about an hour before kickoff. Some guys get rubdowns by trainers before putting on their pads and stretching their uniforms over that exo-skeleton. Scooter gets his kit on and sits at his locker, staring straight ahead. He thinks through the plays and play calls, scrolling through the playbook in his mind's eye.

Coach Peregrine struts into the room with a clipboard in one hand. He is, as always, wearing Dickies and has on a bright red windbreaker, with a white baseball cap with a big "W" on it. He stands in the middle of the locker room. The players sit in front of their lockers. Peregrine waits for complete silence. As he does, he slowly turns around the room, looking every single player in the eye. He finishes with Scooter and then starts speaking softly.

"They think they're better than you." He shakes his head as he says it, softly, almost sadly. He says it a little louder, at a conversational level. "They think they're better than you." He goes on repeating the line, getting a little louder each time until he is practically screaming it, gesticulating wildly, his eyes swimming around the room, his face getting as red as his wind breaker.

"Well, I have never seen a goddamn better team than sits in here right now!"

Scooter can feel the goosebumps creeping up his legs and down his arms.

"I would go to battle with you men any day. Show them. Show the fucking world! This is the best football team in the country. Let's get out there and take what is ours. Bring it in!"

By the end, everyone is standing in the center, jumping up and down and screaming. The players would storm the beaches at Normandy behind their coach without a stutter step. They run through the tunnel and onto the field like primitive warriors eagerly facing a sure death. As they break through into the sunlight, the piercing brass sound of the trumpets from the band shrieks across the stadium and the roar of the crowd builds. Everyone in the stands is on their feet, all in red.

Scooter steps up to the line for the first play. He can hear the Michigan defensive lineman lined up only a few yards away from him. They are all big, strong, and fast. They grunt like stallions, reined back, waiting for the bite of spur into their sides. Scooter calls out an option left. He can either run the ball or flip it to the running back. As he takes the ball from the center, he already knows what he is going to do. He runs down the line, turns upfield, and lowers his shoulder into the sternum of a pursuing linebacker, knocking him backward. As Scooter's shoulder meets the linebacker's chest, the crack of plastic pads is audible in the stands. Scooter can feel and hear the air from the linebacker's lungs rush out of his body. He sees surprise in the other man's eyes. The game is, for all practical purposes, already over. Maybe it always was.

BY THE TIME THE FINAL WHISTLE BLOWS AND THE BAND storms the field, along with the students who are pushing down from the top of the stands, the excitement is over for

Scooter. It was really over after that first play. After that, he knew he would win. The bouncing fans and band members slapping him on the shoulder pads seem trite to him.

But Scooter plays the part. He smiles, gives high-fives, puts his arm around Ed, and smacks Butch on the ass. He looks for the opposing quarterback and half-looks for Luke, but it is a complete mob scene on the field. The band is now playing the Bud Song, but not in formation, just kind of polkaing in random spots as students run around and muster an attack on a goal post. Scooter has his helmet in his hand and starts walking toward the tunnel to the locker room. He looks over to the sideline and sees Harrelson's eyes bordered by a latticework of wrinkles. Harrelson gives Scooter a wink.

Scooter sits down at his locker. Breath and tension flow out of him. He strips off his jersey and unlaces his pads. More players are running into the locker room whooping, jumping, throwing Gatorade in the air. Scooter lets it swirl around him and smiles. Ferris sits at the locker next to Scooter's.

"We are going to get shitfaced tonight!" Ferris screams.

Coach Peregrine gives a solemn speech explaining to them the importance of what just happened. After their showers, the players slather on Aqua Velva and Stetson with Boston blaring from the team room stereo. Plans are made and circulated, and the excitement of the game is replaced with the anticipation of the night—they will be celebrated as heroes. That is what most of them want out of this.

WAITING BEYOND THE PLAYER'S ENTRANCE ARE SCOOT-er's mom, who is speaking to Diana, and his dad standing to the side, leaning against something. Other parents and players and a few reporters are milling about too. His dad is impatient.

"Jesus, you could have hustled a bit, we still have a drive, boy."

"Sorry, dad," Scooter smiles.

"Well, I guess those Michigan guys are softer than I thought."

Scooter smiles more and his dad smacks him on the back. Pierre is fidgety with energy. Scooter can tell his dad is excited from the game but also ready to get back to the farm that he is seldom allowed to leave. Scooter kisses his mom and puts his arm around Diana as they march toward the parked pickup that will carry the Lariouxs back to Famechon Ridge. Scooter walks to the driver's side of the truck as his parents get in.

"Donny'll probably have burned the whole place down, time we get back," his dad says with a shake of his head.

"Tell him hi," Scooter says.

"Will do."

And with that the brown pickup navigates its way out of the parking lot, dodging tailgaters as it has dodged loitering cattle before. The truck turns west and drives toward the already setting sun, finding the road back to Prairie.

Scooter puts his other arm around Diana and kisses her as he picks her up off the ground. She laughs. They set off toward Birch.

"Where is this all going, Scooter? What can't you do?"

He winks. "Well, I suppose I can't do most things other than play football."

Chapter 14

SEPTEMBER 7, 1986

S cooter has always been famous. Every day of his life he's been around people who know who he is. In Prairie, even if people didn't know Pierre, and most did, they knew of Scooter. As he grew, the talk at lunch counters, gas stations, and feed mills spread about the man-child living up on the ridge. So the week after Michigan isn't exactly a surprise to him, or even that new. It is just that the magnitude is that much greater. He catches teachers staring at him in class and can't make it out of a building without someone yelling his name. He isn't surprised by it. He doesn't admit to himself that he likes it.

He has found routine in the schedule that at first seemed so frantic, but now is like breathing. Practice, class, read, nap, practice, study, Diana…

Northern Illinois is their next opponent. After the climax of beating Michigan, it is hard for the Badgers to get that motivated for a team that is just hoping to not get shut out. In the quarterback-receiver practices, they work on new plays and put in different formations and personnel packages. What everyone expects to be a rout will be a good time to expand the playbook and get more players some experience. That could help later in the season.

Friday before the game, Scooter opens the door to his room at Birch to find Ferris ripping bongs to the scratchy island rhythms of Bob Marley and the Wailers. Ferris is wearing only sunglasses and cutoff jeans. The reggae party clashes with the autumn scene outside—the early setting sun and the yellow and red leaves collecting in the corners of the parking lot below. Scooter just laughs and shakes his head. Ferris tips the bong toward Scooter and raises his eyebrows; Scooter shakes his head.

"Mon, someday, you're gonna find out that this is your salvation, mon, me and you mon. Ire mon…what's going on, you gettin' stoked for tomorrow?"

"Yeah, feeling ready…" It's not that Scooter isn't excited to play. But he has never gotten caught up in the fanfare. He is not someone to get stoked to play; to jump around and thump his chest. He doesn't need to do all that.

"I can only imagine what it is to be you." Ferris is actually trying to be serious now. "You come from Hicksville to this school and without even missing a beat, you put us in the conversation for the national championship. Every guy wants to be you. Every girl wants to fuck you. You are a living god; you should enjoy it! And let me enjoy it with you mon!"

Scooter smiles politely. He has heard versions of his spiel before. The thing is, he doesn't really care about what all of this means to anyone else. He didn't choose to be who he is. It just happened. He doesn't play football to reap some reward given after he wins. He would play anyway. He is meant to do it. He knows that. He's good at it. The best really. He likes to run around and hit people. It is that simple to him. Or at least, that's what he thinks.

Ferris looks down and shakes his head. "What is this? Are you complaining, or moping about all this…"

Scooter starts to interrupt him, because he's not. He likes football and he likes being good at it. But Ferris doesn't understand. Everyone has an opinion about what Scooter does at any given moment. There is very little he can ever decide for himself. He's pissed that someone like Ferris, who does whatever the fuck he wants, would not only not see that, but would now, like every other fucking person on the planet, try to tell him how he should feel about being himself. But before he can try to explain all that, as if he could, Ferris continues.

"You have an unbelievable gift that many would give their right nut for. You have amazing opportunities because of it. If you are feeling sorry for yourself for a single minute, cut it. The fuck. Out." He hands Scooter the bong. "Seriously, you need a hit of this because you need to change your mind state."

Scooter shakes his head in frustration, but takes the bong anyway—it seems easier than getting into a big discussion—and kisses his lips to the weathered, resin-tinted plastic. Ferris lights the bowl and Scooter starts to suck. He has seen Ferris do this enough times to know how it goes. Ferris moves the lighter away, and after the tube fills with smoke, he slides the bowl out. Scooter pulls his head back and puffs out a cloud of smoke.

"No, no, no, mon!" says Ferris. "You have to inhale. You have to pull the smoke down deep into your lungs." Ferris demonstrates by taking exaggeratedly big breaths. He points at his belly moving out and then in. "It's all in the diaphragm, mon!"

Scooter tries again. This time, he breathes in deeply with his mouth at the top of the bong. The smoke rushes into Scooter's huge lungs. It feels like a chemical attack, like he has inhaled nettles. He coughs. He can't stop coughing. He spends the next hour wondering if he feels high or not.

The next morning, Ferris and Scooter are roused from their slumber by the smell of grilling sausages and the noise of trucks, campers, and cars jockeying for position in the sea of parking lots between the dorms and the stadium. It is eight o'clock, and they have an hour to get dressed and get to the stadium for the team meal. Scooter rubs his eyes. Ferris is up out of his bed, queuing up a Grateful Dead bootleg.

"It's a wonderful day to kick some Illinois ass—Northern Illinois ass at that. Let's get some!"

Scooter shakes the cobwebs from his head, finds his way to his feet, and puts on his sweats. Ferris takes the bong and pulls a couple of quick hits and then hands it to Scooter.

"Right Ferris, let's at least keep up the appearance of propriety. You may have caught me at a weak point last night, but I'm not getting high on game day."

"Suit yourself, Kemosabe."

Lot 40, the expansive lot just south of the lakeshore dorms, is fuller than one would expect at eight o'clock for an eleven o'clock game. At least some of the tailgaters are clued into the possibility that Scooter might be walking through that very parking lot on his way to the stadium. It makes for an interesting walk. Scooter, for the most part, keeps his eyes down and his hat brim low. Ferris takes a slightly different approach, yelling back at each cheer or shout of encouragement.

"Go get 'em Scooter!" some yell.

Ferris responds, "Goddamn right, he's gonna gettum!"

"Good luck, Scooter!"

"Luck?" Ferris shouts, "This boy don't need luck! Look at 'em, he's like a Brahman Bull. You should be asking him to take mercy on all of us!"

Scooter can't help but laugh at that. By the time they get to University Avenue and wait to cross the street, there are a good twenty fans surrounding them.

Inside the locker room everyone is loose and excited, joking about weekend plans or this or that cheerleader, or making bets about the score. They load up on pancakes and fruit and bacon and eggs and juice and coffee. It is obvious that this is not a pressure game. Northern Illinois has never beaten the Badgers in eleven tries. This is not the year for exceptions, not with a team that's a preseason contender for the Big Ten Championship pleasantly and surprisingly gifted with a seemingly invincible quarterback who just ran through what everyone thought was the best team in the country. Even Coach Harrelson is joking around. Having just stepped in from burning a heater, he regales the players with his Nixon impersonation, holding his two fingers up, mirroring the V of his arms above his head, jutting his head with his turkey neck forward and shaking his head from side to side.

"I. Am. Not. A. Crooooook."

Everyone laughs. Ferris about spits out his coffee.

Then Coach Peregrine steps into the room. He is wearing deep maroon Dickies. They are so tight that despite the thickness of the material they are essentially flush with his flesh. His shirt is a clashing red polo with crease marks as if it was just taken out of plastic wrapping. He looks around and throws a cup of coffee against the wall.

"You pansy asses want to be embarrassed?! Do you want to embarrass me? Is that what's going on here? Is that what you're up to?"

"It's like he's a paranoid schizophrenic, thinking that we are all conspiring against him," Ferris whispers to Scooter.

Scooter waves him off and sees Peregrine's eyes dart in their direction, detecting noise and perhaps dissenting opinion.

"There are some big men, as big as you puny fuckers, in the other room over there." He gestures wildly to the wall separating the visiting and home locker rooms. "Right now, they are punching their lockers, eating red meat, swearing at their mothers, ready to tear your fucking limbs off and beat you to death with them."

Ferris is trying desperately not to laugh at this point. The weed is starting to kick in. He starts coughing to cover the laughter about to spill forth.

Peregrine slams his fist on the Formica top of one of the round tables, rattling dishware and silverware and spilling coffee.

Harrelson rushes to clean it up.

"Leave! It! God! Damn! It!" Peregrine sweeps the plates and cups off the table with his arm and they crash to the floor.

Ferris can't handle it. The laughter is about to explode out of him. He uses his tried and trusty method of faking a bloody nose by suddenly tilting his head back and putting his palm up to one of his nostrils. He rushes into the bathroom area of the locker room.

The rest of the team stares at Coach Peregrine with their mouths wide open. The room is silent, except for the sound of Ferris turning on water and occasionally stifling a cough from the bathroom.

The coach regains his composure and tries to make eye contact with each of his players. Ultimately, inevitably, his eyes come to rest on Scooter. Coach Peregrine gets quieter.

"It feels good to have reached the mountain top. Doesn't it? Men, you can't act like you're there. You can't enjoy it. They are all trying to take it from you, every fucking one of them. Every day you need to prove yourself. Every fucking day. Now, these fuckers from Illinois. These FIBs. They aren't in your league. They aren't as good as you. Shit, Scooter you could probably score a touchdown carrying Eddie over your shoulder. But you know what? They will try to kill you. They will try with everything in their pathetic bodies and souls. You can't let them. You must fight. Let's take what's ours. Let's win this shit, goddammit. LET'S GO!"

With that Coach Peregrine slams his meaty fist down again on the same abused table, rattling what's left of its contents. The team starts making rhythmic, guttural grunts. Butch starts headbutting a locker. Everyone is getting to their feet; jumping, letting the energy flow through them. Coach Peregrine starts heading to the tunnel. The players are practically excreting adrenaline. They gather their helmets and control their rage and energy enough not to stampede their coach as they surge through the choke point of the tunnel leading to the field. As soon as they emerge from the tunnel onto the field, the crowd noise erupts, Coach Peregrine peels to the right, into the ranks of the band, and the marauding horde behind him spreads and surges across the field screaming like possessed, wounded warriors ready to make their last stand.

THE WORLD CHANGES ON THE FIRST PLAY FROM SCRIMMAGE. It starts out typically enough. Scooter drops back and looks at Ed, running a short out route. He is locked up by double coverage. There is a linebacker floating in the middle of the field watching Scooter's eyes. Scooter pumps and the linebacker takes a step back. Scooter rolls to his right as the right defensive end breaks contain and starts running toward him. Scooter sidesteps the left end and breaks to the outside. The left outside linebacker runs with him toward the sideline and then dives at his feet. Scooter, gracefully, jumps over the linebacker and turns his body in midair, ready to explode down the sideline with nothing but fearful, gnat-like cornerbacks in his path. As he lands, Scooter's left foot twists slightly and catches a loose section of turf, his cleat snags. His body continues forward, but his foot stays where it is, caught in the carpet. Scooter goes down. His knee hurts. But not a catastrophic pain. It feels like the pain of a dentist filling a cavity and just barely touching a nerve. There is a spark, a twinge; something is wrong. But it is not catastrophic.

Scooter trots back to the huddle.

"You okay, champ?" Eddie asks.

"Yeah, no big deal."

But it is. On the next play Scooter steps back and plants to throw. The knee moves. Not buckles but moves to the side. The throw is wild, and Scooter grabs his knee. He falls back onto his butt and closes his eyes. He can feel the afternoon sun and smell the cut hay. He can hear and smell the diesel engine from the tractor and just see the back of Pierre's John Deere cap silhouetted by the sun as he pulls the haybine down another row. Then Scooter sees Diana's tanned, long legs running through the fields.

He opens his eyes and the vision evaporates. Staring at him are 72,093 sets of eyes. Everyone is quiet. The trainers are running toward him, and he can see, to his horror, Luke on the sideline flip back his sandy bangs and put on his helmet. Luke is bouncing back and forth from foot to foot like a dancing orangutang. Scooter imagines ripping the bangs right off the phony's head. Then, the trainers are upon Scooter like wolves on a wounded deer, grabbing his calf and pulling it away from his upper leg.

"Feels like an ACL," they say and nod and sigh.

The trainers help Scooter to the sideline and hoist him into a golf cart. He is whisked into the training room with its leather-covered examination tables and cabinets full of bandages, wraps, salves, balms, and needles.

AFTER THE GAME, FERRIS FINDS SCOOTER SITTING IN A metal tub filled with ice water. The tub reminds Scooter of the galvanized water troughs scattered among the ravines between the pastures at home. Scooter has a distant gaze in his eyes. Worry lines crease his brow and his jaw is set, the jaw muscle moving up and down as it flexes.

"How's it going, champ?" Ferris asks.

Scooter heard the PA call the game as he was being examined and then summarily dumped in the icy water and knows that Luke stepped in to throw four touchdowns in an absolute rout.

"They say it's probably my ACL. More tests and x-rays tomorrow, but it looks like I'm on ice and in ice for a while." Scooter speaks in between the clenching of his jaw in total deadpan. He can't believe this has happened. His body has never let him down before. He has never even thought about it.

Ferris pats him on the shoulder a couple of times and walks back to the main locker room to change.

Scooter watches in a disembodied stupor as the trainers help him out of the bath, put an icepack on his knee, and wrap it to keep the ice in place. The trainers give Scooter crutches and strict instructions to ice again before bed and return to the training room first thing in the morning. After the trainers finish, Coach Peregrine steps into the room. He has on slacks and a red V-neck sweater with a W embroidered on the left breast. No doubt he is on his way to the University Club to enjoy a rib eye, some old-fashioneds, and some "Attaboys." Peregrine looks down at Scooter on the training table and sighs.

"Tough break, kid."

Scooter looks up to meet his eyes. Peregrine says nothing more. The look in Peregrine's eyes tells Scooter everything he needs to know. Peregrine has already moved on. The freshman who seemed too good to be true turned out to be just that. Peregrine nods a few times and then walks out to his Saturday night victory celebration.

The wind is up, carrying a musty smell coming from the lake. Scooter's knee is cold as he negotiates the crutches and the bundled leg out the back entrance with Ferris next to him. Diana is sitting on a bench waiting. When she sees Scooter crutch out the door, she lets out an audible gasp. She comes over and touches his arm as if he might break.

"Babe, what is it?"

He can see tears welling up in her eyes. Scooter says, "My knee."

She has no words, only watery doe eyes and disbelief. They make their way slowly to Birch. No one says a thing. Scooter sits on the bed. He shakes his head and stares at Ferris's Grateful Dead '72 poster on the wall, looking for some kind of sign.

"Listen, if you guys want to go to the party, I'm fine. I won't be any fun anyway, and I need to ice this thing again later."

Diana is next to him with her hand on his good leg. "I'll do whatever you want babe, we will get through this. I will help you."

Scooter half-smiles, tightly. He doesn't know what to make of any of this. He just knows everything has changed. "Well, I am definitely staying in tonight. And I won't be any fun. I just need to let all of this sink in," he says.

"Whatever you want, babe." Diana seems relieved as she moves to get up.

Ferris lies down on his bed. "No way, Kemosabe, I'm not going anywhere. Plus, the last thing I want to do is watch the extent to which those fucking phonies, like Butch and those other meatheads, lovingly kiss Luke's entitled ass."

"Suit yourself," Scooter says.

"I'll be back tomorrow morning. Sleep well baby, this will all be fine." Diana kisses Scooter and pulls a white sweater over her bare shoulders as she heads out the door.

Ferris reaches into the cabinet under the sink and pulls out his bong and a plastic sandwich bag filled with weed. "There is only one way that we can get through this Kemosabe, and we're going to do it together." Ferris packs the bowl and hands the bong to Scooter, who is still sitting on his bed.

"Well, I guess I have nothing to lose at this point." Scooter takes a pull from the bong and passes it back while reclining on his bed. He both sees and hears the individual notes plucked by Jerry in some arena a decade or so ago as Ferris turns up the volume and pulls a couple of beers from the dorm fridge.

Chapter 15

SEPTEMBER 14, 1986

The sweat on the back of Scooter's neck is glistening in the morning sun by the time he hobbles on crutches from Birch to Camp Randall and into the training room. Josh is there, along with other trainers whose names he doesn't remember. Josh looks earnestly into his eyes as if Scooter is some kind of refugee kid or something.

"We will get through this together; you will be back stronger than ever."

Scooter just looks at him. He hasn't even thought of the future given all of this or what any of it means. He's still just surprised it happened.

The trainers and team doctors come over, and Josh steps back as they again grab Scooter's lower leg and start manipulating it. Scooter lies back on the table and closes his watering eyes, letting the trainers do their thing. Finally, the prodding seems to diminish, and Scooter feels a hand on his shoulder. The head team doctor, Dr. Englund, who is wearing a white coat with a stethoscope around his neck, speaks to Scooter now almost as earnestly as Josh did before.

"Scooter, I am sorry to tell you that I am reasonably certain that you have torn your anterior cruciate ligament, which is a ligament in your knee that is important for stability. We are going take you to the hospital now for some additional testing, but I can tell you with a high degree of confidence that our recommendation will be surgery. I want to prepare you for that."

They haul Scooter into an athletic department van and drive the few blocks to University Hospital, where they put him in a wheelchair and negotiate the labyrinth of floors until they come to the orthopedic department. Scooter goes through more testing, with the doctors using all their strength to grasp his mammoth calves and yank on his leg. After an x-ray and a CT scan, the diagnosis is confirmed, and Scooter sits in an examination room with a high-strung surgeon and Dr. Englund.

"Without the surgery, you will never play at the same level you did." The surgeon, Dr. Matzke, is talking a mile a minute. "We have gotten much better at this type of reconstruction and have seen athletes return to the playing field within eighteen months at almost full speed. I suggest you talk to your parents and decide quickly. We would like to do this next week."

Scooter sits on the examination table having an out of body experience. The hospital gown barely covers his massive frame. He tips his face down into his hands feeling the two days of stubble, now almost soft on his fingers.

What the fuck? How is this happening? he thinks. He picks up his head and nods at Dr. Matzke and Dr. Englund to signal that he understands what they are saying. The truth is, Scooter's not sure what he feels. He doesn't feel sorry for himself, mad at the world—none of that. He just feels numb, and not just a little surprised that his body has failed him. If he's honest, he thought that this kind of thing couldn't happen to him.

A WEEK AND A DAY LATER, HE IS ON THE SAME FLOOR, in a similar room, with the same astringent smell, surrounded again by Dr. Matzke, Dr. Englund, and various nurses. As the initial sedatives start to set in and he relaxes, he sees them peering down at him as if he is some rhino just toppled on the African Savanna. He can feel the cool sting of isopropyl alcohol on his left leg as they prepare him for shaving. A nurse washes him with an iodine solution as the anesthesiologist helps him count backward from ten.

He wakes up to see Diana fumbling around with some balloons and Ferris awkwardly trying to make small talk with Scooter's mom as his dad gazes out the window. He has seen that gaze before. It is the ten-mile stare of a man who wants to be somewhere else. Now, in early fall, Pierre should be harvesting corn or putting it up for silage. There is work that needs to be done, and he helps no one sitting in a hospital room waiting for his broken son to wake up. Diana sees Scooter stir. She comes over to his side and gives him a kiss. Everyone turns his way.

"How are you feeling, baby?" Diana says through a forced grin.

Scooter's throat is dry and scratchy. He asks for water. He is tired. "I can't feel my leg," he says.

"Well, we told them it would be just as simple to lop it off." The crow's feet around Pierre's eyes crease and dance, and the narrow blue eyes spark like flint.

"Why aren't you at work, old man?" Scooter ventures, the crushed ice loosening his throat.

Pierre's voice is a little quieter now, a little less playful. "Why aren't you?"

Chapter 16

OCTOBER 4, 1986

Scooter is in Birch trying to get through the reading that has piled up during his convalescence. It is still warm enough to have the window open. The slight chill that has come with the turning leaves is superior to the dank smell of sweaty laundry, bong water, and dried beer. Outside, Scooter hears a commotion. It sounds as if someone is screaming the *Star Wars* theme. He grabs a crutch and moves to the window.

His entire leg is in a nylon and steel brace that extends up to his hip. It is connected to a boot over the foot and lower leg. The doctors told him he could put some weight on it, but he should be careful and use crutches when walking for the first few weeks. The leg feels odd. He feels pinpricks of pain from time to time and a sort of sticky sweet ache that pulses through his bones. He hates the whole appendage.

He reaches the window. Sure enough, someone is screaming the *Star Wars* theme. Ferris is on a matte-black Honda scooter, revving the engine and spinning the back tire while riding around and around the circle drive in front of Birch. He sees Scooter in the window.

"My liege," he screams, "your chariot awaits!"

Scooter shakes his head and sits down at the desk. *How did I wind up with this freak?* He wonders. He picks up *Light in August* and tries to find where he left off when Ferris bangs open the door.

"Dude, come check it out!"

Scooter just stares at him. Ferris is wearing a tie-dyed T-shirt with cutoff sleeves and khaki pants also cut off just above the ankle. For some reason, he is also wearing wristbands and a headband.

"I got some guys to throw in an old moped and took a couple hundred off their QP."

This is gibberish to Scooter, but he assumes it refers to selling weed. Some connection of Ferris's had driven out from California and dropped off a duffle bag full of pot that Ferris had been quickly distributing all over campus.

"This is perfect for you to get around while you're in that brace. No more crutching it, champ!"

Scooter shakes his head at Ferris's enthusiasm and begrudgingly reaches for his crutch to head downstairs.

It occurs to Scooter that Ferris might be right. The moped could be the answer to Scooter's prayers. He has to wear the full boot for at least the next three weeks, and the prospect of continuing to gimp around campus (or riding in Ferris's Grand Marquis) is a little worrying.

Ferris holds the moped handlebars as Scooter lowers his bulk onto the long seat. The moped sinks about six inches but doesn't bottom out. If Scooter sits at the back of the seat, he can just fit his booted foot onto the running board without having to flex his knee. He turns the key and the little engine starts with a whine. Scooter twists the throttle and with a few wobbles negotiates around the circle drive.

After lunch and his agriculture class, Scooter meets Josh in the gym at the Nat. This will be his new routine. Class and afternoon training/rehab with Josh and occasionally Dr. Englund. Because Scooter is stuck in a brace and a boot, there is not much rehabilitation he can really do. Not much aerobic work he can do either. He crutches across the room as Josh turns up the boombox churning out the opening power chords of "Walk This Way."

Josh pumps his fits in the air and points rhythmically at Scooter. "Okay, champ! Today is the day we start to build the new terror that is going to come back and tear through this league like a freight train!"

Scooter starts at the bench, warming up with presses of two hundred and twenty-five pounds. Between sets, Josh adds weight until he eventually gets up to four hundred and fifty. It feels good to use his body again. It feels good to know that he is still strong; stronger than anyone else in the gym.

The sweat drying on the moped ride back to Birch cools Scooter down. He negotiates the stairs to the cafeteria without showering first. He takes two pieces of chicken-fried steak and a ladle of creamed spinach from Mrs. Winchester. The disappointment and unadulterated sadness are apparent in her eyes. Scooter smiles at her, but she just looks away, unable to meet his eyes. *What a nut*, he thinks. As he sits and eats, Ferris comes in.

"How is the Millennium Falcon, my captain?"

"Actually, it is helpful. What can I do to pay you back?" Scooter asks. Ferris's mouth pulls into a half grin.

"Funny you should ask. I can't be everywhere at once. I need to make some deliveries. Plus, those guys are coming back in a couple weeks or so. I need to get them their money and they are dropping off more shit. So it will be busy and I need help."

Scooter pauses for a beat. Fuck it, what does he have to lose? "Sure man, just tell me where to go and what to do."

Scooter is a little embarrassed pulling up to the apartment on Spring Street. *Are these guys going to recognize me? I am fucked if someone gets busted; everyone will remember me. Just two weeks removed from injury and now I'm fucking distributing drugs. How the mighty have fallen.* These are the thoughts banging against the front of his skull. He steps over, or more like swings his braced leg, over four bikes and countless beer bottles piled on the porch and knocks on the door. When the door is answered, Scooter thinks to himself, *well this guy isn't going to recognize me.*

He is a skinny, ratty thing with spiked hair, cutoff jeans, and a The Clash shirt that looks like the sleeves have been gnawed off by squirrels. He holds a large fork stuck into the middle of a still-bleeding steak. He looks up at Scooter and flashes his two broken front teeth.

He dons a British accent, "Top of the mornin', guvneh. Delivery for me?"

Scooter hands him a brick of herb wrapped in a plastic bag inside a brown paper bag. The Johnny Rotten lookalike hands him an envelope with five hundreds in it. Scooter counts it and starts to turn back toward the porch.

"Fancy a pint?" asks the wastrel as Scooter turns.

"Why not?" Scooter says, thinking that it is funny sometimes how people surprise you with friendliness.

The punk holds out his hand and says, "I'm Torbjorn." He leads Scooter through the living room, which is devoid of any furniture but for a badly battered leather sofa, toward the kitchen. Torbjorn hands Scooter a Point beer and continues walking out the back door to a gravel parking lot. There are six equally skinny and similarly dressed guys cooking steaks on a little hibachi grill in the middle of the gravel parking lot. They are squatting around the grill poking at steaks like the chimps in *2001: A Space Odyssey.* "London Calling" is blaring from a huge silver boom box.

Torbjorn pushes two of his compatriots to the side, picks up a fork, and stabs a steak with it. He rips it in half and hands half to Scooter. Scooter takes it and nods his appreciation. He is kind of hungry.

Torbjorn yells at him over the music, "You know, mate, we could use more of this shit," holding up the paper bag, "Anytime you're holding, drop by and pay a visit to me and the boys. We will take whatever you can get."

Scooter nods. "Good to know. I'll let Ferris know too."

Torbjorn says, "Any friend of Ferris is a friend of ours." He gestures dramatically around the parking lot as if it is a royal hall. Scooter downs his beer and chews on the steak. He tries to nod to the music but thinks everyone can tell he's not quite into it. He thanks Torbjorn and walks out through the apartment.

Chapter 17

OCTOBER 24, 1986

L inda Slama is a lifeguard at the Nat who Ferris has managed to pull into his orbit by sweet-talking her between
strength training and rubdowns. Linda lives in a six-story
walk-up apartment above Wando's, a campus bar that serves
drinks in fishbowls with multiple straws.

There is a fire escape that runs the length of the side of
the apartment building that overlooks a two-story bar, the
Red Shed. The fire escape stops at the fifth floor. At the last
fire-escape landing, there is a ladder mounted to the wall.
The ladder extends to the roof. The ladder is encircled by
a cylindrical cage-like cover that is closed at the top with
metal bars on a hinge secured with a padlock preventing
anyone from simply climbing up to the roof.

Linda decides to host a kegger on the Friday that Ferris's California connection is expected to roll into town.
Ferris and Scooter wait at Linda's for Ferris's weed delivery.
They take a couple of plastic chairs, a pitcher of beer, some
plastic cups, and a four-foot bong out onto the fire-escape
landing outside of an apartment window and sit in the fall
evening listening to the sounds of the city in full swing.
About halfway through the pitcher, the small talk runs out,
and the two sit staring at the roof of the Red Shed and its

perplexing trademark covered wagon. (Why is it there? This is Wisconsin, were there ever even covered wagons here? Why is it there?) Ferris, fed up with such unanswerable mysteries, stands up and looks at Scooter.

"This view sucks." He walks up to the fifth floor landing and climbs the ladder until the top of the cage stops his progress. Ferris contorts his torso outside of the cage, grabbing the concrete parapet that extends up above the roof. He swings his leg up over the side of the parapet and kind of rolls onto the roof. About two seconds later, he yells down, "C'mon man, it's awesome up here. Bring the beer and the bong!"

Scooter is somewhat less graceful hoisting his giant frame and bad leg, which now only has a knee brace, onto the parapet. He manages to swing his legs, one at a time, over the side and rolls, landing on his butt, onto the recessed roof. He stands up, dusts off his pants, and looks around. The roof is devoid of any structure or appurtenance. It is just a sun-bleached asphalt surface, with practically 360-degree views of the city, including the main thoroughfares and the masses of students walking among the various establishments that line those streets. The two hoist the chairs and bong up to the roof and sit with their feet propped on the parapet. They rip bong hits and climb down from time to time to fill the pitcher. Their movements grow more natural with each ascent and descent.

The party is starting to pick up, and there are about a dozen girls and guys (all Linda's friends) circulating through the apartment. Linda lives with an ex-diver, Sharon. She has a gymnast's body that her mom calls petite. It is petite enough that she can still ride the kiddie rides at the county fair. What she lacks in stature, she makes up for in confidence. The alcohol has enhanced this trait and induced a bouncing mania in her. She seems to be everywhere at once. She especially wants to be wherever Scooter is. She finds a way to make contact with some part of his body at every possible opportunity.

On one of Ferris and Scooter's trips down to refill the pitcher, she bounces into the two.

"Ferris, what is going on up there? I want to come!"

"Sharon, it's not an easy climb up there. There is no way you can reach. We'll try to go up sometime when you are sober, and I can show you how to do it."

Sharon gives Ferris puppy dog eyes while seductively pressing her ample bosom into Scooter.

"Seriously Sharon, do not try to come up. Enjoy your party."

The California dudes show up dusty and bleary-eyed from their cross-country trip. One has a big canvas backpack slung over his shoulder. They shake hands and slap shoulders with Ferris, who introduces them, Ronny and Jonny, to Scooter. They both look like surfers, with long hair and open shirts with shell necklaces. Ronny is the smaller of the two and does all the talking. Jonny is bigger with a build that says he surfs but also spends some time lifting weights. The four of them grab a couple of pitchers of beer, and Ferris and Scooter show the guys how to navigate up to their rooftop oasis. Ronny opens his bag, revealing several bricks of light green marijuana wrapped in clear plastic. The weed is still moist enough to have some spring to it when squeezed. The smell has a skunky note, but not too strong, as if there is a dead skunk on the side of the road but you haven't passed it just yet.

Ferris hands Ronny a wad of cash and they count it. Ronny hands Ferris a couple packages of weed, and Ferris puts them into his own backpack. Then everyone shakes hands. They pass the bong around. Jonny digs into his pocket and pulls out an empty cigarette cellophane. Inside it are tiny pieces of paper, like miniature stamps.

"You guys want to trip?"

"Yes, please," says Ferris, holding out his hand.

Scooter is nervous. He has obviously never tried anything harder than weed, and he has heard that LSD can make you insane. But a little voice inside his head says, "What the fuck? What have you got to lose?" He watches Ferris put the paper under his tongue, and he does the same. Then they all sit at the edge of the roof and watch the biker bar across the street fill up, waiting for the inevitable mayhem to break out.

At some point, Scooter realizes that the sharks he thinks he has been watching circle smaller fish in an urban reef environment are not that at all. They are cop cars doing laps around the parking lot across from the biker bar, also waiting for the mayhem. The sun is just now setting, and the colors are like nothing Scooter has ever seen. A deep orange line on the horizon seems to connect right to his stomach and sends warm waves through his body. He feels connected to the night. Connected to everything. He starts laughing.

They have gone through another pitcher of beer. Scooter feels no effect from the alcohol but cannot get enough to drink. He feels parched. He takes the pitcher and climbs over the side again, swinging onto the fire escape with a sort of reckless abandon he has not felt since his injury. Through the fire-escape window, he sees Diana. She looks amazing.

Her still tan legs telescope out of tight white denim shorts. She is wearing a cropped red Bucky Badger shirt with seemingly nothing underneath. She notices him, as does everyone else in the room, as he negotiates fitting his giant frame through the open window. He goes in headfirst. He puts his hands down on the floor and walks them into the room, never bending his braced knee. As he starts to stand up, he sees her staring at him in horror. *I must look a fright, all weird and wild and crippled,* he thinks. He is a shadow of the Adonis she fell in love with in high school.

He tries to mitigate the situation. He forces a huge grin onto his face and tells himself to act natural. His body interprets that message as an order to act anything but. He moves toward her like a lumbering robot. He is trying to control the movement of every muscle. As he gets closer, he says, "Hi babe, glad you made it," in kind of a theatrical whisper. He deliberately forms the words with his mouth to make sure he is correctly enunciating. This also doesn't work. The expression Scooter sees on Diana's face suggests she is looking at something crazed and wild. She leans away from him as he approaches.

"Scooter, you look like a mess. I can't be around you right now. I think I am going to head over to the Double F. I'll find you after the game tomorrow." She ducks his hug and straightens her top.

The heartbreak lasts one piercing instant. Then he shakes it off. He is having too much fun. He nods at her and gets the beer, then returns to the roof. Ronny and Jonny are loading up the bong. More partiers have found their way up to the roof, following Ferris and Scooter on one or another of their laps for beer. Eventually, there is a crowd of about twenty. Someone has brought up more plastic chairs, pilfered from makeshift porches on the fire-escape landings outside apartments.

As darkness falls, the party picks up in the apartment below and the night takes on an inky blue with electric accents vibrating all around them. The fire escape is crowded, like the line to make the final ascent on Everest, as partiers go up to the roof and back down for refills. Ferris finds a fishing pole in a closet and ties a beer can to the end, lowering it to the sidewalk to "fish" for bar hoppers. Scooter is lost in the aquarium of the night, watching the man o' war-shaped tentacles of light drooping from the lamps and the creatures swimming from place to place below in the inky blue depths of the night.

Suddenly the scene is shattered by Ferris yelling in deep, guttural staccato bursts from below.

"Get the fuck off the roof! Get the bong off the roof!"

Everyone scrambles and Scooter runs over to the fire-escape side of the building to see what is going on. Ferris continues to yell.

Scooter looks over the edge and sees Sharon lying flat on her back on the roof of the Red Shed, splayed out just behind the covered wagon. Scooter can't help but think that she looks like a settler caught unawares by a wild team of horses. His next thought is: *she must be dead.*

Ferris runs two levels down the fire-escape stairs and without breaking stride jumps over the side, clearing a railing and rolling onto the roof of the Red Shed. He gathers himself and runs toward Sharon, his lifeguard training kicking in.

Scooter finds the bong as the revelers scurry over the side of the roof like rats. Next to the bong are two backpacks. One has his and Ferris's weed—two pounds. The other is

Ronny and Jonny's, containing additional quantities, presumably to distribute on their cross-campus tour of Middle America. Next to that is the fishing pole. Scooter loops and ties the fishing line around the two backpacks. He puts the drag on full and casts the loot over the side of the building. He visually measures the distance of the bags from the ground to make sure that no mere mortal could reach the loot. Then he jams the pole into a crevice at the base of the parapet. He grabs the bong and rolls himself over the side of the building onto the fire escape, landing on his right leg to protect the braced one. He finds an empty planter on one of the landings and puts the bong inside it, concealing it with a garbage bag left out on another landing. He continues down another flight, grabs the fire-escape railing and swings over the side, lowering himself as far as he can. He drops down, landing one-legged on the roof of the Red Shed. He limps over to meet Ferris on the roof.

"Is she alive?" Scooter asks as he reaches Ferris.

Ferris is on his knees. He has one forearm under Sharon's head and upper neck and is stabilizing her neck while making sure her airway is open by using his thumb and forefinger to tilt back her chin. Just as Scooter asks, he can hear Sharon moaning.

"Don't move, Sharon, you are going to be fine," says Ferris.

A beam of light starts bouncing around them and blasts Ferris in the face.

Scooter stands up to his full six-foot-four frame, looks up at the fire escape, and yells, "Turn off that fucking annoying light."

The light stops moving and tips up, eventually resting on the face of a Madison police officer who peers at Scooter with narrow eyes and says, "You don't get to tell me what to do."

Scooter winces and says under his breath, "Well it is a fucking annoying light."

Within seconds, Scooter and Ferris are adrift in a sea of police and fire-rescue personnel. The fire-rescue crew takes over Ferris's position stabilizing Sharon's spine, and Ferris and Scooter take a couple of steps back to give the responders room. Miraculously, none of the cops ask for their names and conveniently they all fail to notice that Ferris and Scooter are tripping their balls off.

One of the officers even looks back at Ferris and says, "Nice job."

The responders stabilize Sharon on a backboard and hoist her up to the fire escape. In a matter of minutes, or even seconds, the police and the firemen and Sharon are gone. Scooter and Ferris are left standing on the roof of the Red Shed looking at the covered wagon.

Scooter sees a look of panic sweep across Ferris's face.

"Where are Ronny and Jonny and what did you do with my weed?"

Scooter smiles. "I don't know the answer to your first question but follow me."

They find toe holds and hoist themselves up the wall of the Wando's building back onto the fire escape. As they walk down the sidewalk, Scooter sees the backpacks and points them out to Ferris. They are hanging about eleven feet up, well above the heads and out of reach of the pedestrians walking below, none of whom even seem to notice the bags are there. Scooter starts limping faster, almost skipping. As he comes under the booty, he tips himself forward onto his good leg and explodes into the air. He can just reach and grabs a fistful of one of the bags, snapping the fishing line. Scooter and Ferris each strap on a backpack and head off to look for Ronny and Jonny's VW van.

Finding a VW van in a crazy city full of hippies and drunken revelers while on acid proves more difficult than one might think. They wind up on the east side of the Capitol at about two in the morning.

"I need to pee," says Ferris.

They are in front of an unassuming bar with a pink neon sign that says The Paradise. They pass the bouncer and enter a smoky, crowded bar with "I Wanna be Sedated" by the Ramones blaring over the jukebox. The bathroom is filthy, and something weird is going on in the single stall.

They wander the streets a bit more but find no trace of Ronny and Jonny or their van. Scooter sits down on the beautifully manicured lawn in front of the Capitol, stretching his braced leg in front of him and leaning back onto his elbows. The Capitol is lit in pale white and looks like it is carved out of alabaster. The crickets are chirping desperately against their imminent death, mere weeks away. Scooter becomes lost staring at the golden statue on top of the dome depicting a woman holding a sphere with an eagle perched on it. It seems as if she is looking down at him, indicating a path for him to take.

Ferris starts talking. "My astronomy professor was going on this riff the other day about how there are an infinite number of universes like this one, but all a little different. Like, every time we have a choice, like choosing to go up on the roof for instance, there is another universe where we make the opposite choice. Like, in some universe maybe you never hurt your knee."

Scooter takes his eyes off the Capitol and turns to Ferris. "That's stupid. Everything else being the same, why would anyone make a different choice?"

Ferris looks at Scooter and stares for a second. He scrunches his brow. He looks up at the Capitol.

Just before dawn they drag their weary and gimpy bodies back across campus to Birch. They empty the backpacks onto their beds. In addition to the two pounds Ferris paid for, there is another ten in the other bag.

Scooter looks at the pungent flora spread across the room and says, "What have you gotten me into Ferris? I was the starting quarterback on the number-one football team in the country, and now I have a felonious amount of weed on display in my room, a bad leg, and only a slight hold on reality."

"Don't worry about it Scoots, you're welcome."

Scooter doesn't laugh.

"Seriously," says Ferris, "Ronny and Jonny are solid guys. They will be back, and all this will be out of your hair. Have a couple hits and let the sweet stylings of Toots and the Maytals soothe your troubled mind."

Chapter 18

OCTOBER 25, 1986

S cooter and Ferris are tired, but it is game day after all, and even though only one of them is playing, they are both expected to be at Camp Randall for breakfast. Not risking oversleeping, they don't even bother lying down and instead, after a couple of bong rips, grab their toiletries and strip down to their underwear and walk the length of the floor to the bathroom. Scooter, not having shaved since the surgery, admires the black beard staring back at him in the mirror. After showers, they put on their gray football team-issued sweats and red T-shirts and walk down to the basement to see if Mrs. Winchester has made coffee yet.

She has, and they sit in the back corner eating sweet rolls and drinking cup after cup of coffee.

"Thank god this is an early game, we can catch a couple of hours after," says Scooter. "Are you okay to kick?"

Ferris looks at him as if he is deeply insulted. "Are you kidding, man? This shit is automatic. The results are inevitable."

Scooter just shakes his head and takes another slurp of coffee. The last thing he wants to do is fall asleep on the sideline and give Peregrine a reason to completely give up on his non-operational freshman quarterback.

Scooter gets on the Millennium Falcon and slow rides it next to Ferris as they head across the parking lots toward the stadium.

"The Lord has blessed us with another fabulous day for football." Ferris's sarcasm is thick, but he is right. It is in the midfifties, with just a hint of wind and nary a cloud to be found.

"You know," Scooter says, "I don't miss all the phoniness and the ra-ra bullshit that goes along with being on this team, but a day like this makes me wish I was playing. Putting on the pads and being the right temperature and just waiting to hit someone, to hear that crack. I do miss that."

Inside Camp Randall, the tables are laid out for breakfast and the coaches are strutting around like lonely peacocks chirping encouragement here and there, trying to fire up the energy in the room. Peregrine sees Ferris and Scooter come in and quickly glances at a table in the back of the room, indicating they should sit there. The coach has no time to deal with a lame quarterback and wild-ass kicker. Scooter exchanges nods with Ed and then heads to one of the back tables. He stretches his braced leg out on an empty chair and grabs a couple handfuls of pancakes from a stack in the middle of the table. Ferris has disappeared into the training room to begin stretching and warming up his leg. Scooter sits alone, scowling at his pancakes and just wishing the stupid game and especially the "ra-ra bullshit" that precedes it were over.

DIANA IS WAITING OUTSIDE THE LOCKER ROOM AFTER the game. Scooter is one of the first players out since he doesn't have to shower or change. They hug awkwardly.

He can't stand still. Hands in pockets, not in pockets? The Velcro in his brace is irritating the back of his knee. He keeps fidgeting.

"Did you wind up going to the football party?" he asks.

Diana's eyes look heavy. *I am letting her down,* he thinks. *But what does that even mean? What do I owe her?*

"Yeah, it was the same old thing. Butch did this monster keg stand and everyone thought he was going to puke."

She is still looking at him with those eyes. She stays more than an arm's length away. Something has changed between them.

"What is your plan for the night?" Scooter asks glumly.

"Probably head over to the Double F again and maybe the KK or The Irish or something. I was hoping you would come?"

"Yeah, I'm not really up for hanging out on Langdon, watching Butch do stupid shit and hearing about how great Luke was today, especially when they only won that game because Ferris kicked a fucking forty-six-yarder. I was hoping you might want to just stay in and rent a movie or something."

Her eyes go dull. "Listen, Scooter, everyone knows how great you were…"

He stops listening right there. All he hears is the word "were." It's like it is echoing through his mind, like some Eddie Van Halen wa-wa pedal reverbing its way out into the cosmos. *Has she given up on me? Fuck that,* he thinks. He tunes her back in and hears her say something about Luke being a good player, even if not as great as Scooter was—that past tense again—and a really "nice, down to earth guy," too. *Yeah. Fucking. Right.*

"Well, anyway, I have to run a few errands." He winces

as he says the word "run." "Maybe I'll find you at The Irish later."

Her eyes are back. She just says, "I hope so, Scooter."

He hops onto the Millennium Falcon and swings the bad leg over the duct-taped seat.

He rides across the parking lot, trying to put Diana out of his mind. The next worry that pops up like a rogue cloud on a sunny day is the weed sitting in his room. It is impossible not to worry about how ten, no twelve, pounds of weed in his dorm room could affect his scholarship. Who knows when Ronny and Jonny are coming back, or if they are. They can't keep the shit in their room. It already smelled like weed with Ferris around—that was somewhat concealable—now it's like there is a skunk in the closet. They can't throw it away. Ronny and Jonny will probably come back, and they will want their property. They need to sell it. *Torbjorn said he would always take more. Maybe there are others like that out there. Why is any of this his problem?* He shakes his head. He thinks of Misty. *A girl like that probably knows something or someone. Fuck, I need some sleep.* Scooter falls onto his bed and into the bliss of unconsciousness.

Scooter straps on Ronny and Jonny's canvas backpack and hops out the door and onto his trusty steed. He doesn't know if she'll be there, but if there is one place he would bet a chick like her would hang out on a Saturday night, it's there.

When Scooter steps past the bouncer, heads turn, and he slightly wishes he had changed out of his athletic department sweats and at least put on jeans or something. Everyone is seemingly wearing torn jeans, leather, and punk band T-shirts. The Paradise is the bar for the musicians, the artists, the political dissidents, the wannabe writers, skateboarders, and any other misfit who likes to drink and doesn't mind screamed lyrics. This is not the bar for scholarship football players. He is an affront to all that these people hold holy. But he spots her in the corner of the bar and limps over to her.

"What the fuck are you doing here?" Misty asks without so much as attempting not to look pleased.

"Looking for you," he says. From Misty's face, he realizes it's the right thing to say. "I need your help."

"The rock star quarterback needing something from little old me…?" she bats her eyes and tilts her head. "What, pray tell? I wait with bated breath." She rests her chin on folded hands and bats her eyelashes at him again.

"Uh, yeah…I have some marijuana I need to sell, and I thought you might know some people to buy it."

She looks disappointed and laughs. "That's not the kind of help I was hoping you were looking for. How much are we talking?"

"A few pounds," he says.

She pauses and gives him a curious look. "Have a drink and let's talk business." Scooter orders a Jack and Coke.

Chapter 19

OCTOBER 26, 1986

S cooter wakes with his head pounding. The window is open, and the high-intensity whine of a street sweeper is making life quite uncomfortable. He opens his eyes. Everything is ethereal and white. He is in the nicest apartment he has ever seen. The ceiling must be twelve feet high. He feels the coolness of pristine sheets sliding against his skin. He rolls over to his side and sees Misty, naked, putting on jeans. In a show of mock modesty, she covers her breasts with her hands and turns back to him with a twinkle in her eye.

"Good morning, beautiful," she says.

He groans and rubs his eyes. She jumps on the bed and covers his body with hers, kissing his face. She giggles and slides under the duvet next to him, now on top of him.

THEY SIP COFFEE AT HER DINING ROOM TABLE IN THE middle of a huge room that opens on one side to a kitchen and the other to a balcony overlooking State Street.

"How the fuck do you afford all of this?" he asks.

Misty takes a pull from her morning grit. "Mom is a dermatologist to the stars," she says without any self-consciousness.

"What does that even mean?"

"Well surely, Scooter, you know what a dermatologist is? 'Derma' refers to the skin. 'Tologist' means what it means. I assume you also know what a star is. I'm not using the word in the literal sense, but as a term to describe celebrities. You know, people on TV, movies, live in Hollywood, that kind of thing? My mom makes them beautiful. And for that she is well compensated." She says it all with a playful condescension. Scooter can't help but smile.

Misty pads off to the bathroom, and Scooter steps onto the balcony. He looks over the street still glistening from the street sweeper. There are a few homeless people sleeping on the benches and bus stops that line the curb. The sidewalks still bear the detritus of the previous night's excesses—cans, plastic cups, gyro wrappers, spilled burritos, cigarette butts. The storekeepers are just starting to open things up and hose down their entryways.

Misty comes up behind him and puts her arms around his waist. She presses her face into his back just below his shoulder blades. She whirls him around and stands on her tiptoes to kiss him.

"Let's do some business!" she says.

They take an elevator to an underground parking lot, and he follows her to a black convertible BMW with California plates. The leather seats are worn to a shine, and the inside is littered with cigarette packs and fast-food wrappers. It smells like vanilla air freshener. He slides the passenger seat all the way back and gets in.

They pull out and head east on Johnson Street away from the university. The neighborhoods get funkier with each block as they travel east of the Capitol. They pass Bernie's Rock Shop hawking crystals and beads to string on rawhide bracelets and necklaces. Every food store is some kind of collective. Discarded couches from moving day still line the curbs, waiting for a special trash pickup that may never come. Hints of patchouli and incense spice the air.

The house is at the end of a thousand-foot-long driveway with just the tire tracks paved. Tall bushes scuff the sides of the car. At the end of the drive is a ramshackle Cape Cod house with the wood-shingle siding so aged that it is almost black, as if it has started to rot. There is moss and lichen adding pops of green to the dark wood. Wind chimes and prayer flags hang from the rafters over a deep front porch with several couches that look as if they were pulled from the curbs Scooter and Misty passed along the way. The windows are open, and the falsetto of Jackson Brown welcomes them. Misty raps on a thick wooden door, the varnish stretched tight and crackling. A bearded man with long light-brown hair, a worn flannel with a geometric Navajo pattern, brown corduroys and sandals opens the door. He looks at Misty, crinkles his eyes, and gives her a hug.

"Well, Misty. To what do I owe the pleasure?" He turns and walks back into the house with a casual wave over his shoulder, beckoning for his guests to follow.

There is a large open room with brass incense holders scattered about a random collection of dark wood end tables in between overstuffed leather chairs. In the middle of the room, there is a step down to a sunken sitting area with cushions lining the floor. Beyond the sitting area, opposite the front door, is a row of floor-to-ceiling windows with a central French door opening to a deck with steps descending to a flagstone path that bisects a deep backyard on the shore of Lake Monona. There is a faded white pier stretching into the lake with a boat hoist holding a sparkly Mastercraft above the lazy waves. Just off the deck, on one side of the flagstone path, is a concrete basketball court. On the other side is a huge hot tub bubbling and steaming. The path continues toward the pier bisecting a giant garden fenced in chicken wire with two rows of raised boxes containing trellises, tomato cages, and a variety of plants. The tomato plants are desiccating in the fall air but still bear the last few fruits of a long summer. The gardens give way to a grass lawn about one hundred feet from the shore where the path splits, circling a large fire pit with faded Adirondack chairs. A couple of guys and girls sit around it passing an ornate glass bong.

Spencer, he who led them from the door, offers them ice-cold long necks of Miller High Life pulled from an ancient refrigerator with rounded corners plugged in on the porch. The fridge is full of beer and various root vegetables with clumps of dirt evidencing their recent extraction from the earth. They join the others around the fire pit and look out over the lake as it sparkles and laps at the shore. A few fishermen in Alumacraft boats with outboard motors search between the piers for Walleye or Northern. Spencer packs a fresh bowl and ceremoniously hands the huge bong to Misty.

"Visitors first," he says.

Misty puts her lips to the end as Spencer lights the bowl for her. Misty passes the bong to Scooter, who struggles to look graceful with the geometry of lighting the bowl and keeping his mouth on the end. He is sure he looks like a fool. He isn't exactly experienced at this, despite the deep waters in which he finds himself. After managing to take a hit, Scooter passes the bong, presses into the angled back of the chair, and looks out over the lake. The cicadas buzz their dying songs in the oaks shading the sides of the yard.

Misty launches in. "This is my friend Scooter." She takes a beat and looks around the fire circle, meeting everyone's eyes. She then focuses on Spencer. "Scooter is actually a very good friend of mine; he's actually a classmate of mine, aren't you, Scooter?" Scooter nods a little nervously. "Turns out, Scooter has come into quite a plentiful supply of ganja and would like to bestow it upon you for a fair price. How much can you take and what would you pay?"

Scooter looks out at the fishermen and shakes his head, wondering how he got here. He wonders what Pierre would think. He would be disgusted no doubt. But it's not like Scooter really has a choice in all of this. He needs to sell this weed. He takes a pull on his High Life and opens the bag at his feet, then tosses one of the wrapped pounds to Spencer. He realizes that there is more that needs to be said and that he is the only one who can say it.

"I know you don't know me from Adam, and this is a pretty weird spot I am in, but things have taken quite a turn since my injury."

They all just stare at him. It dawns on him that again, like with Torbjorn, he is in the rare circumstance of finding himself in a group of people his age who have no idea who he is. He fights the urge to chuckle, realizing that would not help his cause here.

"Um, sorry. I should have introduced myself and maybe this will go a ways toward you understanding that I am not a narc, but probably not make this any less weird. For me, at least, if not for you. I am a freshman, so I haven't been here that long. I was the starting quarterback on the Wisconsin football team and then blew out my knee. Basically, I had an odd weekend, and for reasons that I would like to not get into, some acquaintances of my roommate seem to have skipped town and left this marijuana in our possession. I would prefer not to store it in our room—especially given that I am here on a scholarship—but also don't want to look at these guys empty-handed when they come back."

Spencer picks a little hole in the side of the bag and lifts the bag to his nose.

"I would prefer if you got into why these guys left."

Scooter rubs his eyes and takes another swig of beer. "We were on LSD, hanging out on the roof of an apartment building and this girl fell off the roof and landed a couple stories down, on the roof of a bar, and the guys with the weed got scared, probably because most of the police and fire department showed up, and we don't know where they ran off to."

Spencer suppresses a grin. "Onto the roof of the Red Shed, right? We were *in* the Red Shed at the time. People didn't know whether it was a nuclear war or an earthquake!" Spencer looks toward one of the guys at the fire pit. "Caleb here hit the deck and rolled under one of the tables. He screamed 'Save Yourselves!' Real hero, that guy." Everyone chuckles; Caleb shakes his head.

"Not true," says Caleb, "a little spooked is all."

Spencer turns back to Scooter. "Okay, $1,000 dollars a pound. I'll take all you can get."

"Sold!" Misty yells.

At that moment Scooter realizes he has no idea what to charge, but he has no choice but to trust his ride. "I guess, okay then," says Scooter, "Deal."

Scooter turns his palms up to the fall sun. He is relieved. Amazed really. This problem is solved. He sighs and takes in the setting. His eyes linger on the concrete basketball court. He notices that the backboard is Plexiglas. He thinks back to the old wooden backboard and rim that Pierre nailed to the back of the granary. Scooter spent nights in middle school and his early high school years dribbling on the hard-packed dirt and gravel, practicing pivot moves— faking one way with his shoulder to fool his defender into committing and then pivoting back the other way to get the easy layup. Eventually chores and football took over. Scooter liked basketball, but it would never win over a sport where you could deliberately hit the opposing player.

He looks at Spencer. "You hoop?"

"Almost every day," says Spencer. "Feel free to come over and go at it any time."

"I would like that." Scooter winces as he says it, remembering his knee and wondering when he will be able to play any sport again.

Misty and Scooter walk, well Scooter mostly hobbles, through the beachy compound and back to the car parked at the edge of a front yard in desperate need of mowing.

Scooter says, "Who are those guys?"

"Spencer's dad owns some oil company or something. He bought that house for them. They are all loaded but live like hippies. I guess rebelling against their parents. Aren't we all," says Misty.

"Okay, but what are they going to do with ten pounds of weed? If they're so rich, they shouldn't need to be selling this stuff."

Misty keeps her eyes on the road. "I don't know, Scooter, they have a lot of parties, they have a lot of friends, maybe they want to make some of their own money so they aren't under Daddy's thumb. Maybe they want to be rebel drug dealers so they can break completely free of their prep-school upbringing? But you shouldn't look this gift horse in the mouth. You just solved your problem and made $10,000 dollars. Maybe your California friends won't come back."

There is a little glint in Scooter's eye. "I could get used to this money."

Misty smiles and drives.

Chapter 20

NOVEMBER 14, 1986

D r. Englund has cleared Scooter to take off the brace and lifted all restrictions on his rehab and conditioning. Ferris wants to go out and have a beer to celebrate. It is only six o'clock, but already dark. Ferris parks the Grand Marquis on Lake Street, so they have a couple of blocks' walk to get to The Irish. Despite the chill, Scooter is wearing shorts. The cold air feels good on his knee. He is now walking with no discernable limp. The knee is still a little achy, and he gets an occasional nervy tingling down his leg, but he almost doesn't even notice it anymore.

The Irish is dark, and there are spots open at the bar. The green shaded lights make the centers of the tables in the back glow, painting the faces of the patrons. The lighting hides the lack of cleaning, but it can't hide the stale beer smell. Scooter's shoes stick to the floor as he and Ferris make their way to the bar.

Scooter stops in his tracks. Diana. She pushes a piece of hair behind her ear with her index finger. She is smiling, her chin tucked, looking at her hands, wrapping them around her drink. It's a cocktail of some sort, judging from the fruit and the straw. *She never drinks cocktails*, Scooter thinks. She has on jeans, with a red flannel tied around her waist and a white tank top. She looks a vision. Something smooth, shiny, and perfect inside such a broken-down place. Across the table, face also aglow, is Luke.

Two things happen inside Scooter's body at once. He feels a superheated surge of acid climb into his esophagus—a physical manifestation of a primal rage that only bashing in the skull of his rival will assuage. At the same time, his stomach drops like he is on a rollercoaster, or perhaps more accurately as if he is free-falling into the abyss. It is the feeling of going too fast over the ridge road in a Trans Am with someone with whom you expect to spend the rest of your life. He squeezes his eyes closed.

Between gritted teeth he says, "Let's go to The Plaza instead."

"Got it, amigo," says Ferris quickly and they turn and leave.

Scooter cannot get his head right. He feels a pressure in his chest and an emptiness in his stomach. He wants to scream at her. He wants her to understand what he is going through. What he has been through. But mostly he just wants her to want him and only him. That's what he wants. That and to bash Luke's fucking brains in.

They sit at the sticky linoleum bar with annoyingly bright lights and order PBRs. Ferris shrugs his shoulders and clinks Scooter's frosty mug.

"Fuck it?" Ferris suggests with a shrug.

Scooter tips his glass back, lets the golden nectar pour into his mouth and down his chin like a raging Viking, and slams his glass on the table. "FUCK IT!" he yells.

Everyone turns and sees the enormous guy (hey, isn't that the quarterback that got hurt a while ago?) and turns back to their drinks or darts or whatever. Scooter laughs and orders another beer.

Over his shoulder he notices someone approaching and wonders if they are going to take a shot at him for his boisterous revelry. He turns quickly, ready to attack and smash, and Ferris turns too.

"Ronny and Jonny! Long time no see, compadres," says Ferris with a huge smile.

Ronny and Jonny look wild. Their eyes are scanning the room and their hair is dusty. They haven't showered for a while.

"Pull up and have a beer and tell us of the wondrous adventures you two travelers of the universe have undertaken since our last meeting," Ferris says.

Ronny speaks in a shaky, stressed-out voice, "Hey man, did you guys, uh, happen to recover the stuff that we left here? We kinda need it back and the people that we got it from are kinda sweating us."

"Huh," says Ferris, "do you hear that, Scoot? These guys say they left something here. Pray tell, what is this thing, describe it for me please. Use detail." Ferris assumes a mocking smile and puts his elbows on the bar with his hands cradling his chin as he stares at Ronny.

"Very funny, man," says Ronny. "We owe these Mexicans $5,000 for that shit, and if we don't get it to them soon, they are going to start breaking bones. No es bueno."

"Relax," says Ferris. "We'll pay you $6,000 for it. We can pay you tonight and send you boys on your merry way in your wagon of the people."

Ronny and Jonny visibly relax at once, as if Stooges in a silent film.

"Thank fucking god," says Jonny. "I guess I will have that beer." They both pull up stools at the bar, and Jonny holds up two fingers.

Ronny takes a sip of his beer and looks at Scooter, then Ferris. "So, that shit with the girl really freaked us out—by the way, is she okay?" Nods satisfy him and he continues, "So, my dudes, we were both tripping balls—well, I guess you know that—and when that shit went down it went to a really dark place."

Jonny sighs, takes a big swig of his beer, and nods. Ronny continues. "We ran down the fire escape and into the van and hit the road, headed west. But as we were just getting out of town, this fucking cop came screaming up behind us. Turns out the cop wasn't after us but some speeder up ahead, but I didn't know that at the time. They actually taunted us with that fact as they arrested us."

Ronny leans into Ferris's face. "Dude, I was freaking the fuck out. I took a fucking right turn off the road and kept driving through a cornfield. Well, the cop didn't think that was okay, so he gave chase. When the cop found us, we were both going batshit crazy, thinking the corn was attacking us. It took four officers to chase us through the cornfield and eventually pin us down. They checked us into Mendota mental institution. Thought we were both crazy, and we've been there ever since. Just got out today and called home, and found out the Mexicans have been looking for their money. Duuude. Not good. What a fucking whirlwind; one minute, we're hangin' with you dudes on a roof, having a really nice time, next minute, I'm doin' crafts with Ed Gein… That guy can make a lampshade."

The vibe at The Plaza mellows, and the beer eases Scooter's mind from the Diana situation. Or at least distracts him. The conversation touches on topics like belief in aliens, the best beer in the land, and Ferris's thesis on the subtle differences between punk chicks from So-Cal and the Bay

Area. It has a lot to do with eye makeup apparently. Scooter doesn't really follow.

By now it's almost midnight, and Scooter has his first nonbrace session with Josh after morning class. They pay the tab and head out to their respective vehicles.

Scooter says, "You know the Blue Moon? It's on the west side of campus on University Avenue. We'll meet you there. Give us a few minutes to stop at our dorm."

Scooter and Ferris walk into The Blue Moon and see Ronny and Jonny on the second-level balcony looking down on the action below. Before ascending, Scooter stops at the bar and orders a burger, and both Ferris and Scooter order Leinenkugels on tap. The mugs are hefty and frosty. They climb the stairs. Scooter leans heavily on the railing. He wears a backpack with $6,000 in fifties and hundreds inside. The balcony is abandoned. Scooter sets the backpack on the table and eases his chair against the back wall. He takes a long sip of the Leinies and slides the backpack under the table.

Jonny puts his hands under the table and unzips the bag, quickly scanning the contents and running his hands through the bag. He zips it back up and nods and smiles at Scooter. Scooter's order is called and he goes down to get the burger.

Ronny reaches across the table and pats Ferris on the shoulder and says, "You guys really saved our asses. If we had to move this stuff this quickly and then get back and pay our amigos, it would not have been good. And, I'll be honest with you, this is more than we can get for this shit on the West Coast. What do you think about us coming back in a couple of weeks with more? We would front it, of course."

Ferris nods and looks at Scooter as he ascends the stairs, burger basket in hand. "I am in if Scooter is. He lined up moving this shit."

"I'm in," says Scooter, "I might regret it, but I'm in. And I think we could move twice as much if you can get it." As soon as he says it, he can't believe he has.

Chapter 21

NOVEMBER 17, 1986

Scooter keeps running his tongue around the inside of his mouth, trying to get the juices to quench the desert of his soft pallet gone hard. The combination of weeks on pain meds, weed, and a weekend of drinking is not exactly contributing to his overall hydration and health. He has a dull ache in the back of his head. The weekend is a blur. He can't feel his knee. This first workout without any restrictions is going to suck.

Sure enough, Josh is bouncing up and down like a hungry Labrador puppy as Scooter walks into the gym. Josh gets down on his knees and genuflects as Scooter walks up. Scooter hopes to god he doesn't still smell like beer.

"The prodigal son returns; prepare the fattened calf at once!" Josh claps his hands twice for emphasis. "Looking good, buddy!" he says, "You look almost as good as new."

"Well, let's not get ahead of ourselves, but it is nice not to have that smelly brace driving me insane from itching every fucking minute."

"Dr. Englund will check your progress today, and we will come up with some rehabilitation type exercises to start working on, but first, get on that bike and pedal for fifteen minutes."

Scooter nods. Josh walks over with him and lowers the resistance to almost the lowest level. Scooter starts out pedaling slowly. The joint is stiff and there is a bit of an uncomfortable feeling, but no acute pain. By the end of the fifteen minutes, he feels that he is pedaling at a normal pace. Josh beams with pride and keeps patting Scooter on the back.

Dr. Englund joins them and invites Scooter to sit on the end of a large massage table, where he starts manipulating the leg.

"It looks pretty good. Swelling has almost completely subsided," he says. He uses both hands to grab around Scooter's calf, and he repeatedly straightens the leg and then pushes it toward Scooter to see how far it will bend. "You are still a little decreased in mobility. There is definitely some scar tissue in the joint that we will need to break up. Biking is a great first exercise. We want as much repetitive motion as we can without putting a maximum load on the joint. Josh will also…" Before Dr. Englund can finish his sentence, his beeper goes off. He retrieves it from his belt and looks at the screen. "I will be right back; I need to make a call."

"Today is back day!" Josh yells excitedly at Scooter as the doctor walks away. "We will do a circuit. Seated rows, supine rows, and then pull-ups. Start with ten reps each, ten seconds in between sets and one minute in between each round. Add one rep each round until you can't do any more."

Scooter puts the pin in the bottom of a big stack of weights and sits on the floor with his feet pressing against the base of the weight machine and his back ramrod straight and starts cranking out rows. He then lies on his stomach on a raised bench with two 75-pound dumbbells beneath him and cranks out reps of reverse flies. Slamming the weights down, he strides to the squat cage, grabs the bar at the top, and rips off ten pull-ups. He then sits down on the bench for his minute of rest. Dr. Englund returns.

"Sorry about that; I had to call the hospital. I have another patient getting an ACL repair this afternoon. Any questions for me?"

"Yeah, doc," Scooter says, "how does that pager work?"

SCOOTER MAKES IT TO FIFTEEN REPS. THE FIRST ROUNDS wring the beer and hangover out of him. The sweat is dripping from his forehead and pooling on the mats below. Embarrassingly. But he is as focused as he has been in a while. There is a light at the edge of his vision, a point of light, something on the horizon. He focuses on it and pulls his head up over the bar again…and again…and again. Josh is screaming and cheering him on. The light glows and pulsates, blocking out any pain and fatigue from his body, letting him push further and further until the muscles no longer work. On the last round of pull-ups, Josh is screaming. Scooter is too. Scooter is not even conscious he is doing it, but as he finishes the set, he notices a low, guttural, primal yell and realizes, he is its source. Scooter doesn't see him, but Harrelson, hearing the noise, peeks in. In the end, Scooter simply cannot pull his body up high enough to do another pull-up. His lats and his biceps feel like pieces of dry twine, stretched to their limit, about to break.

After, the euphoria and the exhaustion collide in the shower. Scooter is spent in a way he has not been in a long time. His leg free from the brace, the doctor telling him it is healing well, the ability to really push himself in the gym—it all feels good. For the first time in a long time, he feels physically powerful. He feels that he will make it back. He feels himself.

Professor Wachter is Scooter's most practical professor. He essentially teaches how to run a small business. The class is completely straightforward and not theoretical at all.

"This week, each of you will file papers to incorporate a business. Let's talk about what you need to do that."

For the rest of the class, they go through the processes and the forms necessary for incorporating a business in Wisconsin and the differences between an S Corp. versus a limited liability corporation. The students will file the papers to form one of the two. Scooter works through the materials and decides that he will create an LLC. It seems to him that for most farms, filing as an S Corp. is clearly the better move. There are tax advantages for an S Corp. because the owner only pays income tax on the value of his services. But LLCs can be created much more anonymously. His burgeoning agricultural business is not exactly conventional, and it's not as if he is actually going to pay taxes. Anonymity is key.

He gets back to Birch and, as usual, Ferris is communing with his bong. He is sitting cross-legged in the middle of a rug they found in the basement of Birch. The stereo is cranked, and Steely Dan is lazily and jazzily coasting through their jams. Ferris does not move a muscle when Scooter slams the door.

"Ferris, I need your help with something."

Ferris opens one eye. "My copy of *The Kama Sutra* is on the second shelf of my bookcase. I am happy to roleplay if that is what you need." A brief smile flashes across Ferris's face before it returns to its forced placidity.

"Good to know. Do you know of anyone that can make a good fake ID?"

Ferris opens both eyes. "I don't think you'll ever have a problem getting into the bars, Scoot. No one cares."

"It's not for that. I have a plan to keep us under the radar with this new shipment."

Ferris's eyes are fully open now and his eyebrows theatrically raised. "Do tell, wise leader..." he says.

"I will explain it all to you, but first, I need a very good fake ID."

"But Scooter, everyone here knows who you are. Your physical dimensions are somewhat, como se dice...unique."

Scooter nods. "You have a bit of a point there. Do you have a decent fake?"

Ferris smiles and pulls out his wallet. "Oui. I have a fake that is so good it's real."

"Do you have a second form with the same address?"

Ferris bats his eyes. "I am embarrassed that you underestimate my commitment to being a degenerate." He pulls out a library card. Both IDs list him as Malcolm Giddens with a Madison, Wisconsin address: 1506 Forest Lane.

"Fire up the Grand Marquis, Ferris. I am taking you to the post office."

No one questions the fake. Ferris rents a post office box under the name of Malcolm Giddens. Scooter then has Ferris drop him off at the Ag library. Professor Wachter has left the requisite forms for the students to create their own Wisconsin LLC or S Corp. at the research desk. Scooter fills out documents for the incorporation of Famechon, LLC. He lists the business address as the PO box they just rented. All he needs is an agent for service and a physical address. Scooter uses Malcolm Giddens as the registered agent. For the physical address, he includes the 1506 Forest Lane address from the fake ID. Scooter brushes aside any pangs he has about falsifying documents. If this ever blows up, he will say he thought he was just doing it for a class.

Within a half hour, all the forms are filled out. He walks back to Birch and takes the Millennium Falcon back to the post office, where he sends the forms via certified mail.

That done, he finds the name of a pager company in the yellow pages. He calls and asks what he needs to get a pager service for his company and how much it is a month. Turns out all he needs is a mailing address for the bills. The cost for two pagers is twenty-five dollars a month. Scooter asks that they send the contract to his business, Famechon, LLC, to the PO box at the South Madison Post Office.

Chapter 22

NOVEMBER 21, 1986

T he wind pulses through the streets and blows already fallen leaves into swirling piles along the curb. Scooter is on his new multicolored Raleigh mountain bike that he bought at Bicycle Exchange for five hundred dollars. Green, teal, and blue are airbrushed to seamlessly fade from one color to the next. It looks like a blue moon snow cone. It is the biggest frame size Raleigh makes. It is pure aluminum and so light Scooter couldn't believe it when he took a test ride, dodging in and out of traffic and popping up over curbs. The handlebars have diamond-plated chrome horns extending out from the tips so that Scooter can stretch out in an aerodynamic position and let his legs churn.

A southerly breeze has brought up an improbable Indian summer, confusing birds and humans alike. The sun still goes down early, but it is summer-hot and humid with thunderstorms forming in the afternoon, highlighting the end of the day with strobes echoing blue inside giant puffy clouds.

Scooter rides up Monroe Street, past Mickey's Dairy bar and Stadium Barbers, where Peregrine's flattop gets leveled almost daily. Just north and west of the stadium on Monroe, the businesses transition into small, run-down houses that students lease. It is sort of a sleepier version of the houses just to the east of campus. But nicer too, because Wingra park is nearby, as is the zoo.

The streetlights are just coming on. Scooter broke a sweat about a mile ago. But the harder he pedals, the stronger the breeze, and he tears through the neighborhood like a fugitive. His hair is getting long, and his black beard is long enough to stroke. He is like the biker of the apocalypse, but on a mountain bike.

He pulls around the back of the house where the party is and nods at some of the guys smoking outside. There is a grill going with the ubiquitous brats squealing away, squirting fat onto the coals. There is a pony keg too with some microbrew beer. He stops and fills a cup before opening the back door. It is painted a crackling blue with a lace curtain covering the window. There are steps down from the back door to a basement from which the sound of a crowd and Motley Crue's "Shout at the Devil" is pumping.

There are some more kegs against one wall and a crush of people in the middle of the floor, moving to the music with cups raised in the air. Misty is in the middle in a small white sundress. She sort of spins and sways at the same time, flipping her hair from side to side with her eyes closed.

Scooter walks up and says, "Hey."

She turns and smiles—a relaxed, content smile. She grabs his free hand and slides it around her waist as she keeps moving, pressing her body into his. It's nice, this unexpected adjournment in the procession of fall and winter and this warm place, with happy people.

They stay for a few hours. Scooter meets a bunch of cool people who are into things like Ultimate Frisbee and hacky sack and motorcycles. (And, wouldn't you know it, drugs.)

At around ten or eleven Scooter asks Misty if she wants to get some air. They head outside.

"I know a place to go," she says. "It's not too far."

Scooter straddles his bike and holds the handlebars firmly. Misty puts one hand on his shoulder as she positions her dress between her legs with the other and situates herself on the seat. Scooter stands up and pedals while she directs him to the parking lot of Michael's Frozen Custard that dead-ends and then leads to a park and a boat launch on the shores of Lake Wingra.

There are no houses on Lake Wingra. The park has a playground and a soccer field. During the day, the boat launch rents canoes and kayaks. The UW Arboretum occupies the whole south shore. There are also no boat wakes allowed. At this time of night, even on a Saturday, no one is in the park and the lake is a piece of black glass reflecting the orange harvest moon. Next to the boat launch is a large, low, flat pier that extends about fifty feet into the lake. They sit on the end, holding hands, looking out at the calm water, listening to the birds and the last of the surviving insects that are surprised and disoriented to still be alive and just celebrating that. Scooter eases back; there is a cacophony of frogs from the shore. He smiles.

"Listen to that. Now what do you think has got those frogs so fired up?"

"Only one thing can probably do that," says Misty. She slides her hand under his shirt and rolls over onto his chest.

Scooter smiles as they kiss, and it's like the frogs and the crickets are singing harmonies, getting louder by the minute. He eases his hand under her dress and realizes she has nothing on underneath. He peels the dress up over her head. Misty is working on his belt.

THE HARVEST MOON IS SETTING AND THE MILKY WAY IS rising. Scooter thinks that this is how life should be. There are light ripples across the water lapping at the edges of the pier. Misty sighs and presses her head into Scooter's chest. He engulfs her in a big hug and playfully rolls back and forth on the pier. He feels something brush his leg.

"Oh shit, sorry babe."

Misty picks up her head and sees her white dress descending like an apparition through the dark water. Scooter jumps up and walks to the end of the pier. He looks down at the sinking dress and shakes his head.

"Shit." He slowly lowers himself into the water, wincing all the way. When the water gets to his crotch, he lets out a high shriek. The water is up to his chest and it is freezing. He dives his head under and feels along the sand bottom. He finds the dress, brings it to the surface, and flops it on the edge of the pier.

"My hero," says Misty.

"Avert your eyes young lady, that water is cold, and I don't want to put any disappointing visions in your head after things seemed to be going so well."

She giggles and mockingly places her hands over her eyes. Scooter boosts himself onto the pier and grabs his boxers. He quickly yanks them on over his wet legs. He hands Misty his T-shirt.

"You can wear this."

She smiles and slips it over her head. It is long enough to be a dress but billows a bit at the sides. She has to pinch the back behind her and secure it with a hair tie.

"Well, I suppose we should get going before I manage to destroy all of our belongings," says Scooter. "I swear I didn't mean to do that," he laughs.

Scooter again straddles his bike, balancing the handlebars, and Misty gets on back. Scooter feels amazing pumping his legs with his chest bare and Misty's warm hands holding onto his sides as the leaves crunch under the tires. He drops her at her place on State Street and bikes past the Union and up over the hill, past the Observatory and past Diana's dorm.

It is two in the morning by the time he walks up the stairs at Birch. He smiles as he crests the last step and smells the acrid burning-leaf smell; likely Ferris still torching into the night. His smile disappears as he looks down the hall and sees two bare bent legs with arms wrapped around them. Diana's back is against the wall next to his door, her head dropped between her knees. She looks up as he walks down the hall. She has tears in her eyes and shakes her head at his lack of shirt and generally wild appearance.

"What happened to us, Scooter?"

He hates seeing her cry. He has only seen it a few times before, and he tries to think of ways to fix this and make everything okay, but his mind is spinning out of control. And then there is that bite of anger that he feels as the vision of her and Luke at The Irish flashes into his mind.

"I guess things changed, Diana. I guess I let you down. I got hurt. Maybe I went off the rails a little. Maybe we aren't the perfect couple we used to be anymore..." And here it is, that little bite of anger rising "...and maybe you felt you needed to be with the starting quarterback."

She lets out a squeak. "I'm pregnant."

Two words. He never thought that two words could have such a devastating effect on him, but then the next five make them almost irrelevant.

"I don't think it's yours."

He nods and sighs, defeated. He slides down the wall to sit next to her. He puts his arm around her and feels the sobs ripple through her body. His anger gives way to a defeated sadness. He feels like he did sitting on that field after his knee gave out—numb with the knowledge that everything has changed. That his life will never be the same.

Eventually they go inside and find Ferris passed out on the rug with his head awkwardly propped up against his bed and the bong water spilled on the rug as usual. They get into the small bed, not sure, maybe for the first time in their lives, of what their futures hold and what they mean to each other. Scooter lies awake listening to Ferris's snoring and perseverating over what he has lost. Occasionally, his mind gives in to his body and grants him the mercy of sleep. But the sleep is short-lived. He wakes several times to Diana's muffled crying and rhythmic sighing.

HE IS STARTLED BY SOMETHING AND OPENS HIS EYES before dawn has swept the deep blue from the sky. At first, he only remembers that something bad happened before he went to bed. He then looks over at Diana, who is finally asleep, and remembers exactly what that thing was. It occurs to him that she never asked where he was last night and why he was shirtless and wet when he got home. He sort of feels like he got away with something, but he sort of feels like he hasn't. He leaves before Ferris or Diana are awake and rides to the Nat with a different kind of conviction than he has had before. He wants to push something or hit something, but not for the sport of it. He wants to use his body to escape his mind.

Josh is standing with one hand on the bench bar, coffee in another hand, and a big grin on his face.

"We're going to see what you can do today big guy. Hop on the bike for twenty minutes and meet me back here."

When Scooter comes back, he is in full sweat. The gray cutoff sweatshirt he has on has a dark gray crescent from his pecs to his belly button, like a roughly drawn smile. There is lather on his hands from rubbing against the handlebar grips.

"What do you think your max is right now?" Josh asks.

Scooter shrugs. "I guess close to five," he says.

Josh puts two plates on both sides and tells Scooter to do a warm-up set with good form and not too fast. Scooter rhythmically pumps the bar ten times. Josh puts another plate on each side and stands behind Scooter's head with his hands on the bar, ready to spot. Scooter presses up once and then again, and then sets the bar back down. Josh loads an additional plate on both sides and again gets into place behind the bar.

It is hot in the room; the Indian summer combines with the boilers already turned on for winter. Sweat runs off Scooter's arms and onto the floor to mix with ancient sweat stains and rust marks left by countless athletes doing exactly as he is now. The smell of rust, mildew, and body odor combines into a potpourri that acts as a smelling salt calling the body to action.

Scooter pushes the bar off the rack and lets it descend under control to his chest, and then accelerates it back above the rack where it rattles back down, shaking rust free from the metal bars. He lets out a small grunt as the bar ascends from his chest and sighs once the bar is back in its cradle. Scooter is staring at the ceiling now, with its maze of rusty-brown-painted pipes and conduit carrying liquids and electricity to god knows where. He is in a trance, oblivious to the trainer's actions. Josh again adds weight. This time, Scooter's grunt is louder as the bar comes off his chest, but it does so without hesitation. The bar slams down into the cradle supports that rattle the bench.

Others in the room and even in the adjacent weight rooms are noticing something now. They look and whisper. Josh puts another plate on each side of the bar. Scooter's gaze hasn't changed, but he is now panting, hyperventilating to prepare his body for the lift.

This time as the bar comes off his chest, his arms tremble a bit and pause, and he yells as loudly as he can as the bar achieves liftoff and overcomes the gravitational pull of the gym and the weight of his life and the problems of this world. The bar slams into place and Scooter sits up, stands up, shakes out his arms, jumps up and down, and yells again. He looks around the gym and sees, peeking around a corner, Peregrine, who nods and goes back whence he came.

Chapter 23

NOVEMBER 28, 1986

F amechon LLC is up and running. Scooter and Ferris have circulated instructions to Spencer, Torbjorn, and their other customers that when they are ready for a delivery, they are to call a pager number, punch in a number where they can be reached, and then wait for a call back to receive a location somewhere in the Madison area to pick up the herb and leave money. Scooter came up with this arrangement after sitting in on some Criminal Law lectures at the law school. He told his adviser that he might be interested in becoming a lawyer, and the adviser told him that under-graduates were welcome to attend some of the law-school lectures, including Criminal Law.

Scooter's takeaway from the lectures was that to be convicted of selling drugs, the state has to prove that the accused possessed drugs with the intent to deliver them. The way Scooter sees it, even if cops somehow got onto the scent of the operation, as long as the drop location is never the same, the cops would never be able to actually witness or otherwise document Scooter, or any other member of his team, possessing the drugs. And aside from the customers they have already dealt with, like Spencer and Torbjorn, there was no need to give anyone their names. Even if the cops busted someone who gave up the pager number, or otherwise found a way to narc the number out of someone, they couldn't link the number to any actual person, and they would bang their heads against the wall trying to find the identity of the nonexistent Malcolm Giddens.

Their biggest risk was that they let the customer get the product before Scooter got the money. Scooter's solution, albeit imperfect, is what he called a "show." After receiving the page, Scooter would call back the buyer and tell him to go to two locations in sequence, both near one another. At the first location, it was understood that the buyer would be observed from afar and "show" that he is there with the cash to make the trade by simply lifting a bag containing the money. After standing around and being observed for a few minutes, the buyer would proceed to the actual drop point to pick up the weed and leave the cash.

This process did three things to keep the deal honest. First, it let the buyer know he was being watched and could be followed or recognized if he shorted the payment. Basically, it let the buyer know that he was somewhat vulnerable. Second, if the cops were onto them, the narc would have to show his or her face without ever seeing the seller. Scooter expected that undercover cops would be reticent to agree to such a situation. Finally, if the deal looked sketchy, Scooter could bail without ever being seen.

Scooter pushes his mountain bike to the top of a glacial drumlin overlooking one of two parking lots on either side of the UW Arboretum on the south side of Lake Wingra. In between the parking lots is a gravel trail for bikes or pedestrians in the summer and for cross-country skiers in the winter that winds its way through several miles of arboreal forest maintained by the university. The show is to take place on the back side of a warming hut. Scooter has a clear view from the top of the hill. He is in dark clothes, positioned behind a tree, and has binoculars up to his eyes. He starts laughing as soon as he sees the buyer.

It's Spencer, and he is twirling around as instructed on the phone call, holding up a Jansport backpack and pointing to it. He alternates between pointing at the bag and holding up his middle finger. The idea is that Scooter will bike to the next parking lot and leave the five pounds of weed he has in his backpack under an overturned garbage bin. But fuck it. He knows this guy.

Scooter throws the binoculars into his backpack and slings the backpack over his back. He hops on the bike and dodges oak trees down the hill and flies across a natural prairie that was recently burned bare and is now charred grasses and ash. His hands and teeth chatter as he rattles across the ground that is not yet frozen but getting hard. Spencer is initially a little startled by the sound, and then sight, of a 240-pound man rattling down the hill and straight toward him in the middle of a pretty big drug deal, but he is laughing too as Scooter slams on the back brake and slides about twenty feet sideways on the bike until he and the bike are resting comfortably in the charred grass at Spencer's feet. Scooter stands up and dusts himself off.

"Seemed stupid to go through the whole security protocol with you," Scooter says.

"I appreciate it," says Spencer, "and despite my gestures of protest, I actually don't think it's nonsense, and I get that what you are doing protects me too. Let's go get a beer!"

Scooter retrieves his binoculars and they trade bags. Spencer gets into a beat-up Porsche and Scooter gets back on his bike, and they both press their respective pedals. Their vehicles carry them over cracked and potholed asphalt around Lake Wingra and to the parking lot of The Laurel Tavern, which welcomes them with the smell of salty, slow-cooked beef sandwiches and fresh popcorn.

With frosty taps of Point beer in front of them, Spencer asks, "So you're really doing this huh? Star football player turned major drug dealer."

"I don't know. I guess something like that. I can't do anything about getting injured. That happened and maybe spun me out of control. But weirdly, I feel like I can control this. My dad's a farmer, and he bitches about that life, and trust me, I get it, I don't miss having to get up to milk cows. But he has always been someone who controlled his own world, did things his way, never had a boss. I am getting a little taste of what that feels like doing this. No coach. I am calling the shots. As weird as the whole thing is, I like it. You're playing a big part in this too, by the way."

Spencer acknowledges the comment with a nod.

"Anyway," Scooter asks, "why do you need all this weed? From what Misty says, you don't need the money."

"Everyone needs the money, Scooter. I don't give this away. That may be what Misty thinks, but I am making money doing this. Trust me. Your deal has helped greatly with that. Doing this allows me to live my lifestyle without asking Daddy for handouts. Or more handouts at least."

"What lifestyle? Aren't you in school?" asks Scooter.

"Yeah, but I have the house. And school is what I do to appease Dad. I don't want to go into business or become a lawyer or some shit when this brief time is over. I do a lot of gardening and woodworking. That's what I'm really into; that is the thing that really makes me happy. Someday, I am going to build the coolest house you've ever seen. Everything custom."

"Sounds like you have it all figured out."

"Well, I don't, Scooter. But I have been at this a bit longer than you, and I will tell you to set boundaries and be careful. Like what you are doing with the pager and not meeting buyers in person. Stay smart. Anyone who buys or sells something that is illegal plays by their own rules, and you may find people who have rules that differ from yours. There are some rough dudes out there."

Scooter nods but thinks, *what could anyone do to me? I would like to see someone try.*

THE AIR STINGS SCOOTER'S CHEEKS AS HE STARTS TO pedal. He is on the lakeshore path behind the dorms. He has on his thick Wisconsin Football hoody and fleece-lined, windproof pants. So, other than his face, he feels pretty good as he pushes the bike into the complete blackness of the path as it rounds University Bay away from the dorms and toward Picnic Point, a peninsula on the west side of the campus that juts into University Bay. Picnic Point has a large gravel path down the center of it, with campsites and fire pits and a network of smaller footpaths scattered on either side. The main path circles a massive sunken fire pit with benches stepped out above it at the tip of the peninsula. The fire pit is the drop.

The show is about a third of the way from the tip of the peninsula, where there is a beach with a lifeguard stand, which is really more of a wooden shed with lifeguard supplies inside it and a lifeguard chair on one side. West of the beach, near the lakeshore, is a shelter with bathrooms and a few picnic tables. The front of the shelter is the show.

Scooter is about half an hour early. He parks his bike on the east end of the lifeguard stand and climbs the lifeguard chair and pulls himself onto the roof of the shed. It is dark. The moon hasn't risen, or it is a new moon, and it is hard to make out the shelter a couple of hundred yards to the west. Scooter lies on his back on the roof of the shed and looks at the stars, which are seemingly brighter and crisper, as if the crisp air has clarified and hardened everything in the world. He inhales at the sight of the Milky Way and looks for Orion. Finding it, he thinks of Diana and wonders if she has seen it tonight too.

Scooter hears the scraping of footfalls along the pea-gravel path toward the beach. He hears their maker turn toward the shelter and walk away from Scooter. Scooter slides on his belly across the flat plywood roof of the shed. Just at that moment, fingers of fog start rolling in off the lake and settling in low areas, including right in front of the shelter. Despite the bright stars above, it is dark. As he looks out, he can barely make out the figure holding up a bag and twirling around, much less what he looks like. *Shit*, Scooter thinks. But there is nothing he can do, unless he just calls the whole thing off. He scrambles off the roof and quietly pedals his bike on the grass and dirt edge of the path to avoid the sound of crunching gravel. With the bike in tow, Scooter drops down among the rocks at the very edge of the peninsula, below the fire pit tucked into the small amphitheater. He takes off his backpack with three pounds of weed in it and lobs it into the center of the fire pit, which hasn't been used in months.

Scooter conceals himself among the rocks and waits. After a few minutes, he hears steps and can now, from his position, better see his buyer reaching for the bag and leaving another. Scooter hasn't seen the guy before. The buyer has short hair and wears a leather jacket. He is compact but moves well. He is looking around, always checking behind him. He is twitchy. Something doesn't seem right to Scooter. Up until now, every drop, every deal has been casual, easy, informal, and kind of fun. This buyer projects a different energy. He isn't menacing per se, but he is looking around a lot. Like he is looking for Scooter's location.

Before the buyer's footfalls are out of earshot, Scooter scrambles out of his hiding place and grabs the bag from the fire pit. Sure enough, it is short. There is maybe five hundred dollars inside a bag that should contain $3,000. He is not sure why the buyer even bothered to include that much.

There is a small trail on the south side of the peninsula that is parallel to the main trail. It accesses two lakeside campsites. The smaller trail is dirt, covered here and there with wood chips, and is somewhat concealed by trees and the fact that it sits lower in elevation to the main trail.

Scooter takes off sprinting on the side trail, turning his head, searching the darkness through the trees for the silhouette of the buyer. Scooter has not sprinted since the knee injury, and it occurs to him that he feels pretty good. After about thirty seconds of running flat-out, he makes out the shape of the buyer on the main trail above him, walking, but quickly and with purpose.

Scooter slows to a jog. He takes off his sweatshirt as he runs and turns it inside out. He puts his hood up and ties a handkerchief from his back pocket around his face. The two trails merge after maybe half a mile. Scooter hopes he can make it to the convergence point before this asshole.

Scooter starts sprinting again. He slows to a walk as the main trail and the lakeside trail come together. He steps into the brush just off the main trail. He crouches behind a tree and sees two new figures walking down the path toward him. "Fuck!"

They are big guys. Taller than six feet and thick. But they do not move that quickly. Probably high school lineman. Scooter probably played against them. One of them has on a leather jacket and the other a North Face ski jacket—yellow and black. Their hair is cut tight to their scalps. The leather-jacketed one has a baseball bat.

The good news is that they are walking toward him, which means Scooter has gotten past their stupid comrade. There is no question what they are here for. They will pick up their friend and escort him back to the parking lot, paying close attention to anyone coming up the path behind them. No doubt, they will be looking over their shoulder for Scooter approaching from the tip of the peninsula.

Scooter moves deeper into the dense brush between the trail and the water until he is below the path, just along the lakeshore. He starts moving as quietly as possible. The peninsula is about a mile and a half long. He figures they are a little more than a half mile from the tip, a little less than a mile from the parking lot and beginning of the path.

After about a minute of moving quietly but quickly through the brush toward the parking lot, Scooter pauses. He can hear footsteps on gravel moving quickly, but not running. It sounds like they are moving toward him. They are all behind Scooter now, but not far behind.

Scooter begins to jog along the lakeshore. The ground is hard-packed dirt and sand. He makes good time running quietly. Up ahead the elevation of the main path drops to be almost even with the edge of the lake, where Scooter runs now. At that point, the main path narrows and there is no brush or side trails between the main path and the lake on either side. There is an old-fashioned water pump used to fill water bottles on hot summer days on the north side of the path. There is a large lone tree growing next to it. Scooter slips behind the tree. He presses his body against the side that is facing the parking lot and waits. He can only hope that they pass close by to the tree and are walking close together. He's betting the latter will be true.

Scooter hears panting and clumsy feet moving quickly down the path. He thinks to himself that these guys probably thought this was a good plan; *they isolate me on the end of the point, essentially cutting me off. But what they didn't think through is how long a walk it is to get out of there. And they know nothing about me,* he thinks.

Scooter bends his knees and puts one hand on the ground, grinding his feet and hand into a three-point stance. He faces the path, perpendicular to it, concealed by the tree. He watches the path, waiting to see the first bit of shoe.

As soon as he does, he explodes forward, thrusting with his legs, keeping his back low and straight and stretching his arms wide. His shoulder hits the rib cage of baseball bat-boy and slams him into the buyer and their downhill skiing buddy, taking all three down hard, like dominoes. Scooter rides the bat-bearing thug down. Scooter brings his left hand back as his right shoulder drives the thug into the gravel. As they fall, Scooter slams his left fist into the thug's jaw. The biggest threat is out cold.

Scooter pops up onto his feet quickly as the buyer starts to rise. Scooter kicks him in the balls, then turns to focus on the other muscle in the North Face Jacket. The buyer writhes on the ground in pain as the skier crawls away from Scooter toward the side of the path. Scooter beats him there and knees Mr. North Face in the temple, knocking him out as well. Scooter turns back to the moaning buyer, grabs him by the collar, and hauls him up. Scooter rips the backpack with the three pounds of weed from the buyer's hand. The buyer recoils to protect his face.

"Two questions and answer carefully or you sleep underwater tonight. Who are you and how did you get the number?"

The buyer is sweating and looking over his shoulder, hoping his larger friends will come to and rescue his ass. But he is also not an idiot. "I'm Jason." As he says it, he calms down, as if he has deflated and surrendered. "Some guy in a bar gave me the number. I was buying people drinks and asking for weed and this guy told me, but I don't even know his name."

"That better be true," said Scooter. He reaches into the buyer's pocket, takes out his wallet, and pulls the driver's license. "I know who you are, Jason, and if I ever hear you are talking about me, looking for me, or otherwise think- ing about me, I will hunt you down and what I've done so far will feel like your mother cradling you to sleep by comparison. Do you understand?"

Jason nods yes.

"Okay, here is what's going to happen, Jason. I am going to turn you loose, and you are going to go back down to the end of the point while I babysit your friends. You made me leave my bike down there and I need it back. It will also give you time to think about the error of your ways. If you are not back in under five minutes, I will smash your friends' faces in with this here baseball bat..." Scooter releases Jason's shirt and reaches down and picks up the bat as Jason stumbles backward "...so, I suggest you at least break into a light jog. The bike is among the rocks leading down to the water below the fire pit."

Jason starts running on his errand and Scooter prods the two knocked-out goons with the bat. They are coming around and moaning, grabbing their heads. As they open their eyes, they have a look of momentary confusion. The look changes to concern as their brains start working, recalling their situation and appreciating how fucked they are.

"Stay down, boys," Scooter says as he slaps the bat. I want you both to tell me in ten words or less what brought you out here tonight, what your name is, and what you are going to do after this."

They look at each other, a little unsure, and then the guy who brought the bat says, "I'm Ray. We came out here to protect Jason. After this we go home?"

"Good answer as far as it goes, Ray," says Scooter, "but what I want to hear from both of you is that if you are allowed to leave this place at all and without further damage, you will never speak of me or tonight's unfortunate events to anyone. Is that clear?" He points the bat at the other thug and draws small circles in the air.

"Um, um, I'm Ryan," says Mr. North Face. "And, yes, we can keep quiet."

Scooter puts the bag with the five hundred dollars inside the backpack with the weed. He steps behind Ray and Ryan, who sit on the path. Soon Jason returns, slowly jogging alongside the bike, pushing the handlebars. Scooter takes the bike and throws Jason's driver's license back to him. Scooter rides down the path toward the parking lot without even looking back. In the parking lot, there are three girls leaning against a Chevy conversion van with rust spots accenting the dirty white paint. They are smoking cigarettes and talking, but they stop talking as he rides by. He still has the handkerchief covering his face and his hood up. "Have a good night ladies!" he says as he accelerates back down the path toward campus and Birch.

Misty is sitting on his bed, and Ferris is sitting on the rug with the bong out in front of him on the floor. As soon as Scooter walks in, Misty looks straight at his hand with its bleeding knuckles and grated palm from the road base on the trail.

"What happened!?"

"Our first real obstacle, I guess," Scooter says, "The dude shorted me, and then two of his buddies showed up to jump me. Didn't turn out so well for them." Scooter throws the bags on the floor. "Do you think Spencer will take three more pounds? We can give him a hundred-and-fifty-dollar discount on each."

Chapter 24

DECEMBER 23, 1986

S cooter's eyelids are heavy and he shakes his head to keep himself awake as he plods through a textbook on investing in futures contracts to protect from milk-price volatility. The phone ringing is a welcome distraction.

"Hey," Diana says. She sounds defeated.

"Hey," Scooter says. He hasn't seen her in the month since she stayed over at Birch. He assumes she is with Luke, and while he doesn't like it, in some ways it makes things easier for him.

"I wanted to let you know I am not going home for Christmas," she says.

The thought had never crossed Scooter's mind. He had just assumed they would go home.

"I told my parents," she continues, "and it wasn't a great conversation. They are shocked that it is not yours."

Scooter, too, is somewhat shocked by that being stated as fact. Another thing he had assumed but had not confronted as a reality.

"And anyway, I just can't deal with the stress of that on top of everything else right now."

"I get it," Scooter says, but he really doesn't.

"Plus," Diana says, "I am going to California with Luke

to meet his family between Christmas and New Year's. They are actually excited."

Scooter wants to pound the phone through the skull of the smug quarterback. He vows to himself right then that he will take back the starting job and humiliate Luke in the process. "Ah, that's great. I hope you have a nice time," is the best he can muster.

"I'm sorry, Scooter, you can drive the Trans Am if you would like."

He hadn't thought about that either, but no fucking way is he going to drive his ex-girlfriend's car home after she got knocked up by some two-bit, pretty-boy, javelin-throwing, wannabe football player. "Nah," he says, "I'll figure it out."

He hangs up the phone and grabs one of the paper bags lying about with wads of bills inside. He bikes to Randy's Autos, a small used-car lot weirdly located in a residential neighborhood near Lake Wingra in a defunct gas station. He parks the bike in a conveniently placed bike rack near the entrance to the gas station. As he peruses the offerings that range from Gremlins to a pretty nice Mercedes C Class, he sees a 1985 Chevy S10 in all black with a bench seat and cloth interior. It has a few dents, but it's not bad and it has four-wheel drive. He sees someone, presumably Randy, struggling to tuck in his shirt around his massive girth while lighting a cigarette as he waddles toward this fly caught in his web.

"Can I help you, son? Nice-looking truck, isn't it?"

Scooter asks, "How much?"

Randy takes a drag on his cigarette and sidles up to the car to look at the tag he has on it. "$7,500."

Scooter looks at him and blinks. "Is there any discount if I give you cash?"

Randy says, "Well, we usually take cashiers' checks from banks; you know, that's better for taxes and such."

"I can get one of those too," Scooter says, "But I can give you $7,000 in cash right now if I can put my bike in the back of this and drive away." Scooter opens the paper bag and hands it to Randy.

Randy adjusts his belt and says, "Sold! Let's go get the paperwork done."

Driving back to Birch, Scooter feels oddly nervous. He never imagined being able to just go to a dealership and buy a pretty sweet truck. Pierre still drives the same beat-up Chevy that he bought used a decade ago. Scooter isn't quite sure what he will say to Pierre about the new truck, but he is sure he will be asked. At the same time, it feels fucking awesome to be driving his own S10 down the streets of Madison.

THE FIRST WORDS OUT OF PIERRE'S MOUTH AS SCOOTER strides up the walk with a duffle bag over his shoulder are, "How did you pay for that thing?" pointing to the pickup. Actually, he just points and says, "How the fuck?"

Scooter has his lie ready and says that he has been picking up extra cash working as a bouncer at some campus bars.

"If you can do that, you can get your ass back here and help with chores on the weekend. I am about three weeks behind."

Scooter just nods.

Pierre grabs Scooter's arm as he walks by and looks directly into his son's eyes. "I want to have a nice Christmas and I'm not going to say anything else about this, but if you are not playing football, you are coming back here to help on the weekends, and if you lose your scholarship, I cannot pay for you to stay, do you understand me? I am not trying to be mean, son, but that is just the way of the world."

Scooter looks his dad in the eyes and nods. "I hear you."

Pierre spits a long strand of tobacco juice into the snow and they walk to the back porch.

As Scooter opens the door, his mom peeks back into the porch. She pushes her hands down her flour-covered apron and gives her son a big hug, grabbing him behind his neck.

"I missed you so much," she says.

The house, filled with Christmas decorations, smells like mincemeat pie and roasting turkey. Scooter takes his duffle bag up the narrow stairs and down the hall to the last door on the left. His bedroom, with its single bed and posters of John Elway and Michael Jordan, is untouched. Pierre keeps the house a blazing eighty degrees, periodically stoking the wood-burning furnace in the hand-dug basement. Irene has left one of the windows in Scooter's room cracked, knowing he will never sleep in the heat. Through the open window, Scooter can hear a cow wailing in the pasture across the road.

It is just after noon on Christmas Day, and the entire family will be coming up the hill around four or so. His little cousins will bask in the majesty of the tree in the corner of the living room (a room where Irene allows no food or drink and, as such, no one ever really uses, except for Christmas) with presents stacked above the lower branches and spilling out throughout the room. The children will wait impatiently for Pierre and Scooter (and Donny) to finish milking before they can open their presents.

Scooter takes off his street clothes. He puts on long underwear and a worn cotton button-down work shirt over the top. He presumes (correctly) that his coveralls are still hanging on one of the hooks on the back porch. He goes downstairs to find Pierre snoring in his La-Z-Boy chair with the farm report playing on the radio next to him. Irene continues to prepare food for the feast, monitoring the turkey and ricing some potatoes while she waits for loaves of dough in tins covered with dishtowels to rise. Scooter sits on one of the barstools on the end of the large island.

"How is Diana? Did you two come home separately?" Irene asks.

Scooter knew this was coming too and has been dreading it. He doesn't want to have this conversation with anyone, much less his mother.

"She didn't come home."

His mother stops ricing and looks up at him with raised eyebrows.

"We broke up, Mom, or drifted apart. Anyway, she has a new boyfriend and stayed back with him."

Irene comes to him and puts her hand on his back.

"I am sorry son. I am so, so sorry. Are you okay?"

Scooter shrugs. "I'm fine. She was my high school sweetheart. People don't stay together forever like you and Dad anymore."

"Oh, honey," says Irene.

AROUND TWO THIRTY, PIERRE AND SCOOTER START GET-ting ready for milking. They sweep the lime that was spread after the morning milking into the gutters and run the gutters again to get everything missed out of the barn. Scooter goes up into the haymow and throws down some bales of hay to distribute in the troughs in front of each milking station. He then takes a milk crate full of giant bottles into the tank room, opens the spigot at the bottom of the huge stainless-steel tank, and fills the bottles with thick, creamy milk. He stretches big rubber nipples across the opening of each bottle and takes the crate upstairs to the calf stalls. He puts each one on a hanger on the outside of each calf's stall and watches for a moment as the calves greedily suck down the milk.

Donny pulls the manure spreader away from the barn with the old John Deere tractor. Scooter can hear the chugging engine making its way up the road and then across to spread the fresh manure onto the frozen fields, leaving the promise of an aromatic spring thaw. Scooter follows his dad out to the cluster of silos next to the machine shed. His father cranks a handle attached to a steel cable and then flips a switch. Silage starts flowing into the free-stall barn adjacent to the milking barn. After about five minutes, the central trough of the free-stall barn, just below head level for the cows, is filled with a sweet, sticky corn and hay mixture that smells like molasses. Pierre flips the switch and the motor turning the auger stops rumbling. They can hear each other again, but there is nothing to say.

They walk across the cow yard and open the big gate that opens out to the ridge road. The cows are gathered at the gate on the other side of the road that opens to the pasture. The wind whips across the road and stings their cheeks. A few light snowflakes are falling. They have on insulated green John Deere caps with flaps that fold down over their ears. The coveralls and long underwear they wear render the Wisconsin winter more of an inconvenience than a discomfort. At least on most days.

As Scooter crosses the road behind his dad, he feels the winter on his cheeks and thinks about how far from this life he knows so well he has ventured. It is as if he is an imposter here now. A sinister visitor to this Norman Rockwell Eden.

By the time the morning milking is done the next day, the snow has been cleared with the old Bobcat and the temperature has dropped, freezing everything in place. Pierre and Irene walk down to see Scooter off. His mom gives him a hug and hands him a brown bag with sliced turkey and crescent rolls inside. Scooter gets into the pickup, and his dad motions for Scooter to roll down the window.

Pierre leans in and says, "Remember what we talked about. If you have enough time to make money for yourself, you have enough time to get back here and help me with chores, especially now that you have a vehicle. Also, no football, no go. I am barely managing here."

Scooter nods again and starts the engine. He turns left out of the driveway to take the back way along the Wisconsin River bottom. He is in third by the time he reaches the crest of the first hill east of the farm. He slams his boot into the floorboards and feels weightless as the wheels briefly, for just an instant, leave the road. It makes him crack a smile. He has no intention of abiding his father's command. He can make enough money in a month to pay the note on the farm for a year. He just can't tell Pierre that.

Chapter 25

DECEMBER 27, 1986

Scooter is up and at the Nat by six o'clock. No one is there. He finds the barely functioning stereo system and turns it on. It is tuned to 101.5 WIBA FM. Keith Moon's drums are Scooter's metronome as he starts working out. He alternates from the squat rack to bench to deadlifts then pull-ups, then curls, triceps, and back to squats. He moves through the exercises over and over, adding weight from round to round. He is moving weight at a frenetic pace as if he is slinging bales of hay onto the back of a moving trailer. When he can't add any more, he lies back on the bench. Boston's "Foreplay/Longtime" is on the radio rattling through the weight room. It occurs to him that he has never been there alone before. The song is making him feel nostalgic, or lonely, or something. His light gray sweats are dark, wet, and heavy.

This is how he moves through life over the next three days. He works out as hard as he ever has twice a day. On his own. Every day, he commits to remaking himself as even stronger than before the injury. His knee is almost back to normal, and he can squat almost as much as he did before the accident, but there is still an odd twinge or a weird step here and there. He uses that uncertainty to fuel his determination to get back to what he was and better. He grits his teeth, his legs shaking under the weight of the bar.

Mrs. Winchester is off for the long weekend, seeing as how essentially the entire campus is on break. Scooter has plenty of cash and alternates between Parthenon Gyros and La Bamba Burritos—burritos as big as your head—for dinner. Mickey's Dairy Bar is still open, and after his morning workouts he washes down a scramble of eggs, cheese, bacon, and hash browns with a thick chocolate malt. He feels full almost until dinner.

Sunday afternoon, Ferris shows up after driving solo home and back to California for Christmas. When he stumbles into the room, he looks as if he has been up all night. He throws a duffle bag onto the floor. "Take a look in there, amigo, this is a whole different animal. 'Kind' bud. KB. No more selling pounds of Mexican brick weed. People will pay four hundred an ounce for this. Ronny and Jonny are giving it to us for half that. Ten pounds every two weeks. No one has this kind of shit. No one, man." With that, Ferris flops down on his bed and passes out immediately. He almost instantly begins a high-frequency snoring.

Scooter opens the duffle bag and is overcome by a combination of skunk and citrus unlike anything he has ever smelled. He grabs a large Ziploc bag of the stuff and heads out as Ferris's sleep cycle shifts into second gear and his snoring reaches another level of harmonic convergence. The windows are rattling.

Scooter pedals east along the lakeshore path, his shadow long in front of him. The cool air chaps his face. He merges onto the street at the Union and speeds down an empty State Street toward the East Side and Lake Monona. He walks his bike around the back of the ramshackle Cape Cod and finds Spencer sitting around the fire pit in front of a huge bonfire with a near freezing beer in his hand and a blanket over his shoulders.

"Scoot!" Spencer says. "Grab a beer and a chair. Good to see you, man."

Scooter takes off his backpack, sits next to Spencer, and hands the Ziploc to him. "Take a look and a sniff inside."

Spencer does so. "Can we smoke some?" Spencer asks with a grin.

"Sure," Scooter says, "I think we should use a clean bong though."

Spencer walks the stone path into the house, and Scooter follows him into the kitchen and grabs a beer. Spencer opens the dishwasher, which contains a sparkling, freshly washed glass bong. They fill it with water, pack the bowl, and head back to the fire circle. Spencer takes the first hit. He smiles deeply and hands the bong to Scooter. Scooter has never tasted or experienced anything quite like it. He closes his eyes and sees gold and yellow and orange and giggles for the first time in as long as he can remember.

They spend the remaining daylight hours working up a winter sweat on the basketball court playing twenty-one. They talk trash and trade games. Spencer played in high school—at some prep school back east—and has a nice jumper that he can hit, even though Scooter has the height advantage. In between games, they drink beer around the fire and discuss whether the Parthenon or Zorba's has the best gyros in Madison and whether everything is being controlled by aliens.

Spencer buys the bag, a pound, for $6,400. There is no negotiation, just offer and acceptance. Scooter rides back through the city and down State Street in the cold dark. The air is so clear, he thinks he can make out individual beams of light. He gets back to Birch and opens the door to find Ferris sitting cross-legged on the floor with his eyes closed, listening to some sort of classical music.

"This stuff is amazing," Scooter says as Ferris turns to look at him with a wide smile. "I sold a pound to Spencer, $6,400, no questions asked." Scooter tosses the backpack to Ferris, who opens it up and takes out the bills and nods.

"Righteous!"

Scooter sits down on the floor with Ferris, who pulls a couple of Sierra Nevada Pale Ales out of the mini fridge. They load the bong with KB, and each take a couple of hits. Ferris turns on The Dead.

"So, how was the drive, man?" Scooter asks.

Chapter 26

MAY 12, 1987

Misty's BMW skids down the steep hill, the asphalt of Lake Mendota Drive having transitioned to loose gravel as soon as they turned off the road. They are west of campus, where there is a swath of lakeshore that is still wild. The wild area serves as a buffer between the campus and Shorewood Hills, with its large old houses and manicured lawns lining the lakefront. As is typical, there is no one parked in the almost-hidden parking lot. At the west end of the parking lot is a path to the lake that is blocked by a massive log to keep out any wheeled vehicles. The path is hardened dirt and rutted. It descends steeply down to the bank of Lake Mendota, which rises considerably higher on this side of the lake and in some places is sheer sandstone. The path then curves and follows a sort of ledge above the lake with a drop of maybe twenty feet. After two miles or so, it meets up with the wide gravel path to Picnic Point.

The well-traveled path leading to the east and eventually to Picnic Point is frequented by dog walkers and day hikers. But there is a fainter path that goes west. This is the trail that Scooter and Misty follow.

It looks like a deer trail. There is just a narrow strip of dirt and matted-down grass and even ferns pushed aside or bent by gentle, infrequent foot traffic. The trail dead-ends at a circular ledge on top of a cliff, the lake some fifteen feet below.

Scooter and Misty sit on the ledge with their backs to the sandstone, looking out at the lake. The light of the day is expiring. Scooter pulls a pipe and a lighter out of his jeans pocket and they both take a couple of hits, telling the stories of their day. Scooter leans over and kisses Misty on the neck as she laughs about the naked models in her painting class and everyone trying to be mature about a dude disrobing and straddling a bench buck naked in front of a class of mostly female painters. As she tells the story, Scooter works his way down her neck, kissing and unbuttoning as he goes. Misty runs her hands through Scooter's hair and continues down his back, pulling his T-shirt over his head. They stand up, each undoing the other's belt, and Scooter leans down to put his mouth over Misty's. She sighs as he turns her around to face the cliff face. Her hands are on the rock face; she presses back into him.

THEY LIE ON THE MATTED GRASS ATOP THE LEDGE GAZING out over the lake lit now only by the moon. A loon wails a ghostly cry over the lake. As if waking suddenly from a trance, Scooter kisses Misty and abruptly stands up. He runs and jumps off the ledge, grabbing a rope left at this perfect spot by some unknown fellow traveler from who knows when. He swings away from their perch and lets go, falling into the cool, black water of Lake Mendota. Misty follows a few seconds later, whooping as she lets go, soaring above the lake. They embrace in the water, splashing and playing in their secret spot, unseen.

The dicey part is getting out. The drop-off from the ledge is too steep to ascend, so they have to swim about twenty-five yards along the shore to a little beach area that opens between two cliff faces. Scooter and Misty wade to shore and stealthily negotiate the trail back to the parking lot. It is not particularly taxing from a physical standpoint, but they are completely naked and have no way of avoiding any evening dog walkers or bird watchers looking for owls, or other couples like them looking for a secluded spot away from the world. They sprint up the hill, laughing the whole way, and make it back to their spot unseen. They put on their clothes and walk up to the car hand in hand. Misty drives Scooter back to Birch. It is almost eleven o'clock. She kisses him goodnight. As he closes the car door and walks toward the dorm, he gives thanks for his life.

He hears the phone ring as he puts the key in the lock and opens the door. He shakes his head wearily as the skunk smell smacks him in the face. *We need to find another spot to store our ganja,* he thinks to himself. They could easily get busted by even the most laid-back RA. He picks up the receiver and says hello. He hears his mother's voice breaking on the other end.

"He is gone; you need to come home."

"What's wrong Mom? Who is gone?"

"Your father has died. You need to come home." This is all she says, and then she starts crying.

Scooter keeps asking questions, but there are only sobs on the other end of the line. "I will be home in two hours. I love you," he says and hangs up the phone.

Chapter 27

MAY 12, 1987

He returns home to find his mother shattered. It is 1:21 in the morning. She is sitting in a worn armchair opposite Pierre's La-Z-Boy. She is wearing a threadbare floral nightgown and a robe. She stares toward the kitchen and barely looks up as he walks in from the back porch. He walks across the room, kneels in front of the chair, and hugs her.

"What happened, Mom?" he asks as gently as he can. She is slow in answering.

"I had to call the Sawmill to find Donny."

Whether intended or not, Scooter feels a little ice dagger jab into his heart.

"He didn't come home. I didn't know where to look. Donny called 911 and they found him. He was in the back pasture at the Snopes' place."

Scooter looks down at the carpet, the gravity of this happening in his absence pulling at him. "How did it happen?" he asks.

His mom just shrugs. "You'll have to talk to Donny," she says.

"I'm so sorry Mom."

She nods with tears in her eyes, and he hugs her again. "Let's get you up to bed."

He helps her upstairs. They both close the doors to their respective rooms. Scooter spends the night staring at the ceiling. He thinks about his mom, in that bed, alone for the first time in what, twenty-five years, in silence, the absence of Pierre's snoring a constant reminder of something lost. Scooter knows she will not sleep.

He gets out of bed at four thirty and puts on jeans and a work shirt. He walks down the path past the driveway. Donny gets out of his truck upon hearing the approaching footsteps. They work in silence, doing the same things they would have done with Pierre: getting the barn cleaned and ready, filling the troughs with hay and silage, starting up the milking machine. They cross the ridge road, open the gate, and serve as crossing guards for ninety-eight milk cows. Scooter wonders if the cows wonder where Pierre is. He doubts it. The radio is tuned to the same station it always is. The cows usher themselves into the parlor in an orderly fashion. The first shift is in place, and the milk machine is running. Scooter and Donny stand with their backs to the lime-caked walls, each with one of the soles of their boots flat against the wall.

"What happened, Donny?" Scooter asks quietly.

"Pierre let me have Friday night off, just to blow off steam, you know. It has been hot. The hay is early. We been cutting hay all week. The Snopes' back pasture was the last one. We found him there."

"I know where he was found, Donny, what I'm asking is how it happened."

"He was caught in the teeth of the haybine. He must of somehow fell into the teeth. And his foot was about cut off. There was a chain off a sprocket out on the top of the haybine in front of the teeth and blood all over the top of the haybine. I think a chain must have come off its sprocket and Pierre got mad and kicked it, but the sprocket was spinning and went through his boot and cut off most of his foot, and he fell into the teeth."

"Shit," is all Scooter can say. "Shit."

They finish milking and cleaning and walk up to the house. Irene brings coffee and leftover pie to the back porch for Donny. Scooter comes into the kitchen and finds eggs and biscuits and more coffee. Irene is wearing the same nightgown and robe from the night before. Her eyes are glassy, and there is a set to her jaw. It occurs to Scooter that she blames them—him and Donny. They weren't there. The old man was left cutting hay in a back pasture away from anyone, alone, at night, after a week of cutting hay in addition to the constant drumbeat of caring for and milking cows.

Scooter eats his breakfast and drinks his coffee, then goes up to his room to lie in bed for a few hours. He hears the porch door shut as Donny walks down to his rusted truck to nod off to the radio. Scooter wakes around ten thirty. His mom is standing at the foot of his bed.

"God only blessed me with one child. Lord knows you were all we could handle. This is your lot now. You will run this farm. We have nothing else."

She turns and leaves. Scooter rubs his eyes. His life, as it was just a day ago, is now nothing more than a dream, becoming more distant with every waking hour. He realizes how much he has lost. First football, then Diana, and just when he thought he was putting it back together becoming the invincible Scooter Larioux again, Pierre goes and dies.

Scooter pulls on his boots on the back porch. Donny is leaning up against his truck and throws him a tin of Copenhagen.

Donny says, "I guess we gotta go get the haybine, fix it, finish cutting Snopes' and start picking up hay. It's been almost a week in the field for the first ones cut."

Scooter nods.

The haybine is John Deere green, but now with red blood spattered and dried and sticky all over the platform in front of the operator's compartment, on the teeth that rake up the hay, and on the hay itself.

"Fuck. Could have at least fucking rained for us," Scooter says. He climbs up onto the platform and sees the chainless sprocket. The long chain that fits over its teeth is nowhere to be seen. The sprocket is covered in blood. He reaches down below the bloody sprocket and can just grasp the end of the chain. He finds one of the links broken. He manages to fit the chain over the sprocket's teeth and turns the sprocket until he finds the other end of the chain. He fixes the broken link with pliers. He turns the sprocket manually and it works. Scooter wipes his hands, which are now covered in grease, blood, and dirt, on his jeans. He gets onto the seat of the tractor and starts it up. The haybine starts turning. Scooter watches the sharp teeth, still covered in his dad's blood, spinning up toward him, like the talons of a thousand deadly raptors.

Scooter finishes cutting the field and follows Donny back to the machine shed with the grisly machine. They park it outside and get a power washer, then wash away Pierre's blood. Scooter wonders if they should even bale the hay from that field or if they should rinse that too. Or burn it. The thought of the cows eating hay soaked in his father's blood is a complicated one. He tries not to dwell on it.

Chapter 28

MAY 22, 1987

Scooter and Donny work as hard as they ever have in their lives. They fall into the farm rhythm that was worn into place like the ruts of a dirt road so many decades ago by Pierre. Well, actually Louis. Neither Scooter nor Donny propose any changes to the way they run the farm, nor does it occur to them to do so. By the Friday before Memorial Day, they have the hay baled and up in the haymow. They plow fields and plant corn, on top of the daily grind of milking, feeding, and caring for the cows and calves. Irene keeps them fed and washes Scooter's clothes, but otherwise keeps mostly to herself. Scooter catches a hard stare from her faded blue eyes from time to time.

The family comes up to grill out and for dinner on Saturday afternoon. After his uncles pack up their kids for the drive down the coulee to the river bottom and back to Prairie, Scooter sits at the picnic table watching the sunset and listening to the sounds of the animals that are now all in his charge. Irene bangs the screen door and steps off the front stoop with a banker's box full of ledgers and loose papers and sets it down on the picnic table in front of Scooter.

"This is the farm business, I figure it's time you attend to this. For instance, you need to make sure we have the money to make payments and then actually make them. You also need to think about selling off some of those boy calves, decide whether we can sell hay, and whether to buy any cows. That is usually the kind of thing your father would start thinking of at this time of year."

Scooter has been so busy with keeping up with the physical work of the farm that the business stuff hasn't even crossed his mind. His Agriculture Business class was supposed to be preparing him for exactly this. It was easy enough to apply it to making a weed business profitable and reasonably concealed. But when he thinks about the complications of running a farm—buying feed, selling animals, selling milk, raising crops—he can't seem to bring any of what he learned to mind.

"I'll look through this stuff this weekend and see what I can figure out," he says to his mother with a nod.

She goes back in the house, tidies the kitchen, and sighs up the stairs to get ready for bed.

Scooter goes into the kitchen and dials his dorm. Ferris answers on the first ring.

"Dude, you need to get back here."

It has been more than two weeks since Pierre died. Finals are over, and Ferris needs to pack up and go back home.

"Ferris, I can't leave. This is it for me. I have to run the farm. I have no choice. There is no choice."

"Fucking A, Scooter, I can't handle all of these fucking drops. I have to move out this weekend and everything is chaos."

Scooter groans. "Yeah, that was actually why I was calling. Do you think you can pack up the rest of my shit and drop it here on your way home? I wouldn't ask, but I literally cannot get away from here right now."

Ferris doesn't answer right away. "Okay, man," he eventually says. "I'll show up sometime tomorrow. But you owe me. We need to figure out a plan going forward. You can't just drop everything and become a farmer."

"Maybe this is what I always was."

It is a sight to see the Grand Marquis navigate the loose gravel and ruts of the driveway around the barn and granary, like a boat being pushed this way and that by crossing waves. Scooter is sitting at the picnic table in front of the house, having finished lunch. He has an hour or so before he needs to load some hay and get ready to milk.

Ferris smiles mightily as Scooter strides down the path to meet his friend. Ferris gets out of the car and gives Scooter a big hug. "I'm sorry, man. I really can't believe all of this."

"I know," says Scooter.

Ferris digs out Scooter's suitcase with his remaining clothes and a backpack full of books and hands them to Scooter. He also hands Scooter a couple of grocery bags stuffed with almost $100,000 in cash. Each bag has some loose papers on top to conceal the cash.

"It is a relief to get all this shit out of the dorm," Ferris says. "Believe me, I was sweating bullets when Peregrine showed up looking for you. He knocked on the door like a fucking sledgehammer."

Scooter takes Ferris up to his room first to stash the cash and the hefty package of weed that Ferris concealed in Scooter's suitcase. In the kitchen, Scooter reintroduces Ferris to his mom.

"Mom, you remember, this is Ferris, he was my room-mate, he is the kicker."

"Nice to see you," Irene says, with no emotion in her voice or eyes. "You must be hungry." She hands him a plate with crescent rolls and sliced pot roast that she has reheated in the oven and smothered with gravy. There are mashed potatoes and corn on the side. She pours Ferris a glass of ice-cold milk from the glass pitcher in the refrigerator. Ferris stares at it with a look of bewilderment: the inch or so of cream floating on top of the milk is not something he has seen before. But it is unbelievably delicious, as is the meal.

Sated, Ferris compliments Irene profusely and jokingly says he could get used to farm life.

"I guess you can join me for chores, then," Scooter says.

"Are you staying the night?" Irene asks.

Ferris shrugs. "I guess so."

Ferris is in awe of Donny. "I had no idea you guys were this fucking hardcore out here," he says quietly to Scooter as Donny jumps from the back of the trailer and takes off his shirt in the afternoon heat.

"The fuck is this?" Donny asks as they pass him.

"Donny, this is my roommate Ferris, he is the kicker for the Badgers."

"Oh, okay. Nice to meet you," says Donny. "Is this like some kind of school ride-along program or something?"

The three are picking up bales, and it is a relief to have Ferris there to help. Ferris will take Scooter's typical spot, following the wagon and picking up and hoisting bales to Scooter, who will stack them in the wagon. Donny will assume Pierre's role driving the truck and controlling the speed of the operation.

Scooter whispers to Donny, "Take it easy on him," as he gets out of the truck.

Donny flashes a gold canine tooth.

About halfway through the third row of bales, Ferris has broken a sweat, but he is looking pretty relaxed and not showing any serious effort, getting the bales up and into the back of the wagon without breaking stride. Scooter can feel Donny increase the speed ever so slightly. By the time they reach the last of the rows and the wagon is almost full, Ferris is ragged and soaked in his own sweat. But he doesn't complain. Scooter gets the last bale situated on the wagon and pulls his friend onto the back.

"Nice job, man. This really was a help. I mean that."

Ferris slumps against the stack of bales. He closes his eyes as the wagon rattles over the rutted dirt road. "Man," Ferris says weakly. "Now I know how you got to be you."

Back at the barn, Donny punches Ferris's shoulder. "Not bad," Donny says.

WAKING UP FERRIS AT FOUR IN THE MORNING IS, NOT surprisingly, a challenge. Scooter and Ferris stayed up after Irene went to bed and smoked bowls lying on their backs in the huge yard looking at the endless blanket of stars, searching for fast-moving satellites and elusive shooting stars, the Milky Way like a scar across the indigo, pulsing sky. Ferris moans a few times and rolls around on the makeshift bed on the floor of Scooter's room. Scooter tells Ferris that he doesn't have to help. He can sleep in. Irene will be up in no time to cook breakfast. As Scooter starts out the door, Ferris forces himself up. He pulls on shorts and Chuck Taylors.

Donny takes a fist-size wad of Copenhagen and hands the tin to Scooter, who feels the sting of wintergreen as the softness of sleep shifts to the hardness of day and work.

Ferris drifts behind the two, following them like a sleep-walker as they silently go through their morning routine with the radio switching between scratchy big bands and milk-futures prices.

As the first round of cows are settled and there is a lull in the need for anyone to do anything, Scooter looks at Ferris, who is starting to perk up. "So, I never really asked, what is your plan for the summer?"

"Uh, not totally sure. I'll probably crash with Ronny and Jonny for a while at the beach. Beyond that, I don't really know."

Chapter 29

AUGUST 29, 1987

Managing the farm business is a hell of a lot easier with $100,000 in cash to spend. Scooter buys a new skid-steer loader with several attachments that make moving hay and cleaning out the stalls in the free-stall barn and the cow yard quicker and just cleaner. He pays Donny in cash every two weeks and gives him a 10 percent raise.

When Scooter peels off the bills and hands them to Donny for the first time, Donny says, "Well, where did this come from, Scoot?"

"Does it matter?" Scooter asks.

"I guess not."

Scooter pays Doc Bourne in cash for the annual vaccinations, wellness checks, and antibiotics. He also buys some young heifers that will be milk cows by fall from the Amish, who are always happy to take cash over checks. Finally, he buys a new haybine attachment for the tractor. Fuck if he'll keep working with the machine that killed his father.

Taking care of as many expenses as possible with cash makes the farm suddenly profitable. Just from milk sales alone, the farm banks a profit of $10,000 a month for June, July, and August. But Scooter's stash of cash is starting to run low. On the last weekend in August, he decides to drive down to the Sawmill with Donny on a Saturday night.

As they walk in, Scooter watches Donny put on a jean jacket with its sleeves cut off and a patch on the back with a cartoonish dog underneath the words Hounds of Hell.

"What's that?" Scooter asks.

"Um, that's my motorcycle club. Some of your buddies are riding with us now, Dickie Snopes and Walter Hill, you remember those guys?"

Not sure if Donny is joking or not, Scooter, says, "Donny, I graduated a year ago. It has been a pretty intense year, but I think the brain damage is minimal."

They sit and drink ice-cold Miller Lites and then add some shots of Jack Daniels. Before long, Dickie, Walter, and two other wiry tattooed bikers who could be Dickie's brothers walk in. No doubt at least one of them is some Snopes or another.

Behind the Sawmill, the hot wind is gathering moisture from the great river and sprinkling it over the town like so much fairy dust. They carry beers out from the bar to a back patio looking out over the river and huddle around Scooter, holding up hands to shield the bowl and lighter from the wind. The lighter lights and Scooter hands the fresh bowl to Donny, who inhales as the orange glow of the lighter makes the packed weed crackle. Donny holds the smoke in, smiling and then coughing.

"Holy shit. Holy fucking shit! This shit is unbelievable." Donny hands the bowl to Dickie.

Everyone in the circle takes two puffs and passes. It is just dust and ash when it gets back to Scooter. He takes a bag out of his pocket and packs some more before passing it around again. Donny is literally howling at the moon.

Just then a gigantic swarm of mayflies like a cloud of doom rising from the primordial waters swarms the patio, darkening the lights and covering everyone and everything in bugs. They run inside and sit four across at the bar.

After everyone calms down from the insect invasion, Scooter turns to Donny. "So, do you guys know people who would buy this? If you guys can sell it for $400 an ounce, I can give it to you for $5,000 a pound, which gives you a profit of $1,400 a pound."

"Shit, we could sure as hell give it a shot. I bet half the people in here would scrape up fifty for an eighth," says Donny.

"I'll tell you what," says Scooter. "I'll front you a quarter pound. See how you guys do and let me know if you want me to get more." He turns to Dickie. "I will only deal with Donny. Place all your orders through him. No one mentions my name. Got it?" Scooter looks Dickie right in the eyes, dead serious.

Dickie, who hasn't stopped giggling from the weed and from Walter screaming as the mayflies attacked them, stops smiling for just an instant and nods.

Scooter hands Donny a backpack with the quarter pound in it. "Donny, I'll see you tomorrow morning bright and early then. You boys behave." Scooter chuckles as he leaves, wondering what such a crew will get up to tonight.

Scooter creeps up the stairs and crawls into bed. It is only ten thirty, but it is as late as he has been up in weeks. It also feels a little weird to be high and in the house alone with his grieving mother. The windows in his room are wide open, and he lies on his back listening to the intense chirping of the grasshoppers and occasional noises from the cows. He thinks about Diana. She must be due soon. He misses Misty.

Donny is passed out in his truck when Scooter walks past on the way to morning milking. Scooter stands on the running board and rocks the truck back and forth until the occupant is rattled around enough to pick his head up and run his knuckles over his eyes. Scooter figures Donny has been there since leaving the bar, or a brief stop afterward.

"So, what is it that you do in your little biker gang other than craft projects like sewing patches on jackets?" Scooter asks.

Donny is wiping his face after puking up Budweiser foam. "I don't know. We do what biker gangs do. Ride around and look for places to party and get in fights and find girls."

Scooter nods. "Why, though?"

Donny just looks at him. "Anyway," says Donny, "we sold all your shit, can you get more?" He reaches through the window of his pickup and pulls out Scooter's backpack, now stuffed with cash.

Scooter smiles and chuckles. "Donny, we may just be able to make farming profitable." As he says it, he thinks back to Pierre and his joke about winning the lottery.

Part II

CYRUS

Chapter 30

OCTOBER 13, 2003

Milwaukee, WI

C yrus Jackson sits in front of a large TV in the sitting area of his hotel suite. The carpet is thick and soft. He looks at it and thinks of the word "cashmere." The carpet is cream colored, but with a subtle paisley pattern. There is a fruit basket wrapped in colorful cellophane and a bottle of champagne, also wrapped in cellophane, on the wide coffee table in front of him. He can lay his long frame across the main part of the sectional sofa without touching either end. The furniture, the carpet, the woodwork—it is not new. There are nicks on the legs of the desk, and the plumbing thumps and hums when he flushes the toilet. The hotel, or more specifically, the Milwaukee Athletic Club, is old and battered, but it still maintains an air of luxury and grandness, maybe more so because it is from a bygone era.

Cyrus is amused and slightly awed to even find himself in this situation. It is the kind of space he imagines Nixon watching some TV program about himself as everything crumbled around him and he was left alone by his attendants and advisers, smoking and thinking. Cyrus can't remember if Nixon smoked or not.

Cyrus never thought of himself as rich, but he certainly felt privileged growing up in Madison, Wisconsin. The son of two professors, his mother a professor of Medieval Women's Studies and his dad a Physics professor. He felt that they were well off, whatever that meant. But he has never stayed in a hotel like this, or even ever really thought about the existence of places like this. He knew they existed. They just weren't part of his consciousness. The windows open, although they creak as he opens them, and he notices little chips in the varnish on the windowsill, to a view up Wisconsin Avenue and to the ice-blue lake that presents, it seems for his benefit, a sort of monument to everything right with the world. The view makes him think of those blue-marble pictures of the earth from space. *Here is earth in all its blueness*, he thinks.

His stay at the hotel is completely paid for by a law firm, Earnhardt and Earnhardt, LLP. He is in the first semester of his second year of law school at the University of Wisconsin in Madison, just in Milwaukee for the night to interview the following day. All of this—the big hotel room, the champagne, the expense account—is because he did well on some exams the year before. The firms are now recruiting him, and it feels strange and not really earned.

He spent most of his life in a swimming pool watching the unmoving black line below him and pushing his body off one wall and then, fourteen or so seconds and twelve strokes later, off the opposite wall on frigid mornings and dark evenings and hot afternoons and everything in between, sacrificing so much he thinks now, but he is not sure if he means it. All he knows is it was so much time.

And he excelled. He had always wanted to play basketball, but by the time he grew to a height where that even seemed like an option, he was so entrenched in swimming that it did not make sense to switch sports. He enjoyed the success that swimming brought him. He was considered one of the best distance swimmers in the country at age seventeen. Maybe top twenty, top thirty in the country. Not quite able to reach up to Olympic trials, but certainly elite by any measure. And he was recruited then too. He thought it was amazing at the time. Coaches sent him plane tickets to travel to different schools where he was met by upperclassman swim team members who took him to football games and parties before and after the games. At the parties, they drank beer and played quarters and some of the upperclassmen even told him how much they wanted him to come and be their teammate. He always secretly wondered why they gave a shit. What was he to them? Why did they care? But he was happy to hear the words and just excited to be in a position to go to school for free. But he was even happier, or prouder, or something like that, to be able to know and have other people know that he was an elite athlete.

The swimming recruiting was nothing like the way he is being recruited now. On those college trips, now a decade ago, they put him up in dorms and sent him to cookouts and fast-food restaurants. There was no Dom Perignon in cellophane or unlimited expense accounts or hotel suites that are bigger than his apartment. *How much is this costing?* he wonders. This is his third week of "callback" interviews. He has been to Chicago, Dallas, and New York. Next week he is going to San Francisco for the weekend. He is astounded by the efforts these firms are expending to get him to go work for them. All because he had a good week a year ago. He didn't really even study that hard. He isn't really even sure that he wants to be a lawyer.

He sits down on the couch and flips through TV channels as he absentmindedly begins peeling the cellophane and then the foil off the champagne bottle. He tries to enjoy it, to appreciate the luxury and take it in, to be part of it and be present with it. But it feels forced. He is alone in a hotel room. He pops the cork and takes a pull directly from the bottle. It is four o'clock in the afternoon, and his interviews start at nine the next morning.

The bottle is gone before he knows it, and he is standing in the small elevator pressing the down button, fixing his hair in the reflection of the mirrored brass doors. He likes the way he looks in a well-worn blue polo shirt with a red logo. His straw hair is straight and chopped in front revealing his youthful face—the beauty mark on his left cheek and his light-brown eyes.

The elevator opens to a lobby that has a faint smell of cigar smoke and radiates a certain old-world opulence. The building is, he supposes, of the art deco style. There are geometric patterns above the door frames with light sconces that look like deconstructed gemstones. The entrance has a large metallic awning that makes him think of some theater in New York, like where David Letterman shoots his show. There are vast Oriental rugs on the floor covering a patterned parquet that was likely first scuffed before prohibition. There are huge oil paintings on the walls—dark and heavy with gilded frames and lit by overhanging lights with translucent green shades.

He walks across the lobby into a bar/restaurant that opens out to the street. The building is just two blocks north of Wisconsin Avenue. Cyrus sits at the bar, which is empty. The bartender presents him with a bowl of mixed nuts. The Brewers are playing the Twins on the two TV screens that bookend the bottles of bourbon, scotch, and vodka that are framed by the bar, which has inlaid wood in a sunburst pattern, as if the bottles are radiating their good cheer and brightening the dim room. Cyrus orders a Guinness and asks for the chicken wings. He settles into the plush leather barstool and his thoughts melt away.

AFTER DINNER, HE FINDS HIMSELF CLIMBING THE SPIRAL staircase past giant oil paintings. The alcohol has made him recede into himself, as if he had taken two steps back behind his eyes and now sits at the controls of a complicated machine navigating its surroundings. There is a crystal chandelier that hangs above the staircase, breaking up the warm-colored light and scattering it over the vast and varied space. The staircase ends on the third floor. It opens to a ballroom. Across the landing is another, smaller room.

There is a nameplate above the doorway that reads Bali Room. The Bali Room has a large oval-shaped bar in the middle of it. The walls are adorned with a mural that apparently depicts life in Bali. In the mural at least, all the women in Bali are topless.

He is the only one there. Geometrically arranged around the room are about a dozen four-top tables. Some four paces from the bar, the tables scatter to provide space for a pool table. Cyrus wins the bartender's attention away from polishing pints and rocks glasses.

"How much is it to play pool?"

The bartender smiles and gestures broadly. "Have at it. What can I get you?"

Cyrus shakes his head in a sort of disbelieving haze at his good fortune and orders an old- fashioned, sweet.

THE NEXT MORNING, CYRUS TAKES THE ELEVATOR DOWN to the sixth floor, the men's athletic department. An attendant shows him to a guest locker. He changes into a speedo and walks along a walkway that is also a balcony overlooking the pool. It is twenty-five yards long; he can tell that just by walking its length. On the wall opposite the walkway and stairs he now descends is an expansive mural with a Greek-island landscape.

As he reaches the pool deck, he grabs a kickboard, a pull buoy, and a towel. At seven thirty the pool is empty, save for an attendant who keeps popping in to arrange a lunch buffet on the pool deck.

Cyrus slips into the pool and knows that it is above eighty degrees; too warm to really work out. All the competition pools he ever swam in were kept somewhere between seventy-six and seventy-nine degrees. Even in seventy-nine-degree water, his cheeks would start to flush with any sustained effort. The pool, on this day especially, is a luxury. The warm water is not the usual jolt to the system that is often the most difficult, at least mentally, part of any swimming workout. Getting into this pool is like sliding from one aspect of comfort to another. He bobs up and down a couple of times and spits on the inside of his goggles before running his fingers along the lenses. He then pulls the goggle strap over the back of his head. He swings his arms out in front of him and behind him, clapping his hands behind him as he does so. He jumps up one last time and lets his body drop down into the water. He pushes off the wall, stretching into a streamline position and exhaling as he glides below the backstroke flags.

His body fights the first five hundred yards. His mind is squirrely, thinking of a way out of the activity, a reason to go take a sauna, or just a long shower. Maybe he should cut this short and prepare for the interviews. His mind focuses now on a pinch in his shoulder, now on the tightness in his triceps. His breathing is choppy. At about five hundred yards, his thoughts melt away. He stretches out his stroke and begins reaching further, rolling more from side to side as he smoothly knocks down length after length. His thoughts are indistinguishable from the water he moves through and the motion of his arms and legs that move him through it. He pushes hard against the wall and stretches his hands up above his head, his right hand overlapping his left hand with his thumb hooked around the outside of his palm to keep the hands tightly sandwiched together. He squeezes his ears with his biceps and extends as far as he can, gliding and starting to kick as his momentum slows. He breaks the water with his right elbow after his hand finishes pulling the water down to his hip and flicking it toward his feet.

Chapter 31

OCTOBER 31, 2005

Cyrus crawls into bed, moving slowly, trying not to disturb Lucy. Biggie growls and shows his teeth as Cyrus gently pushes him with two hands; one pushing on the side of his neck and one at his haunch, trying to slide him to the center of the bed. It is three in the morning, and Cyrus has spent the last fifteen minutes in the shower trying to scrub the cigarette smell off his body and out of his hair after going out to "have a beer" after work with his associate mentor, Grayson Asher. Things got a bit out of hand.

Sliding Biggie out of the way pulls at the duvet, which falls to the floor leaving Lucy naked and uncovered. Cyrus scrambles to pull the duvet back up over her, so as not to wake her. He loses his balance and finds himself on top of her.

"What the hell, Cyrus?" she says groggily, waking slightly.

Cyrus strokes her thigh and then kisses her hair. "Sorry, go back to sleep, it's almost morning."

She rolls toward him and pushes her face into his chest, her hands sliding down under the covers. "I'm awake now," she says with a little smile.

He wakes up hours later. Lucy is gone. Biggie is asleep

at the foot of the bed. It must be a little after seven. He hears the train rattling in from Chicago. His mind braces for the coming blast as the train crosses the Milwaukee River and turns west to enter the station, allowing for a brief but perfectly timed moment when the full force of the whistle is aimed directly at his bedroom window. The piercing sound manifests itself more as a vision than a sound. He thinks he can see spears of light shooting into his eyes.

He thinks of the word "desiccated." He pictures a dried-out corn husk blowing around a dirt road. That is exactly what he feels like. He runs the tap and shovels water into his mouth using both hands. He huffs into his hands in the shower, trying to detect any off-gassing of ethanol that he needs to be wary of before entering an elevator or conference room. He can't tell. It's probably just pouring out of him and he is inured to it.

He stops at the Voyageur coffee shop before backtracking to the office. Lucy is wearing tight black jeans and a cotton V-neck T-shirt under a white apron. Each item of clothing seems stretched to its limits. She gives two blasts on the steamer as he approaches the counter.

"Well, if it isn't the party boy off to work."

Cyrus gives a meek smile and mumbles, "Cappuccino, sorry again, didn't mean to stay out that late…"

"That's what I thought," says Lucy, who turns to swirling espresso and the alchemic mixing of the froth with the brew to create a big heart. She hands the cup to Cyrus and says, "Have a nice day, baby. I have rehearsal tonight, so you are alone for dinner."

Lucy is an apprentice in the Milwaukee ballet. She has a dream of making it as a regular, which means group rehearsals four nights a week and countless studio time on her own, all unpaid.

Cyrus turns and walks back down Milwaukee Street.

There is a scent in the city just before it rains. It is a musty sort of dust smell that tickles the nose. Cyrus wonders where it comes from or if anyone has ever thought to study the phenomenon. But he smells it and sneezes just as he steps onto the sidewalk, and by the time he reaches the 414 building elevator, only a block and a half away, his clothes and hair are rain-soaked and disheveled, and he is shivering.

Just before the elevator door closes, Ed Song, Earnhardt and Earnhardt's top billing lawyer, steps onto the elevator. Everything about him is perfect. His hair is a perfect fade with a little length on top and still unblemished by gray. His tan herringbone suit is fresh and wrinkle-free. His tie has a perfect knot with a tear-shaped dimple below it, and his shoes reflect the ceiling lights. Not to mention that the man still looks like he could play professional football.

Cyrus is freaked out by this level of perfection. He pushes into the back corner of the elevator as far as he can, almost cowering. As soon as the doors close, Song turns around and extends his hand.

"I don't think we've met. I'm Ed Song. You are one of our new associates, right? Looks like you got caught a little unprepared today." He laughs a little as Cyrus takes his hand.

"Nice to meet you."

Song follows Cyrus into his office and sits down in one of the guest chairs. *A bit presumptuous, this guy,* Cyrus thinks. Song sets his briefcase at his feet, neatly crosses his knees, and picks at the cuff of his pants.

"Do you know about my practice, Cyrus?"

Cyrus can't deny that Song smells good. Cyrus has never been a cologne guy, but he starts thinking right there that maybe he could be. This is the scent of someone you want to be around. He just smells good—maybe there is a little pine there, maybe some musk.

"Sure," Cyrus says, "you are the lawyer everyone wants to be. You are the best product-liability litigator in the country."

What Cyrus doesn't say is that of course everyone knows Ed Song and his résumé. He is one of the few African American partners at Earnhardt and certainly the only lawyer in the firm who played in the NFL. The whispers among the associates center around why Ed actually works at Earnhardt. He made a ton of money in the NFL. He walked away from football after suffering his third concussion, and playing three years of a $30 Million contract. He walked right into Harvard law. At least in the minds of the overworked associates, there is no good reason someone like that needs to work, or at least work as hard as Song does. Many years he bills the most hours in the firm. The associate gossip mill postulates that Song must have some sort of financial problem. Gambling is the favorite theory.

Song smiles a weary smile and looks at Cyrus with eyes that radiate into crow's feet honed by countless hours searching the sky for footballs thrown impossibly far, only reachable by a sprinting Ed Song.

"Well, I don't like to put myself into such a narrow category, but I am someone who tries cases and happens to be very good at it."

Such a modest guy, Cyrus thinks to himself.

"I thought maybe, if you have any interest in doing so, you could help me out on a case I have pending in upstate New York. We have a trial date in two months."

Cyrus wonders if he should say yes or ask for more time to think about it. That would seem like the more mature answer; the answer of someone who is legitimately giving the offer some thought and actual consideration.

"Sure, Mr. Song, I would be happy to help in any way that I can."

"Call me Ed," says Song. "That is outstanding. I really look forward to working with you. Let's get lunch tomorrow and I can fill you in on what is going on."

Song's scent still lingers after he leaves the room.

Lunch with Song starts with cigars and scotch. Expensive scotch. They are sitting on the patio of his club in the autumn sunshine. Song's suit coat is laid just so over the back of the next chair over. Song looks to the sky as he savors the taste of his cigar. Cyrus knows it is Cuban and he is impressed, wondering how it got smuggled in and how someone like Song gets his hands on such expensive contraband. Cyrus appreciates the scent, but he can't stand smoking cigars and is trying hard to look like he knows what he is doing and enjoy the thing. He fights with every fiber in his being not to inhale and suck the burning fumes down into his lungs. *What is the point of smoking if you can't inhale,* he thinks. He tries to smile and squirms in his seat in front of a tall, perspiring beer glass.

"It doesn't get any better than this, Cyrus," Song says. "Here we are, being paid to sit in the sun, enjoy a good cigar and this nectar of the gods—Song swirls a glass of Macallan 24—and talk about the important things in life." He pauses and looks down the tenth fairway. The momentary silence makes Cyrus uncomfortable. He tries another puff of the cigar and almost chokes. Song turns back to him and looks briefly troubled by the quality of his company.

"Let me outline the case for you. It concerns a fatal motorcycle accident that occurred in upstate New York. Todd O'Leary was working on the case, but as you know, he is now leaving us, and I need someone to help me get the case ready for trial and to actually try it with me." He takes a sip of scotch and lets it linger in his mouth before continuing. "Our client is the venerable Outlaw Motorcycle Corporation. They make custom bikes, mostly for yuppies, or at least people with money. They build a lot of theme bikes. They will make a bike to match your sports car, or with your favorite team's logo, or make the bike look like a helicopter or an alien." Song sips his drink. "You get the idea.

"The plaintiff's decedent, Mr. Hebert, was a gentleman who was on a ride with his wife and some friends, the Kellers, in the Finger Lakes region, visiting wineries. At the time of the accident, they were following a section of road along Cayuga Lake. They were, I believe, on the west side of the lake where there are some cliffs that drop down into the lake. At the time of the accident, they were on a slight incline. There was a gentle curve to the left, not one that required braking mind you, but a curve nevertheless. The Heberts were staggered behind the Kellers and on the inside of the lane as they started taking the curve to the left. But Mr. Hebert never turned his bike. As the road curved, Mr. Hebert just continued in a straight line. As this was happening, Mrs. Hebert was yelling 'Lake! Lake! Lake!' Over and over.

"Mr. Hebert did not respond. Mrs. Hebert bailed off the bike at the last second. She broke her wrist and got some significant road rash, but has fully recovered. Mr. Hebert continued riding, launching the bike into oblivion over a thirty-foot cliff, the chrome sparkling in the afternoon sun.

Fire rescue pulled the bike out of the lake. Mr. Hebert was still astride it gripping the handlebars.

"I will send you the file number and you can start going through the file tonight. We have some motions in limine to complete and exhibits to prepare in the next few weeks."

BACK AT THE OFFICE, SONG'S ASSISTANT SENDS CYRUS the file number for the Hebert file. Cyrus walks down the hall to locate the physical file. He brings back folders of deposition transcripts, medical records, police reports, and recorded interviews. He spends the rest of the day lazily reading through them, turning the material into a story in his head. He learns what he can about the life of the Heberts before the fateful moment of their accident. From his medical records, Mr. Hebert was slightly overweight, drank too much, and smoked. Cyrus is hardly one to judge. Turning to the depositions, Cyrus constructs a narrative in his head of the accident day.

The Heberts and Kellers planned for a beautiful ride through the Finger Lakes region, stopping at wineries here and there. They started early, before nine o'clock. It was a hot day. Sometime around noon, they pulled over to eat sandwiches and took a quick dip in a lake. Mr. Hebert complained about the heat to his wife and Mr. Keller. Mr. Hebert was too hot to wear his leathers and stashed them in his saddle bags. As the couples remounted their bikes at the last winery of the day, everyone in the group was fatigued and over their day's journey, ready to just get home to their evening routines. The accident occurred just after four that afternoon. The stops at the wineries would have produced a slight buzz that was probably more of an irritant than anything else at that point. Cyrus feels like he was there with them.

He looks up from his reading. It is five thirty. Shit. He was supposed to be at Flannery's just after five for Todd O'Leary's going-away party. Grayson will give him shit, no doubt. Cyrus shakes off the spell that the case is casting and waits for his computer to shut down. He turns off his lights and slinks out to catch the elevator.

Chapter 32

JANUARY 6, 2006

Plaintiffs' counsel, Conrad Gold has his suit game on point for the opening. Somehow, he has managed to find suspenders with the exact same purple paisley pattern as his tie. Cyrus thinks, surprisingly, they are not a terrible match for the metallic gray suit. The judge has greeted the jury and the courtroom is silent. Gold stands to deliver his opening.

"Hello…" he looks down at some notes, "…hi! My name is Conrad Gold, well you know that, I introduced myself in voir dire. In any event…" It is a rambling mess.

After Gold finishes, the judge beckons Song to address the jury with a simple glance and nod. In contrast to Gold, Song is completely composed. He puts on some cheater glasses and glances at his notes, then neatly folds the cheaters into his pocket and looks up from the lectern.

"May it please the court," Song turns and faces Gold. He sweeps his arm toward plaintiffs' counsel's table, "Counsel, Mrs. Hebert," he turns back toward the jury, "and may it please you ladies and gentlemen of the jury. We are here because Mr. Hebert, for some reason, stopped controlling his motorcycle and drove it over a cliff into Cayuga Lake. That is why we are here.

"First, let me thank you for taking the time out from your lives and doing your duty as citizens of this great country to serve as jurors in this case. You are here because we have a disagreement, plaintiffs and us, the Outlaw Motorcycle Company, which we cannot solve. Our Constitution puts the responsibility of solving such disagreements not on judges, such as our wise Judge Bender in this case, or elected officials or bureaucrats or kings, as it was in the past, but in the hands of citizens who can sit in judgment objectively and fairly judge their fellow citizens. I submit to you that civilization falls apart if we cannot turn to our fellow citizens—to you—to decide these disputes that we cannot solve ourselves.

"There are some things that plaintiffs and Outlaw do not need you to resolve in this case. For instance, the parties do not disagree that Mr. Hebert was a fine man, a good husband, and a loving father, and that his loss is felt by many. The parties also do not disagree that Mrs. Hebert is a nice woman, a wonderful mother, and someone who many call friend, and that she suffered a terrible accident and witnessed her husband launch off a cliff into a lake on his motorcycle. That has impacted her life. No, we do not disagree about those things…"

The jury sits in rapt attention. To Cyrus, they look glad that they have been selected for this case. He assumes it is far more entertaining than the routines of their lives. Cyrus can relate.

Song goes through what the evidence will show: that Mr. Hebert never reported any problem with the motorcycle, that the motorcycle was well engineered and meticulously manufactured, that the accident occurred toward the end of a long, hot day when everyone was tired.

In the middle of his opening Song looks at the jury, pausing as he makes eye contact with individual jurors. "Ladies and gentlemen, I want you to pay particular attention to Mrs. Hebert's testimony in this case. She is a very important witness. I expect that Mrs. Hebert will admit and the evidence will show that as the accident was progressing, she yelled the word "Lake!" several times as loud as she could. Yet her husband continued to ride in a straight line and rode straight off the cliff. Mr. Hebert never responded to Mrs. Hebert's cries. Her warnings."

Song emphasizes that no one had a chance to inspect the bike after the accident because it was sold for scrap. He mentions that the court will explain to the jury that the plaintiffs have the burden of proof and without the actual motorcycle, they cannot meet their burden. At this, the judge raises his eyebrows. This is a legal argument, not appropriate for opening statements. But Gold fails to object. The judge lets it go.

Song concludes, "Ladies and gentlemen, at the end of this trial, I am going to ask you to enter a verdict in favor of the Outlaw Motorcycle Company. That verdict will mean that the Heberts will not be awarded any money in this case. This may be difficult for you to do. You may feel sympathy for Mrs. Hebert because Mr. Hebert was a good man whom many mourn and because Mrs. Hebert is a good woman who went through a terrible accident. But if you listen to the evidence and apply it to the law as the judge directs you, it will be the only verdict that justice can abide. It is the only fair result."

Back in the war room; the sun has gone down, and the town is closed up. Song smiles as he pours himself a few fingers of scotch from the back bar. He leans back in his chair, crosses his long legs and swirls the glass. Song, Cyrus, and their paralegal Rachel sit in jeans listening to Bob Marley and relaxing. After weeks of furious preparation, stress, and worry, the trial is underway, they have made their first pitch to the jury, and they have the weekend to prepare for evidence.

Song says, "Well, what did you think, Cyrus, is this all that you hoped it would be?"

Cyrus thinks he catches a slight smile from Rachel behind her laptop. She is making last minute tweaks to the PowerPoint presentation that their liability expert will use to aid his testimony.

"Honestly, Ed, you were amazing. This whole thing is mind-blowing."

Song's satisfied smile and nod of his head tells Cyrus that the sentiment is exactly what Song wants to hear. It also occurs to Cyrus that finances have nothing to do with why Song does this and why he works so hard. He is a winner. He has always won. He enjoys the spotlight. He enjoys winning. Cyrus feels like an imposter.

PLAINTIFFS' EXPERT AND LAST WITNESS IS A RETIRED aircraft engineer named Jim Morgan, who had briefly worked for NASA and could say, and in fact did say, in a transparent attempt to impress the jury about to be offered his bullshit sandwich for lunch, that he was, in fact, a rocket scientist. Cyrus could not suppress rolling his eyes as soon as Morgan disingenuously sneered the sentence to the jury. Morgan chuckles after he says it to disguise the naked attempt to bolster his credibility as modesty. Cyrus quickly puts his head down and rubs his forehead, hoping the jury did not catch his eye roll.

Gold clumsily directs Morgan through his direct examination. Gold starts with the conclusion, asking Morgan to give his opinions in the case.

"The bike was defectively designed or manufactured. The brake line was susceptible to overheating and failure," Morgan mechanically recites.

Gold never asks how Morgan reached such a conclusion. Instead, Gold asks a series of questions about Morgan's time at NASA. He then asks Morgan to describe for the jury the events leading up to the accident and how the accident happened.

Song objects as Gold asks Morgan how Mr. Hebert responded when he felt his brakes not working properly due to a brake-fluid leak. Standing to address the court, Song articulates his objection.

"Judge, this is all speculation. Unprovable, unknowable, and unlikely."

The judge sustains the objection, but Gold continues to ask his expert leading questions, assuming a brake failure and speculating that Mr. Hebert was distracted by the brake failure, causing him to miss the curve. Song calmly reiterates his objections. The judge sustains them. Gold then asks what Mr. Hebert must have been thinking as the crash unfolded. The question is again disallowed. The whole cross-examination is a disjointed, rambling affair. Gold wastes so much time trying to get Morgan to testify as to what was going through Mr. Hebert's mind that he fails to ask Morgan to articulate any basis for his opinion that the motorcycle is defective.

In contrast, Song's cross-examination is efficient and precise. Song leads Morgan down a path to the inevitable conclusion that his opinion is speculative and unreliable. Morgan admits he has done no testing, in fact he has never even seen the bike—it was sold for scrap. He never went to the accident scene, and he has performed no calculations. All he did was look at some pictures taken by an insurance adjuster. Song then asks Morgan to concede that his opinion that the brakes distracted Mr. Hebert is, at the end of the day, guesswork?

"No, I would not say that," Morgan responds.

"How about, conjecture?" asks Song, looking at the jury while asking the question. He can raise one eyebrow at a time to make a theatrical expression of skepticism.

"It is not conjecture," says Morgan, trying to sound and look as convincing as possible. He sits up and straightens his tie as he raises his voice to make the point.

"Would you call it speculation, then?" asks Song.

To this, Morgan tries to look world-weary, like he has heard this old saw before. "No," says Morgan, "it is not speculation; I analyzed the evidence and used my experience and expertise and came to the most reasonable conclusion."

Song has a little glint in his eye. "Sir, do you consider yourself a psychic?"

"Of course not," responds Morgan.

"Well, I just don't understand then how you can give an opinion that requires you to guess as to what Mr. Hebert was thinking just before his accident, with his wife shouting to get his attention and Mr. Hebert driving straight off the road. You couldn't possibly know what he was thinking at that moment."

"Objection!" Gold has jumped to his feet and is staring angrily at Song.

Song looks down, smiles, and nods his head as if to say that he lost himself. He looks up at Judge Bender and says, "Withdrawn, Your Honor."

He then turns, walking slowly back to counsel table, but stops about halfway and turns back toward Judge Bender and says, "Your Honor, I'm just thinking this through, and I think I need to move to strike Mr. Morgan. His testimony is not based on any evidence at all. It is speculative and unreliable."

Judge Bender sighs. He has been around long enough to have seen this routine, or something similar, before. "Motion denied."

Song sits down and says, "No further questions, Your Honor."

Cyrus, Song, and Rachel prematurely celebrate at a local Tex-Mex chain restaurant, El Burro Loco, that conveniently shares a parking lot with their hotel. They sit at the bar side by side. Cyrus cannot remember ever feeling so physically bad. In the war room he gorges on Twizzlers and pretzels as he grinds through drafting motions and highlighting deposition testimony. Every night they eat some flavor of casual fast-food for dinner. There is always a side of fries or nachos or something derived of grease and carbohydrates. He needs a week of purification. At least. His skin is even getting bad. He slides the empty, gigantic, frosty stein of beer away from him and graduates to "The Burro's" margarita offerings. The sugary drink is not exactly the remedy he sought.

"We make an awesome team," Song says at one point during the celebrated euphoria. "Cyrus, I want you to take our expert tomorrow."

Cyrus is blown away. He got to cross-examine a police officer and one of the post-accident bystanders, but to be given a meaningful witness to handle on direct is a big deal and an honor. It suggests that Song sees him as perhaps capable of trying cases on his own soon. It is a step on the path to partnership.

"Thanks, Ed," says Cyrus, thinking to himself that he'd better stop drinking and start preparing.

THE NEXT DAY, IN THE RESTAURANT/LOUNGE OF THE hotel, Cyrus wants breakfast to last forever. There is a slight pain behind his eyes and an overall jittery feeling going on in his body that tells him that he drank too much last night and is probably not on his game. He tries to eat a full breakfast to compensate. Choking down the hotel eggs that are the consistency of a greasy sponge makes him regret that too.

Before Cyrus can get his bearings, Song is swinging the rented minivan into the back parking lot of the courthouse that runs along an old train track a block off Main Street. Song takes their usual spot near the back door. As usual, they are one of the first cars there. Cyrus feels like he is going to puke.

He tries to calm himself and think relaxing thoughts; the black line at the bottom of the pool gliding under his body until he reaches the T just before the wall and flips and repeats, over and over, allowing his mind to get into that trancelike space that got him through so many early morning swimming practices and really twenty years of his life. His breathing starts to slow and deepen.

The expert he will direct is Lonnie Collins. He is a trained engineer, but really just an expert motorcycle rider. He is in his early seventies and has probably spent more hours riding motorcycles than anyone on the planet. At one time, he worked for a motorcycle manufacturer at one of their testing facilities in the desert outside of Las Vegas. The track was three miles long in the straights with huge sweeping turns. Lonnie's job was to ride a motorcycle up to and even over 100 miles per hour, take his hands off the handlebars, and "induce wobble." Which means he had to slap the gas tank as hard as he could to get the bike to start flopping back and forth while flying down the track. Then he was to sit back and let the bike self-correct without putting his hands on the handlebars. This insane exercise was meant to test the suspension to make sure the bike would dampen any wobbles, weaves, or vibrations instead of amplifying them. According to the standards, at 100 miles per hour, the bike is supposed to self-correct within three seconds.

Often these tests were videotaped. Cyrus has seen the videos. They are no bullshit. It is some real cowboy shit. No one does that anymore. No one has the balls. Now it is all computer simulation.

Lonnie has piercing blue eyes and wispy hair ringing a bald dome. He is dressed in a gray wool suit that creases perfectly as he crosses his legs while settling back into the witness chair. He nods at the jury. He is wearing a bolo tie with a huge chunk of turquoise in it. He looks like a grandfather, or like you would want your grandfather to look, or a cowboy, or the last of the motorcycle-crazy mechanical engineers that actually tested their bikes on tracks wearing leathers in the hot sun.

The truth is, he is all of those things. He grew up on a ranch outside of Steamboat Springs, Colorado, breaking horses and driving cattle up into the mountains in the summer to fatten on the extra nutritious grasses the altitude offers. He quips that riding motorcycles was an easy transition from breaking broncs. At least the motorcycles don't fight back. "Well, usually," he likes to say with a sly smile to the jury. After he got his degree in mechanical engineering, he spent a year rebuilding a 1975 Triumph, including machining many parts himself, in his basement. That bike went on to set a land speed record. He is happy to tell the jury about that story as well as his time riding motorcycles in Vietnam as an army medic and other tales of an adventurous life well lived.

Song describes Lonnie as a "plug and play" witness, meaning that the lawyer really doesn't have to do much work to guide him through his testimony. You just ask him a few questions here and there, and Lonnie, understanding what story he needs to tell on the stand, simply talks to the jury and explains why the bike is not defective and what caused the accident instead.

After spending the last few days working with Lonnie in preparation for his direct, Cyrus realized that the "plug and play" Lonnie was the old Lonnie. This Lonnie is still pretty smooth, but all those hours sitting on roaring choppers, whining sport bikes, and growling dirt bikes has significantly diminished Lonnie's hearing, and he misses a lot. Cyrus hadn't worried about it much because he assumed Song was handling Lonnie's direct and they have prepared enough that Lonnie knows all the questions he will be asked.

Cyrus grows a little more concerned as the direct starts. He has to practically yell his questions across the courtroom, and even then, Lonnie sometimes just takes off on an answer that doesn't quite respond to the question asked. Nevertheless, Lonnie's testimony is going fine, and Cyrus is doing a fine job walking him through it but staying out of the way, letting Lonnie talk to the jury.

As is his practice, Lonnie has done some ride testing of the same model motorcycle on the same road and even did so with a disconnected rear brake—the one that plaintiffs say failed here. They play the video of the testing to the jury, demonstrating that there was absolutely no reason to apply the brakes while riding through the fateful curve. Lonnie testifies that simply rolling off the throttle, or at most downshifting, would provide more than enough deceleration given the grade of the road. Lonnie explains that actually applying the brakes would be a dangerous move that would make it more difficult to negotiate the curve and could cause a rider to lock up the rear wheel and skid. The only reason to apply the brakes at that moment would be in the event of some emergency, which no one recalled occurring. Certainly, the Kellers, and Mrs. Hebert for that matter, would have remembered that.

Cyrus watches the jurors as Lonnie testifies. Cyrus feels like the jurors are on his side. They nod at the right time. They do not seem bored. The jurors genuinely seem to enjoy listening to this charming man talk about his life's work and break down a motorcycle accident and what could have gone wrong to cause said accident.

"Well, Mr. Collins, what is it that you think, in your expert opinion, caused this accident?"

Lonnie smiles and pauses, as if caught unawares by the question (which he really is not). "Well," he says, "what I think happened is that Mr. Hebert stopped operating his motorcycle…" Lonnie pauses again. "You know, it was a long day, and that doggone Outlaw is such a good bike, it rides so smooth, I think Mr. Hebert simply dozed off. He just closed his eyes and let the motorcycle go where gravity took it. Unfortunately, that was into the cool waters of the Cayuga."

Gold stands and objects, and the judge sustains the objection. But it is too late, the damage is done, the jury has heard the entire case come together.

"Thank you, sir. No more questions." Cyrus sits down. Song gives him a nod.

As Gold begins his cross-examination, Cyrus reflects that Gold has unquestionably improved his trial technique since the beginning of trial. He is suddenly asking clearer questions, he seems to have focused his case, and he understands what he needs the jury to believe to side with him. Cyrus, condescendingly, thinks that maybe the professionalism of Song and himself have rubbed off. Gold does a decent job pointing out the other cases in which Lonnie has testified on behalf of Outlaw and other motorcycle manufacturers and that Lonnie has never given an opinion that a motorcycle is defective. It is always the rider's fault in Lonnie's eyes. And of course, Lonnie can easily ride the same road on the same bike that Mr. Hebert did without any difficulty or applying the brakes; after all, who is as good a rider as Lonnie?

But the best part of Gold's cross is his use of photographs. He has found one, taken around lunchtime on the day of the accident at a roadside turnoff overlooking one of the Finger Lakes, that he asks the jury to focus on. There is a beach below the turnoff, and according to Mrs. Hebert's testimony, the group took off their leathers and jumped in the lake for a dip before having some sandwiches. There is a picture of the two wives, smoking cigarettes, both sitting sidesaddle on the seat of the Hebert's bike.

Gold has blown up the picture and puts it up on the screen in front of the jury. The blowup of the picture focuses on an area, near the brake pedal, where a small round viewing window into the rear master brake cylinder is just visible. The window is there so that riders can check their brake fluid level without having to disconnect the brakes. Gold then pulls out another picture on foam-core that further blows up the image so that the round window is shown as about about six inches across.

Cyrus is shocked. In the blown-up image, it sure looks like the master cylinder is only half full of brake fluid. It seems unfathomable now, given all of the documents they have pored over and all of the preparation, but neither Cyrus nor Song nor, for that matter, anyone on the defense team, ever noticed that picture, or at least that you can see the window in it. Cyrus can feel his heartbeat and feels the rivulets of sweat flowing from the tips of his hair straight down his spine.

Gold asks, "Mr. Collins, does that master brake cylinder look full of fluid?"

Lonnie pauses and seems to lean forward in his seat as he squints at the picture. "No. It doesn't."

"Thank you, sir." Gold sits down.

Shit. Shit. Shit. Shit. Shit. Shit. It occurs to Cyrus that perhaps Gold has not improved as a lawyer, but that bumbling through the first half of the trial was just an act. Song puts a heavy hand on Cyrus's shoulder and pulls him toward him so that Song's mouth is right next to Cyrus's ear.

Song whispers, "Redirect him. Get him to say that the picture does not mean that the brakes were not working."

"Um, okay." Cyrus gathers his binder with his outline, notes, and his few scribbled redirect questions on it and slowly walks back to the podium. He's not exactly sure how he is supposed to do this but trusts Song that it will go okay.

"Mr. Collins, the picture that Mr. Gold just showed you, I want you to look at that again."

"What?"

This is the problem. Lonnie has no idea what questions are coming and can't hear Cyrus. Cyrus raises his voice and practically screams at Lonnie.

"Mr. Collins, does this image look like a normal Outlaw bike with a proper fluid level?" It is an unartful question, but Cyrus isn't exactly sure how to get Lonnie to say what he hopes he will say.

"No," Lonnie shouts back. "It looks like the brake fluid is low."

Cyrus can feel his palms getting moist, and his eyes are doing the thing that they do when he is stressed and hasn't had enough sleep. They blink. A lot. So much so that he starts to think about how much he is blinking, and that makes him nervous and just sets him off to blink more.

He just stands there and stares at Lonnie, looking for some sign of recognition or elaboration in the sparkle of Lonnie's eyes. Cyrus needs some cue from his expert that if he just asks a different question, Lonnie will answer and put this issue to rest. But Cyrus sees nothing in Lonnie's eyes. Lonnie makes no gesture suggesting he wants to elaborate.

Cyrus has no idea what to do. Should he keep trying? Will it make it worse?...

"No further questions." Cyrus walks back to counsel table and sits next to Song, who is stone-faced and silent.

Chapter 33

JANUARY 23, 2006

Cyrus walks the halls quickly. He feels that the stench of defeat, or even death, follows him wherever he goes. The others can smell it on him. It trails him as if he is dusting crops with a cocktail of chemicals that mean death, despair, and starvation for the countless insects and microbes waiting below. He is that bringer of death and defeat, and everyone in his general vicinity ducks and flees to avoid the despair he brings forth.

But Cyrus pretends to be unaffected. He tells himself that losing means he put himself out there. The irony is that this blow has knocked the laissez-faire out of him. He never set out to be a lawyer representing corporations. But the money was so good, how could he turn down Earnhardt's offer? It's weird, because for all his apathy about his job, now that he has failed, and miserably so, in a public spectacle of flaming dog shit, he actually gives a shit. He is genuinely afraid that this fucking loss will sink him.

Cyrus's coffee is long gone and there is absolutely no news about the escalating war in Afghanistan, the occupation of Iraq, or the public unraveling of Britney Spears, that he has not at least skimmed. Despite his despair, fear of more failure, and newfound desire to succeed, he cannot seem to motivate himself to do anything about it. He has some discovery he could draft, or he could call someone or read a case or something. Instead, he surfs the internet and wallows.

A little before noon, there is a knock on his door. He is relieved. Finally, a diversion. Finally, something new.

John Quinlan leans into the doorway, projecting the patrician air of a gentleman farmer or English professor. Quinlan is an oft underestimated litigator. He lacks the bluster and bravado of someone like Song and for that reason is rarely seen in the eyes of the associates, thirsty for free cocktails and war stories, as someone to put on a pedestal.

"How are you doing, Cyrus? Getting back on the horse, dusting yourself off?" He asks the question in a genuine way. He asks as someone who has lost a trial or two and understands what a blow to the confidence and psyche that experience can be.

"Um, I'm okay, you know. Like you said, trying to shake it off and get back into some kind of rhythm."

"Well, are you interested in helping out on a criminal matter? It might be just the kind of thing that you can dive into and get your mind off the trial. And, of course, you get full credit billing for it."

Cyrus is interested. Song is religiously avoiding him. Cyrus doubts Song will ever give him work after the loss. He needs to find a new benefactor at Earnhardt and fast, before he is labeled a choke artist for good.

"John, I would be grateful for anything that can help build my litigation experience."

It's essentially a bullshit answer to prevent himself from desperately screaming for Quinlan to save him from the defeat and save his career.

"Well, this looks like a pretty interesting case," Quinlan says, "the client we have been asked to represent is sort of a peripheral player in a larger criminal enterprise. You heard about the *Blakely* decision in the Supreme Court? It's a Scalia decision that is riling up conservatives and the entire federal judiciary. That decision calls into question the constitutionality of sentencing guidelines. It provides a path for anyone sentenced based on the guidelines to challenge their sentences. There will be countless appeals and reversals of sentencing decisions that come out of this. It may apply to the sentencing in this case—which seems to be pretty excessive."

The amount of caffeine in Cyrus's bloodstream and his general mindset in these crazy times have made it difficult for him to focus on anything. But there is something about the look Quinlan gives him and the twist of his mouth that makes Cyrus sit up.

"The case is on appeal in the Seventh Circuit. It involves a motorcycle gang called the Hounds of Hell."

CYRUS PACKS TWO BINDERS OF TRANSCRIPTS FROM THE Hounds of Hell trial into his backpack and slips on his suede Solomon winter slippers—he feels like Mr. Rodgers changing shoes—for the quiet walk home through the snowy Third Ward.

He particularly enjoys the winter walk, seeing all of the holiday shoppers scrambling for parking spaces and negotiating the ever-narrowing streets as the mounds of snow that grow grayer and grayer by the day build up on the curbs, constricting everything like plaque in an artery. Cyrus leaps from one rock-hard mound to another. Tonight, there is a light snow falling, the kind where individual crystals are visible in the dry, clear, cool air. He stops at the Public Market and picks up dinner for one—a steak chipotle burrito and a bottle of malbec with enough spice to match the meal.

Cyrus hasn't seen or heard from Lucy since the debacle at Todd's going-away party. She thought he was flirting with a paralegal. (He figures it sort of depends on your definition of flirt.) By the time they were back in the apartment, they were both screaming. Cyrus put a fist through a cabinet door. Lucy left. He assumes she has been with her sister, but the complete silence for months now is shocking when he thinks about it. The abandonment initially made the sting of the trial loss even a little worse, but as the nights wear on he starts relishing wallowing in his misery alone.

Home in his solitude, he turns on the Bucks, digs into his dinner, and watches T.J. Ford sprint up and down the court, outrunning everyone and getting knocked to the floor on every third trip or so. It is exhausting to watch. Cyrus finishes the burrito and is halfway through the bottle of wine when he turns off the TV and pulls out the binders of transcripts. He settles into a recliner with a glass of wine beside him and begins reading.

Chapter 34

JANUARY 23, 2006

After opening statements, the first witness is FBI Special Agent Cecil McGraw. The prosecutor, Assistant US Attorney Joseph Nelson, starts by asking McGraw how the investigation into the Hounds began.

McGraw: Walter Hill was pulled over for swerving shortly after midnight outside of Cedar Rapids on March 15, 2001, by the Iowa State Patrol. He passed a field sobriety test, but the trooper thought something was off. He shined a light into the back seat and saw a black nine-millimeter handgun partially covered by a denim jacket with a motorcycle patch on the back of it. He asked Walter to get out of the car and Walter complied. The trooper then asked Walter if he had any more weapons. Walter told him that he did.

Nelson: Mr. McGraw, how did you become aware of this arrest?

McGraw: I had done some weapons and drug training in Cedar Rapids a couple of weeks before. At those trainings, I always encourage state officers to involve us as early as possible in issues that look like they might cross state lines. Realizing that this was one of those cases, the trooper reached out to me. It was really just a lucky coincidence.

Nelson: What was it about this particular stop that made him think this was a case for you?

McGraw: Well, the trooper popped the trunk and inside he found a shotgun, an AK-47, and a suitcase. He also noticed white crystalline residue throughout the interior of the trunk. The fact that there were Wisconsin license plates and Walter seemed to be heading back to Wisconsin, led the trooper to conclude that this could have an interstate aspect to it.

Nelson: Was Walter Hill known to you before this arrest?

McGraw: Yes, Walter Hill was known to me as a member of a motorcycle….

McGraw's answer is interrupted by an objection and there is a sidebar. Defense counsel reminds the judge and attorney Nelson of a pre-trial ruling precluding the government from using the phrase "motorcycle gang." Apparently, the defense thinks the jury will be so prejudiced by the idea of a motorcycle gang that the defendants will not get a fair trial. Cyrus smiles as he reads the arguments, thinking that there is no way the jury is not already certain that these guys are part of a motorcycle gang. It's not like they are a bunch of yuppies riding their BMWs up to Door County or something.

Nelson: What happened when the trooper contacted you?

McGraw: I asked the trooper to read what the patch on the denim jacket says. The trooper relayed to me that there was a patch on the top part of the back of the jacket that read "Hounds of Hell" and a big patch over the center of the back of the jacket with a picture of a cartoonish dog with its tongue hanging out and Xs for eyes. Below that there was a patch that said, "Prairie du Chien."

Nelson: What does Prairie du Chien actually mean in English?

McGraw: Prairie of the dog.

Cyrus chuckles to himself at the stupidity of the question.

Nelson: How was it that Walter Hill was known to you?

McGraw: For about a year before Walter was picked up in Iowa, I had been investigating methamphetamine distribution in western Wisconsin. Through confidential informants, I had identified Walter Hill, Dickie Snopes, and Donny Jones as individuals who were distributing methamphetamine for payment out of Prairie du Chien.

Nelson: Can you explain for the jury what a confidential informant is?

McGraw: Sure. Yes. A confidential informant is someone who does not work for the Bureau but has information related to an investigation and is confidentially providing information to the Bureau.

Nelson: Did you use confidential informants in this case?

McGraw: Yes, we had several.

Nelson: Did you ever ask the confidential informants to wear a recording device to obtain evidence in this case?

McGraw: Yes, we did.

Nelson: Does the Bureau pay confidential informants?

McGraw: Sometimes we do, yes.

Nelson: If you knew from confidential informants that Mr. Hill, Mr. Snopes, and Mr. Jones were selling drugs, why hadn't you arrested those individuals even before Walter Hill was picked up in Iowa?"

There is an objection and sidebar. The defense counsel are concerned that Nelson is baiting McGraw into telling the jury that several of their confidential informants had gone missing after providing information.

Cyrus is riveted. He had no idea all of this had been going on in Prairie du Chien. He had an aunt that lived there and recalled as a kid visiting an old mansion and fort. He remembers it as a small town, a backwater really, but with a mysterious past that was intriguing to him then. It is even more so now.

Judge Cobb allows the question but excuses the jury and instructs Mr. McGraw that he is not to testify as to the disappearance of confidential informants and especially not to speculate as to what happened to any of them. They take a ten-minute break, and the jury is again seated.

Nelson: If you knew from confidential informants that Mr. Hill, Mr. Snopes, and Mr. Jones were selling drugs, why hadn't you arrested those individuals before Mr. Hill was stopped in Iowa?

McGraw: Well, I didn't think I had enough evidence to make a case, and I wanted to find out where the drugs were coming from and who else was involved.

Nelson: Were you able to answer those questions?

McGraw: Yes, for the most part.

Nelson: Well, for starters, where was the methamphetamine coming from?

McGraw: Mexico.

Nelson: Who else was involved in the distribution of the methamphetamine?

McGraw: The entire Hounds of Hell motorcycle…club was involved, along with Diana Davis, who helped the club with their drug business.

Nelson: Is Diana Davis in the courtroom today?

McGraw: Yes, she is sitting at that table along with Mr. Jones, Mr. Snopes, and Mr. Hill.

Nelson: Thank you. How were you able to determine the source of the drugs and who was involved?

McGraw: Well, after Walter was picked up and I got the report from the trooper in Iowa, we obtained a warrant to put in place wiretaps on Walter Hill's phone and then got warrants for additional taps of Dickie Snopes' phone and Diana Davis's phone.

Nelson asks for the judge's permission to approach the witness and it is granted. He then asks for her permission to allow Mr. McGraw to read the transcript of one of the recorded calls. Cyrus wonders why the defense lawyers aren't objecting to this as hearsay.

Nelson: Please read the transcript to the jury.
McGraw (reads):

Walter Hill: Well, um, I had a bit of a speedbump on the way home.
Dickie Snopes: Yeah, who did you have to kill?
Walter Hill: Funny. I got stopped by the cops in Iowa, just about to Cedar Rapids.
Dickie Snopes: Shit. And they let you go?
Walter Hill: No, Dickie. I am currently booked, and I decided to make you my one phone call. Yes, they fucking let me go.
Dickie Snopes: Well, did they search you?
Walter Hill: That's the weird thing, they kind of did. I think the cop popped the trunk, and then he went back to the squad car, and then he let me go.
Dickie Snopes: Well, I guess it's your lucky day.
Walter Hill: Just the same, um, I think we should tell the Chief.
Dickie Snopes: What is this "we" shit?

Nelson: Thank you Mr. McGraw, would you be so kind as to tell the jury what you know about Walter Hill and Dickie Snopes, their history, etc....

McGraw: Both Walter and Dickie grew up in Prairie du Chien and played football together. They both went to trade school after high school and eventually became motorcycle mechanics. They worked at various shops and motorcycle dealerships over the years, but for the last ten years they worked at Famechon Mechanics on Marquette Street in Prairie du Chien. They are both members of the Hounds of Hell motorcycle...club.

Nelson: Who owns Famechon Mechanics?

McGraw: We don't exactly know. We know that it is affiliated with the Hounds of Hell motorcycle club. Technically, it is owned by a company called Famechon LLC. The last known member of that company was an individual named Malcom Giddens, whom we were unable to find, but the ownership was transferred some time ago to an anonymous LLC based in the Cayman Islands with no members identified.

Nelson: Mr. McGraw, please open your binder to Exhibit 32. What is that document?

McGraw: That is a transcript of a recording of a call by Mr. Hill on March 14, 2001.

Nelson: Mr. McGraw, please read the first page of that transcript.

This time, one of the defense attorneys objects based on hearsay and that there is technically no question being asked. Judge Cobb overrules the objection as an admission by a party opponent. McGraw proceeds to read the transcript of a conversation between Walter and Donny Jones.

McGraw (reads):

Walter Hill: Um, I talked to the Mexicans and um, they are coming up here the first week in April.
Donny Jones: Why the fuck is that my problem?

Walter Hill: I don't know where to put them.

Donny Jones: Call Diana and have her arrange some-
thing. We must have a trailer somewhere or she could
just put them in the Beaver. Tell them this isn't exactly
Vegas and they can't expect the Taj Mahal or some
shit. Does the Chief know this is happening? I assume
they want to meet with him.

Walter Hill: Uh, no. I was thinking maybe, uh, you
could tell him.

Nelson: Did you have an understanding at the time of who
"the Mexicans" were?

McGraw: Yes. Based on phone records and assistance
from the DEA in voice analysis, we were confident that "the
Mexicans" as the Hounds referred to them, and as we have
been in this trial, were representatives of the Los Gatos drug
cartel from Tijuana.

Nelson: Was that surprising to you?

McGraw: It was very surprising. Before this investigation,
we were under the assumption that the methamphetamine
product proliferating throughout the Midwest was homegrown;
that amateur chemists were cooking methamphetamine in
rural makeshift labs using stolen fertilizer and cold medicine.
We had no idea this had become an international operation.

Nelson: Mr. McGraw, did you come to learn when the
Mexicans were to actually travel to Prairie du Chien?

McGraw: Yes.

Nelson: When was that?

McGraw: April 1, 2001.

Nelson: Did you do anything in response?

McGraw: Yes, my partner, Dustin Bradley, and I, set up
surveillance on the Beaver Motor Lodge starting on that date.

We were also up on Diana Davis's phone.

Nelson: How did you know that the Mexicans were going to stay at the Beaver Motor Lodge?

McGraw: Because we were recording Diana Davis's cell phone conversations. We recorded her call to the motel to make the reservations.

Nelson: Mr. McGraw, please describe your surveillance efforts on April 1, 2001, for the jury. Feel free to refer to your case notes.

McGraw: Special Agent Bradley and I rented a room at the Beaver Motor Lodge and also set up in a van in the Piggly Wiggly parking lot, which sits on the high side of the highway, across the street, looking down on the Beaver Motor Lodge.

Nelson: Did you observe a meeting between members of the Los Gatos cartel and the Hounds?

McGraw: Yes. At about six o'clock in the evening on the first, I was in the passenger seat of the surveillance van, and I saw a black Toyota Camry pull up and two men, who looked Hispanic, wearing cowboy hats get out and go to the motel office. They exited the office, returned to their car, and parked in front of room number five. They each took several bags into rooms four and five, met back in front of the car, and then one of the individuals made a call on his cell phone. They smoked cigarettes. About ten minutes later, Donny Jones and Dickie Snopes pulled up on motorcycles.

Nelson: Did you later confirm that the two individuals in the Camry were members of the Los Gatos cartel?

McGraw: Yes. Again, working with the DEA, we were able to positively identify them as two members of the Los Gatos cartel.

Nelson: Mr. McGraw, how did you know it was Donny and Dickie on the motorcycles?

McGraw: Well, look at them. They are pretty much unmistakable. Especially Donny, with his long beard and hair.

Nelson: What were they wearing?

McGraw: They had on wrap-around sunglasses. They were wearing denim jackets with the sleeves cut off with windbreakers underneath. The cutoff denim jackets had Hounds of Hell patches on the back.

Also, they were riding stripped-down Harley Sportsters with ape hanger handlebars and sissy bars on the back of the seats. The custom pipes make the bikes really loud. You can really hear the Hounds before you see them.

Nelson: After Dickie and Donny got to the hotel, what did you observe?

McGraw: They got off their bikes and everyone shook hands and sort of half-embraced, bro hugs if you will, keeping each other at arm's distance. The Mexicans got into their car and Dickie and Donny got onto their bikes, and the Mexicans followed Dickie and Donny down Marquette Street, heading north through town.

Nelson: Did you follow them?

McGraw: Yes. Bradley was driving. He waited a beat, started up the van, and pulled out of the Piggly Wiggly parking lot onto the four-lane road that bisects Prairie running parallel to the river and the train tracks. The tail was pretty easy because the bikes are so loud. Bradley was able to stay a few cars back and out of sight with pretty good confidence that we wouldn't be noticed. We had to be more careful as we got north of town. Traffic outside of town was pretty light. Bradley had to make sure we were not directly behind the Mexicans or visible to the bikes. But we weren't worried we would lose them because we could still hear the choppers.

Nelson: At some point did they turn off the highway?

McGraw: Yes, as the vehicles approached County Road N, known as Famechon Ridge Road, they slowed down. There is a restaurant called The Silver Spring House, a roadhouse—with an exceptional fish fry by the way—across from a section of the Mississippi backwaters, at the intersection of N and the highway. We saw all three vehicles turn off the highway onto Famechon Ridge Road, County N.

Nelson: What did you do then?

McGraw: Bradley continued past County N, to make sure it was not obvious we were following them. He then turned into the gravel parking lot of the tavern. We could still hear the bikes echoing up the coulee. The noise increased, and it was clear they were increasing their speed up the hill.

Nelson: Did you pursue them up County N?

McGraw: Yes. We waited until we were confident they would not detect us following them, and then we drove up the road following the noise of the bikes. When we got to the top of the coulee where the road follows the ridge, they were nowhere in sight. At that point, there was nothing me and Bradley could do. We couldn't exactly go knocking on doors on the ridge, and we felt pretty exposed out there. Bradley turned the car around and we returned to The Beaver Lodge.

Nelson: Mr. McGraw, could you please turn to Exhibit 75 in the binder in front of you.

McGraw: I have located it.

Nelson: Mr. McGraw, please describe for the jury what Exhibit 75 is.

McGraw: Exhibit 75 is a transcript of a recording that a confidential informant made of a meeting at the Hounds' clubhouse, in the back of the Sawmill Saloon in Prairie du Chien, on April 5, 2001.

Nelson requests the court's permission to play the recording rather than have McGraw read the transcript again. One of the defense attorneys objects, again making a hearsay objection and also arguing that the full audio is more prejudicial than probative, but at this point, even in the transcript, his tone seems resigned to accept the fact that the judge will let it in. Ultimately, Judge Cobb allows it.

Nelson: Mr. McGraw, who will we hear first on the recording?
McGraw: Donny Jones.
Nelson: Please press play.

Hey, sorry I'm late, goddamn crazy snow. Some lady went off the road down by The Spring House and the whole fucking road was blocked off for about fifteen minutes. Had no choice but to go in and get a drink. [There is laughter around the room] Okay, we can start the meeting.

Nelson: Mr. McGraw, please stop the recording. Who will we hear next?
McGraw: The next speaker is Dickie Snopes.
Nelson: Please resume.

Report from the meet with the Mexicans. They are upping our price by a hundred dollars a pound. Chief agreed. Not much we can really do about that. It is still cheaper than any realistic option by about half. The shipment and everything else will stay the same. Every two weeks. Next shipment should arrive Tuesday afternoon or Wednesday morning.

Nelson: Mr. McGraw, please stop the playback again. As part of your investigation, did you come to understand how the Hounds were bringing methamphetamine into Prairie du Chien?

McGraw: I did.

Nelson: How did you determine how they were bringing in the methamphetamine?

McGraw: As you heard at the end of the last recording, Dickie said the shipment would arrive Tuesday afternoon or Wednesday morning.

Nelson: What day was the recording made?

McGraw: It was a Thursday evening. So we knew another shipment was coming in less than a week.

Nelson: What did you do to prepare for that?

McGraw: Well, we enlisted the help of several additional agents to stake out places around Prairie du Chien that we knew were typical Hounds hangouts. But then we got a break.

Nelson: What was the break?

McGraw: We recorded a conversation between Walter Hill and Dickie Snopes that gave us more details about the delivery.

Nelson: Do you have that transcript in the binder in front of you?

McGraw: Yes.

Nelson: Please read it for the jury.

McGraw (reads):

Walter Hill: Hey man, when did you say that shipment is coming in? I am super dry and people are sweating me.

Dickie Snopes: Shit, Walter, we're not supposed to talk about this shit on the phone.

Walter Hill: I'm just talking about mayonnaise, I need some for my sandwiches.

Dickie Snopes: You're an idiot. It's supposed to come Tuesday or Wednesday.

Walter Hill: Can you bring my share up to me?

Dickie Snopes: What's wrong with you?

Walter Hill: I guess I have the gout. I can barely fucking move.

Dickie Snopes: God. I guess I'll take the truck in to work and stop up by you after.

Nelson: How did that recording assist you?

McGraw: Well, we now knew that Dickie was going to actually pick up the shipment and then take it to Walter, so all we really needed to do was watch Dickie on April 10 and 11. We also knew he was going in to work.

Nelson: Did you watch him?

McGraw: Yes. Special Agent Bradley and I set up a disguised service van on a street behind Famechon Mechanics. There is a gravel parking lot behind the shop that the employees park in. We parked the van about a half block away, facing the entrance to the shop. We had another agent in a van watching the front entrance to the shop, which also has a small parking lot.

Nelson: What did you observe?

McGraw: That's the funny thing. On April 10, we thought the day was a bust. We saw Dickie pull into work in his Chevy S10 pickup and park in the back parking lot. There were a total of three customers that visited the shop that day. All of them either dropped off or picked up a motorcycle and then left. We did not observe any of them deliver any packages or anything that could contain significant quantities of meth-

amphetamine. Then, at about four p.m., a UPS truck pulled up into the back lot. Dickie met the driver and assisted in unloading several boxes on pallets using a pallet jack.

Nelson: Why do you say that was funny?

McGraw: Well, I meant "funny" like "odd." We thought based on our observation that there had been no delivery of methamphetamine that day. We certainly did not think they were shipping large quantities of methamphetamine by UPS. But then, as Dickie was closing up the shop and leaving, at around five, we observed him carry a duffel bag out of the shop and put it into the cab of his truck. When he got in the cab, we recorded a conversation of him calling Walter to say he was on his way.

Nelson: Were you able to observe Dickie actually deliver drugs to Walter?

McGraw: No, not on that day. We followed Dickie leaving Famechon Mechanics to Walter Hill's house but were not able to see them make contact.

Nelson: Where does Walter Hill live?

McGraw: Well, his mailing address is for a farm on Famechon Ridge, or County Road N, about ten miles from Prairie. That's the same ridge road that we followed Donny and Dickie up when they had the meeting with the Los Gatos cartel members. We had to stay pretty far back. You get up on top of the ridge and it is very exposed. Just fields everywhere and several farms right off the ridge road. We were able to see Dickie in front of the farm that corresponds to the mailing address we had for Walter, but then Dickie's vehicle took a right turn onto a dirt road that cut across some fields. We were unable to pursue him.

Nelson: Based on your observations, did you come up with a plan to determine how the Hounds were importing drugs into Prairie du Chien?

McGraw: Yes. Based on our observations that day and calls recorded afterward, we had probable cause to believe that the Hounds were receiving the methamphetamine through UPS, as crazy as that seemed. So, we obtained a warrant to seize any UPS shipments to Famechon Mechanics within the next three weeks. The warrants allowed us to take possession of and x-ray all shipments going to Famechon Mechanics during that time frame.

Nelson: What did you find?

McGraw: Well, for the first thirteen days, we x-rayed a bunch of motorcycle parts and tools and some leather jackets. But exactly two weeks after we watched Dickie drive a duffel bag up to Walter, we intercepted a shipment of motorcycle exhaust pipes from a motorcycle shop named Famechon Motorcycles in Oceanside, California. We x-rayed the shipment and found that the pipes were stuffed with what looked like packages of methamphetamine.

Nelson: What did you do after making this finding?

McGraw: We allowed UPS to make the delivery to Famechon Mechanics and prepared to raid Famechon Mechanics shortly after the UPS driver left the premises.

Nelson: How many agents did you use for that raid?

McGraw: Eight.

Nelson: Please describe the raid.

McGraw: We had two vehicles in the alley behind the shop and another two on Main Street in front of the shop. We were all in radio contact. Agent Bradley and I were behind the shop, and two other agents were in the other vehicle. We were armed and also had with us a device to forcibly enter a premises, essentially a battering ram. We waited about fifteen minutes after the UPS van left, and then I ordered the agents to proceed to enter the shop. Bradley and I quickly approached the back door. There is a regular door, next to a large roll-up garage door. We checked the door to see if it was open. It was not. I knocked hard on the door and identified myself as FBI. We then used the battering ram to forcibly open the door.

Nelson: What did you find when you were inside?

McGraw: Dickie Snopes and Donny Jones were inside in the center of the workshop with boxes open and exhaust pipes spread out on several metal tables. There were cutting torches on the tables. Both were startled by our entrance, I guess the cutting torches were loud enough that they couldn't hear us knock, and they started scrambling to reach for a couple of nine-millimeter handguns they had on another table at the back of the room. We pointed our weapons and yelled for the suspects to get on the floor, and they complied.

Nelson: Did you find anything inside the exhaust pipes?

McGraw: Yes. Most had pieces of metal welded to the ends, closing off the end, which is strange for an exhaust pipe when you think about it. But Donny and Dickie had apparently used the torches to cut open several pipes, revealing their contents: about three pounds of methamphetamine total in two pipes and about a pound of marijuana inside one pipe.

Nelson: Did you conduct any other raids that day?

At this, one of the defense counsel objects and asks for a sidebar. The defense objects to any testimony relating to the second raid that day, which was a raid on Walter Hill's residence. The defense argues that the raid was illegal because the warrant didn't allow for it. The FBI had a warrant for the mailing address, which corresponded to a farmhouse owned by one Malcom Giddens, whom no one could seem to locate, on County Road N. The defense argues that the warrant doesn't apply to Walter Hill's residence because Walter was living in a trailer over a mile from the farmhouse and farm buildings. Judge Cobb considers the argument but ultimately denies it, ruling that the warrant includes Walter Hill's residence because it is on the same undivided parcel of property as the farmhouse.

Nelson: Do you recall the question?

McGraw: Yes, we also conducted a raid on a trailer that Walter Hill was living in up on Famechon Ridge.

Nelson: Who conducted that raid?

McGraw: Initially, three other agents, not involved in the raid on Famechon Mechanics.

Nelson: At some point did you join them at Mr. Hill's residence?

McGraw: Yes. Shortly after we secured the scene at Famechon Mechanics, we received a call from the agent leading the raid on Walter's trailer. He reported that there were shots fired and that they were holding their position. We left two agents at Famechon Mechanics to process the suspects and record and preserve the evidence, and the rest of us got in our vehicles and drove the ten miles or so to the location of the standoff.

Nelson: Can you describe the location of Mr. Hill's trailer to the jury?

McGraw: Yes. Highway N, or Famechon Ridge Road, is a two-lane road that runs east–west on the top of Famechon Ridge. The road is really hilly with big dips. About four miles east of where the road levels off up on top of the ridge, there is a farm in a dip in between two hills. It has a milk barn, house, and some other farm buildings on the north side of the road, and the south is all pasture. There is a rutted dirt road that goes out into the pasture. A lot of the pasture drops steeply into ravines and eventually Mill Coulee, which goes all the way down to the river bottom. It is heavily wooded in those areas. Walter's trailer is about a mile off the ridge road on a rocky hill that drops off in the back into one of those heavily wooded ravines.

Nelson: What did you see when you got there?

McGraw: Well, we turned off the ridge road and drove down the dirt road to find it barricaded by an FBI SUV. There were three agents at the scene. We were in communication with the agents by radio. We knew that two of the agents were behind the trailer in the woods below it. They had been approaching from below. The other agent was positioned behind another SUV parked directly in front of Walter's trailer. We left our vehicles on the road behind the first SUV and approached on foot, meeting the other agent, who was behind his vehicle.

Nelson: Did that agent have his weapon drawn?

McGraw: Yes, he was in a defensive position behind his vehicle with a long gun. He reported that when he initially pulled up in front of the trailer, Hill had started firing an automatic weapon at the vehicle and a bullet pierced the agent's windshield.

Nelson: What did you do after receiving that report?

McGraw: I took out a bullhorn from the agent's vehicle and attempted to make contact with Walter Hill.

Nelson: What did you say?

McGraw: I said, "Walter, there is nowhere to go. We have Dickie and Donny."

Nelson: Did he communicate any response?

McGraw: Yes. He said something to the effect of, "Fuck off, pigs."

Nelson: That doesn't sound promising. What did you do next?

McGraw: I just kept talking. I told him that we knew about the stop in Iowa; that his phone had been tapped for some time. I asked him about his gout and whether he was again waiting for Dickie to deliver his cut to him. Then he smashed out one of the front windows and started firing, and we all ducked down behind the SUV.

Nelson: Tell the jury how you were able to finally apprehend him.

McGraw: Well, I figured as long as he was shooting out the front, the agents could approach from behind. We were pretty sure he was alone, and there was a back porch off the trailer. I radioed for the agents to approach the back porch and I kept talking to Walter, trying to draw his fire. When the agents radioed that they were in position near the door off the back porch, I returned Walter's fire and hit the side of the trailer. Walter then started shooting continuously. The agents were able to enter the trailer through a sliding door to the back porch undetected. As Walter was firing out one of the front windows, the agents tackled him and secured his weapon and his person before he was able to react.

Nelson: What did you find in the trailer?

McGraw: We found a total of twenty-seven guns. Of all kinds. Handguns, AK-47s, other kinds of assault rifles. Even an old grenade launcher. There was also an inordinate amount of empty fried chicken buckets.

Nelson: Are any of those guns in the courtroom today, Mr. McGraw?

McGraw: Yes. Most of the guns on the table behind the suspects were secured from Walter Hill's residence.

Nelson: Following the stakeouts, wiretaps, raids, and arrests, were you able to sort through everything and piece together how the Hounds were bringing methamphetamine into Prairie du Chien?

McGraw: Yes. The Hounds have a club chapter in Oceanside, California. The Los Gatos cartel would drive factory-grade methamphetamine across the border and deliver it to a motorcycle shop that the Hounds operated there, Famechon Motorcycles. Then, at Famechon Motorcycles, the Oceanside chapter of the Hounds would pack bags of methamphetamine into motorcycle exhaust pipes. They would then weld the ends of the exhaust pipes closed, put them in boxes, and simply send them FedEx or UPS to Famechon Mechanics in Prairie du Chien, where Dickie and Donny would use a torch cutter to take off the welded ends of the pipes and take out the bags of meth. They then cut the meth, usually with baby formula, and distributed it throughout the Midwest for sale.

Cyrus looks at the clock next to his bed. It is two in the morning, and he feels like he hasn't blinked. The transcript is more entertaining than anything he has read recently. It sure as hell is better than reading a bunch of objections to discovery in a civil case or even expert reports on motorcycle engineering. At the thought, he flashes back to the Hebert jurors making eye contact with him as they announced their verdict. He groans, rolls over, and closes his eyes.

Chapter 35

JANUARY 24, 2006

Cyrus has avoided stopping at Voyageur on his way to work and grabs a coffee at the Starbucks near the Public Market instead. It has been more than three months now since he has seen or talked to Lucy, and he can only imagine how awkward or even painful that would be.

The office is dead. Many of the partners are working out of offices in warmer climates. It is the part of winter that rubs the skin raw. The sun is a distant memory hanging out vaguely on the periphery of life. The snow piles in parking lots are now modernist sculptures with a metallic gray color and an equally metallic hardness. Everything is dirt and ice, like a comet drifting aimlessly, or not at all, through the empty vacuum of space.

Quinlan is sitting, long legs crossed at his knees, in the break room. He lifts a small coffee cup to his mouth and blows softly, creating a hole in the foam of his cappuccino revealing the dark espresso below.

"John. Mr. Quinlan. I am glad I found you."

Quinlan looks up from the cup and smiles warily.

"I just wanted to thank you for this Hounds case," Cyrus says. "It is the most interesting thing I have read in a long time."

Quinlan looks pleased, if not surprised. "Well, let me know what you need from me," Quinlan says as he turns back to his coffee, then, as an afterthought, "Have you contacted Ms. Davis? You need to arrange for a visit. I would not put that off until the brief is due. Believe it or not, she may know if something about her trial was off—odd, or unfair. Also, she is your client; she needs to be on board with your defense strategy." Cyrus had no idea this was something he should or could do, and his face betrays as much.

"Right, I will do that right away."

"Okay," says Quinlan. "Just submit your expenses to my secretary once you get back."

Diana is in a federal prison in Virginia, not far from the border of Kentucky and Tennessee and within spitting distance of West Virginia. Cyrus arranges to have a phone call with Diana later that afternoon to introduce himself and to plan for the visit. When the call is connected, the voice on the other end of the phone is quiet. It seems to Cyrus that Diana is unsure of who he is. Cyrus stumbles with how to introduce himself and make it clear that he is friend, not foe.

"Um, I have been appointed by the court to help you appeal your conviction and sentence." There is silence on the other end. "Basically, I am your attorney. It is no different than if you would have just gone out and hired me. I will do everything that I can to help you."

"Oh, okay," Diana says, "everyone I talk to tells me I should not be in here for this. Honestly, I can't believe this is how things have turned out. I sometimes wake up thinking it is all a dream."

"I get that, um," Cyrus is a little cautious with what all he can say. It occurs to him that the call could be monitored or recorded, although he really has no idea, but better safe than sorry, "I think the best thing would be for me to come down there and meet you in person, and we can go through the evidence at trial and your sentence and figure out if there is a good basis for an appeal."

"Um, okay," says Diana with a hint of fatigue in her voice, "I thought that the Supreme Court cases, *Booker* and *Blakely*, meant that I at least get a new sentence. That's what I put in my appeal. Did you read that at least?"

"Yes, of course. You are right."

Cyrus winces as soon as he says it. Probably not the best practice to tell a prisoner appellee that she is right that she should get a new sentence. He is sort of guaranteeing victory and setting himself up for failure. More failure.

Cyrus was vaguely aware of the *Booker* and *Blakely* decisions but had not read them until after reading Diana's handwritten, jailhouse appeal. The cases do give some hope to her cause, or at least something to talk about. Hearing her cite the cases on the phone makes him even more uncomfortable than he already was. He is not all that familiar with criminal law and she, the client sitting in a federal prison somewhere in Appalachia, already knows as much as he does about the arguments he is supposed to be coming up with for her.

"Besides *Booker* and *Blakely* and sentencing, I think we should look and see if you have any other bases to overturn your sentence. But I think we need to discuss that in person," Cyrus says.

"Well, you know where to find me. I'll pretty much just be sittin' here."

Quinlan looks up when Cyrus knocks on the door of his office. The crease of Quinlan's pants is still protectively maintained, but now he has an actual book resting on his thigh that he is paging through thoughtfully, licking his finger from time to time to turn the page.

Cyrus almost snickers. No practicing lawyers read actual bound paper books anymore. They don't even teach you how to do research in books. Everything is online now.

"Sorry to disturb you for the second time in a day, but I am trying to plan this trip, and it doesn't seem like there is any good way to get to this prison. It is in Virginia, on the Kentucky border."

"Ah, yes, the Lee Penitentiary," Quinlan says. "I have been there. Call Timmerman Airport and see how much it costs to charter a King Air Turboprop for a day. It's probably no different from flying commercial, renting a car, and staying two nights, which you'd have to do otherwise."

Chapter 36

FEBRUARY 3, 2006

The sun is not yet up, and there is a fresh dusting of snow as Cyrus pulls up to the small airport surrounded by a sleepy neighborhood. The signs direct him to drive almost onto the tarmac and park next to a hanger that is really just a pole barn with rusted brown metal siding. He goes into a "lobby," which has a couple of seats and an acid bath of a pot of coffee thickening in the corner. An unkempt-looking man in a greasy Carhartt jacket and floppy galoshes rounds the tail of an antique-looking silver plane and bounds into the lobby.

"I'm Randy, your pilot." He seems a little overly energetic. He holds out his hand and Cyrus shakes it, taking off his glove first. "There are some doughnuts on board. And a cooler with water and juice and some soda. Coffee is hot." Randy gestures toward the metal diner-style coffeemaker and pot, which is producing an acrid aroma. It gives Cyrus heartburn just thinking about the liquid sloshing against his stomach lining. Cyrus holds up his latte.

"I'm all set there," he says, forcing a smile.

"The heater works, but it will still be cold up there on a day like today. I hope you have warm socks on."

Around ten o'clock, Randy switches on the intercom and informs Cyrus that they are about to start descending. Cyrus doesn't see any airport. They are flying over forested spines of land that drop into narrow valleys, many with streams at their bottom that sparkle as the sun hits them just so as they fly over top. Here and there the earth of a mountain is exposed by a strip mine with ramps of dirt and huge yellow trucks and earth movers ascending and descending the steep slopes.

The cloud cover increases, and suddenly the tops of the mountains are gone. In their place is a single, smooth white layer below them. Randy starts humming and then presses forward on the controls, dropping the plane into the white fluffy floor. They keep descending, with clouds seemingly whipping the windows until the treetops of a mountain below become visible as if viewed through lace curtains. To Cyrus, the trees seem awfully close and approaching fast. The plane bursts through the clouds. Revealed is a long tabletop of a mountain with its top cut off and a runway paved from edge to edge. Randy drops the tail of the plane, and the wheels bounce as he pulls back hard on the controls and somehow slams on the brakes. Cyrus instinctually presses his feet into the floor. He can feel the wheels biting into the tarmac as the plane tries to slow its forward progress. The end of the runway is like an infinity pool dropping off into the valley below. The plane never actually stops on the runway. Before falling into the abyss, Randy makes a hard right turn that brings them to a parking area just next to a hanger. Randy turns off the engine and takes off his headset.

"These runways are built right on top of old coal mines. After the mine closes, they fill it in and create these flat mountains, perfect for landing."

"Wow, yeah, that was something," Cyrus says and means it.

Inside, the layout is just like Timmerman. There is a makeshift lobby with interior walls extending far short of the height of the hanger. The furniture is old and weathered. There is even a standup ashtray next to a faux leather couch. On the back wall is the same coffee maker with coffee that smells like it has roughly the same Ph as that they left behind in Milwaukee.

Randy's company has arranged a driver to take Cyrus to the prison as part of the cost of the flight. Earl, a mechanic for the airport, steps into the lobby in blue coveralls and a John Deere hat.

He shakes Cyrus's hand and says, "I'm Earl. It's an hour and a half to the prison."

Cyrus follows Earl to his well-worn F-150 and climbs up into the passenger seat.

Earl is not much of a conversationalist, but the ride is fascinating to Cyrus. They twist down an old mining road from the airport and follow a muddy river through a narrow valley. There are occasional houses and a couple of churches. Earl points as they come upon a stoplight.

"Only restaurant for quite some time, if you want something."

"Uh, no, thanks. Maybe on the way back if we have time."

"Suit yourself," says Earl.

They descend roads following old deer, cattle, or coal trails dropping into hollers, running along riverbeds, and then rising only to descend again. The roads mostly follow the rivers along thin spits of flat space between the small, steep mountains filled with coal. The houses are mostly spaced out and have the feel of little farms with animals kept here and there, but no fields plowed. Cyrus figures that the land is too scarce in the hollers and too steep on the mountainsides to plant. He keeps noticing little plastic sheds and pens housing chickens in the yards they pass. They remind him of the little calf huts in Wisconsin, especially western Wisconsin. He recalls his grandfather remarking on the changes in raising cattle from small, concentrated areas inside barns with stalls to little plastic sheds outside where the calves have their own space and are less prone to disease. He wonders if the people of Appalachia are employing this same strategy with their chickens—a new kind of free-range and responsible way to raise poultry.

"Earl, what is the reason for the little stalls for all the chickens? Are these, like, free-range chickens?"

Earl looks at him, confused for a second, and Cyrus wonders if Earl can't understand his Wisconsin accent. The accents at the airport were twangy and distinct. Some almost seemed garbled to Cyrus's ear, and he hopes that is not how he sounds to Earl.

Earl's eyes light up as Cyrus's question finally registers. "Aw them…? Them's fightin' chickens."

Cyrus nods thoughtfully.

CYRUS STEPS DOWN FROM THE TRUCK AND BRUSHES THE dust off his pants. He opens the briefcase and pulls out a letter from Diana's counselor explaining what entrance he should go to and to whom he should speak. Earl has stopped in the middle of a parking lot the size of a typical grocery store parking lot surrounded by a high fence. They had to pass through an outer perimeter of fences even to get into the parking lot. There are guard towers at every corner. The buildings are low and brick and seem too small to hold a federal prison complex. There is a painted path leading to a one-story building in the center of the parking lot toward the front. Beyond that, there are clusters of buildings around courtyards surrounded by additional layers of fencing, these with razor wire. Cyrus has never been to a prison before and isn't sure how this will all work.

He walks to the building at the front of the parking lot, which is a sort of gatehouse that all visitors pass through. Inside, there is a woman sitting behind a Plexiglass divider. Cyrus gets up to the window and says, "I am here to see Diana Davis, I am her lawyer."

The woman looks at him over cat-eye glasses and asks to see a bar card. Cyrus fumbles with his wallet, squeezing his briefcase between his knees to free up his hands, and hands her the little laminated Wisconsin State Bar card with a year and number on it. The woman looks at it skeptically and then picks up the phone. She swivels her chair and talks low into the phone. Cyrus can make out names and a little of what she is saying, but not all of it. She swivels back and points at a door.

"Wait over there. You are going to Attorney/Conference C."

Cyrus marches to the doorway she indicated and stands, like a dog waiting for the next command.

Everything looks polished, new, and there is an antiseptic smell to the place. The door he is waiting at is painted a dull blue. It is clearly metal, and there is a small piece of thick glass just at head level. There is no doorknob. Cyrus hears a loud click and sees the face of a jowly guard with a crew cut appear at the door. The door swings, or not really swings but just pivots a few feet toward the guard. He pulls it open and beckons for Cyrus to follow with a tilt of his head. Cyrus steps through and the door closes automatically. He looks up and sees a camera above the door. He turns to follow the guard and sees another camera at the end of the hall above another door; this one an elevator door. The guard stops in front of it and waits.

"All of the cells here are underground. We are going to level B4, which is the only women's floor and is considered medium security. When the elevator door opens, step out and another guard will meet you. I will accompany you back to the entrance at the end of your meeting."

"Okay, thanks," says Cyrus.

The elevator door opens and Cyrus steps out. He is standing in front of a barred door. The bars are flat metal and there is a rectangular slot above waist level with a short metal shelf. Beyond the door is a hall that leads to another door, like the one he walked through to get to the elevator. He can see a camera at the end of the hall and presumes there is one behind him, but he doesn't look over his shoulder. There is a female guard walking toward him in khakis. Her hair is pulled back tightly, pulling the corners of her eyes toward her ears.

Cyrus follows her down a hall that opens into a large room with several tables arranged like flower petals. They have plastic or Formica tops and built-in swivel seats, like at a McDonalds, that are affixed to the ground. The room is large but empty, and there is a door opposite the one they entered. There are cameras above each door. The floor is some kind of cement, so polished that it almost looks to be metal. The walls are the same. There are two conference rooms with large glass windows adjacent to the door he has just come through.

It is completely silent. Every one of his footfalls crashes as if moving air that has sat inert, heavy, and unmoved since the earth was formed. Cyrus is conscious that they are underground. Inside a mountain. He is also aware of the ever-present antiseptic smell and high shine to every surface. He feels like an insect under glass, inside a vault.

The guard directs him to one of the conference rooms and turns on the light. Cyrus sits down against the wall, facing the big window, and takes out his briefcase. He opens it, taking out a folder and notepad and setting them on the table in front of him. He hears a click across the expanse of the empty and gleaming room. Another guard walks in followed by an inmate, presumably Diana, in orange prison clothes that resemble surgical scrubs. She is wearing slip-on shoes, slightly more durable-looking than slippers. The guard walks ahead of her. Diana's hands are cuffed in front of her prison scrubs. She has straight black hair tied in a knot on top of her head. Despite the circumstances, it looks like she wears a slight smile, and she cocks her head to look around the guard and into the meeting room as if to find what new adventure might be waiting for her there.

The guard brings her into the room and points at a chair on the opposite side of the table as the one in which Cyrus sits, and Diana takes her place.

The guard says to Cyrus, "We will be right outside if you need anything, and you can have as long as you want, but dinner is at five, and if she is here beyond that she will not get fed."

"Can you take her handcuffs off?" Cyrus asks.

"Up to you," says the guard.

"Please take them off."

The guard does, and Diana stretches her arms and flexes

her wrists back and forth, kneading each of her hands with the other before folding them on the table; her hands seemingly relishing their freedom. The guard leaves and closes the door. Both guards stand against the opposite wall, leaning against it. One bends her knee to put the sole of her boot against the wall. They turn toward each other and talk.

Cyrus cannot hear the guards at all. He is surrounded by a thick silence interrupted only by his and Diana's breathing.

He reaches for his case file, puts it on his lap, and looks at her. She is beautiful. That thought takes ahold of him. Her eyes seem to see everything, and there is a little mischief in the set of her mouth. She is thin under her prison scrubs, and her high cheekbones shine in the fluorescent light.

"So, what can I do you for, counselor?" She says it in a playful way.

It is not what Cyrus expected. This is a woman doing thirty-three years for answering a couple of phone calls. When she was convicted, she had twenty-six dollars in her bank account. Before giving up and cleaning house for Donny Jones, she had been fired from her last job selling used four wheelers and deer rifles at Prairie Speed, Field and River. She was a meth addict. And here she is, seemingly enjoying this diversion in her day.

"I'm Cyrus. It's nice to meet you," Cyrus says awkwardly.

"Well, I know who you are. What are we going to do to get me out of here?" She folds and unfolds her hands as if she is waiting for his answer.

Cyrus is nervous again and doesn't quite know where to go with the conversation. "Why don't you tell me about anything that you thought was unfair about your trial? You sat through it. We can start there," he says. As he says it, he thinks, *well, that sounded stupid.*

"For starters, it wasn't fair that I was on trial with them."

"You mean the Hounds?"

"Yeah, I wasn't in any motorcycle gang. I was there watching my life unravel, cleaning Donny's fucking toilets."

Cyrus is a little taken aback by the sudden show of anger. "How did you even get to know the Hounds?"

When he pronounces the word, "Hounds," he sees the mischief return to Diana's eyes and her mouth turns up at one end. It seems like she is suppressing a laugh, or a chuckle at least.

"I've known those boys my whole life." She says it with a sigh. "They weren't always bikers. They were mostly dumb farm kids. Anyway, I knew them from school and stuff. I used to be a big deal. You probably can't see it now, but those boys worshipped me in high school. I went to college at Wisconsin and was even a cheerleader. I got knocked up by the starting quarterback of the Badgers. Do you remember Luke Davis, or were you too young? Anyway, we even got married. My daddy demanded it, and Luke said okay. We had the most beautiful daughter."

Diana pauses here, and the mischief is gone. "We *have* the most beautiful daughter." There are tears in her eyes.

"I was a good mother at first. I tried to make going to school and parenting work. The sleep, or lack of sleep, just killed me. She would be up all night, and I was supposed to wake up and go to English or History or something and I just didn't. But I loved..." she pauses again. "I love, my daughter." Another pause. "Antigone." She says the name as if recounting a dream. "Those days were some of the happiest for me. It didn't matter to me that I was effectively dropping out of school. My parents seemed happy for me and everyone assumed Luke was going to the NFL, so we weren't worried about money, or the future, or whatever.

"But it changed when he got drafted. He went to San Diego and Antigone and I moved out there with him, and it was like I never saw him. He just wouldn't come home for days at a time. It's not like he was actually playing. I don't think he was even the backup quarterback. He was third string or on the practice team or something. I heard things from the other wives—that he was out at clubs and with this girl or that. The other wives were trying to be nice to me. They were trying to warn me. A lot of them had kind of been through the same thing, or so they said. But I was so embarrassed, and I didn't want to confront Luke. I didn't really think I could. I wasn't in a position of power, so to speak. So, I left. I couldn't handle it. I took little Antigone and went back home to Prairie du Chien to live with my parents.

"Am I going on too long? Is any of this important to the case?"

Cyrus stares at her and then blinks. "I want to hear it all, your whole story. I think I need to hear it to understand and best present this case." He isn't sure that's true, but he desperately does want to hear her story.

"Well, I got back home, and it was a relief. It was nice not to have the pressure of trying to make a relationship that wasn't working work. You know? And it was fun for the first few years. My parents had this big, beautiful house in the hills above the Mississippi. Antigone loved it there. There were animals to play with, a pool, and nature. My dad told me I didn't need to work, just focus on raising Antigone. I did. I also did things like volunteer with the school play, work at the library—that kind of stuff.

"The Hounds, the guys that were in the club, were fun too. There was no meth then. They had somehow developed this marijuana business. The cops left them alone. But they had a lot of money. They bought the Sawmill, which is the main bar in town, and they started a motorcycle shop. They also partied a lot, but they were fun parties. I liked to party then. I always did. It was like a continuation of high school, but everyone seemed better off, more important. It was like we were adults, but still having fun."

"Diana, who was the leader of the Hounds?"

Diana pauses after the question as if her focus has been interrupted by this unnecessary detail.

"Oh, I'm not sure there was ever a leader or anything like that. They were still just boys running around and mostly just having fun."

"When did meth get into the picture?"

"I think it must have been around 1991, 1992, but I couldn't really swear to any dates. Antigone was just starting kindergarten. I remember that. That is when everything started going to shit." Diana's voice catches.

"How did meth get into the picture?"

"I'm not exactly sure. The Hounds had these contacts in California—I knew that—who would bring in the weed. There was this guy that wasn't exactly part of the Hounds but hung out with them. I knew him a bit in college; his name was Ferris. He had these California connections, and I think those connections brought in the marijuana for the Hounds. Ferris was the one that bought the Sawmill, I think. But I think he also had the weed connections.

"At some point, these guys who were bringing in the weed from California—they would stay over weekends and hang out with all of us and have parties—and sometimes they would bring shrooms or acid, or even coke, and it wasn't a huge deal. It was fun, and there would be bonfires and campouts. Then, all of a sudden it seemed like...it was meth. At all these parties, there was meth everywhere and it was like someone had stirred up a beehive. Everyone got crazy. They fought about it, the Hounds, I saw that. I think some of them saw they could make even more money selling meth and wanted to do that. Ferris left during that time. I never saw him again.

"For me, that was the end of 'Fun Mom,' 'Party Mom.' It's like I got lost in a snowstorm. I started missing when I was supposed to pick up Antigone. I let my mom just take care of her and I slept all day. I missed so much. Now she has a baby. I missed that too. I missed my baby having a baby."

Diana is sobbing now. Her arms are on the table cradling her head and her back is shuddering with sobs. Cyrus is silent. He looks down at his hands.

Chapter 37

FEBRUARY 3, 2006

I t is cold back in Milwaukee, and Cyrus wonders why he didn't plan to stay the weekend in Virginia. It is late and his car, along with presumably Randy's, are the only ones left at the airport. They are frozen metal. The car seat creaks as he lowers into it. The car emits a grinding sound as he turns the key, but it turns over and starts. He cranks up the heat and sits for a minute, hoping the warmth of the car will melt the layer of frost and ice from the windows without him having to go outside with a scraper.

His phone rings. Lucy. He answers.

"Hey."

"Hey," she says. "Long time no talk."

She sounds down, or resigned, or tired or something, he thinks. *I could have reached out. I could have apologized. I should have.* He feels responsible for her sadness, or whatever, and thinks about what it must have taken for her to pick up the phone and call him.

"I want to see you," she says. "I miss you."

There is some local band playing at The Milwaukee Ale House. There is every Friday, but Lucy is meeting some friends there who know the band, and she wants him to come. He demurs, but he has nothing else to do and he misses, if not her, then human contact, holding someone, being with someone. He has been alone these last months, wallowing in defeat, drinking beer, and watching the NBA on the West Coast until it is way too late to function as a professional adult. He says okay.

Two hours later he is standing at the bar. It is packed. The bar is of a piece with the condos in which many of the patrons live: an old warehouse with wooden beams and reclaimed wood-plank flooring that give it a warm, barnlike feel. The bar is furnished with high-top tables the size of picnic tables spaced sufficiently to allow gathering around and between them. The ceiling is about twenty feet high, and there is a raised stage where the band is plugging in and tuning, spinning the wing nut on the high hat, checking volumes—the usual band stuff.

The band opens with "Every Day is Like Sunday" by Morrissey. Cyrus notices that the drummer has added electronic pads to his standard drum kit to add effects that really make these eighties songs distinct. Cyrus grabs a house-made pale ale and stands at the bar bobbing his head. He is happy to be out among people.

He spots Lucy at a table with friends next to a wall of floor-to-ceiling windows that open into the brewing room and its huge copper kettles. She is wearing a flannel shirt unbuttoned to below her clavicle, and her hair is curled just a little so that it bounces and flows around her head. She is smiling and chatting with her friends. It looks like she is having fun.

Doubt creeps into Cyrus's head. Why is he here? Why didn't they just leave well enough alone? He then notices that he still feels like he is on the turboprop flying through the cloudy night sky. His feet feel unsteady underneath him, and his stomach is churning. The cabin never got fully warm on the trip back, and his toes are still a little numb. If he closes his eyes, he feels the choppy air that toyed with the small craft over Lake Michigan from Chicago to Milwaukee.

He opens his eyes and sees Lucy looking at him. She has a huge grin and is climbing out from behind the bench of the high-top to make her way over to him. He shifts his weight from one foot to the other, trying to feel normal. In that moment he sees their relationship open up before him as if projected on the broad wooden floor boards. He sees her in their apartment, crawling into bed naked, making coffee, waking up to walk the dog. He misses her. She laughs when she reaches him.

"What are you doing over here, daydreaming?"

She gives him a big hug, and it is like she never left. Actually, it's better. At least, for that moment.

"How is it going, Luce?"

"Not bad, except I miss you," she says, and he believes it.

"I miss you too," he says, and he believes that too. "What's new?" After he says it, he chuckles at the absurdity of the situation and question.

"Kind of a lot, I guess. I quit the Voyageur. Maybe you noticed? I got a job basically creating PowerPoints for this businessman, who goes around and gives speeches around the country. He is a big entrepreneur, the guy who just bought Hamms, and he has a bunch of other businesses. Anyway, I am getting way more money than I could ever make as a barista just working on his PowerPoint presentations from home."

"Sounds weird, but kind of cool," Cyrus says. He notices she didn't say anything about ballet.

The night is fine. The band is good, they rock The Cure, more Morrissey, some Depeche Mode, Tears for Fears. It's like watching MTV after middle school. The lead singer gets a little campy and makes it fun acting out some lyrics, pointing dramatically into the crowd. By the end of the night, Lucy and Cyrus are in front of the stage dancing and jumping with fingers in the air to "C'mon Eileen." The whole crowd is behind them singing along, fists in the air, fighting through the emptiness of a winter night.

He wakes up in his bed with Lucy there. He notices her packed bag in the corner. An overnight snowstorm has left the Third Ward quiet, muted. The plows will reach the side streets, their street, last, but he can hear the rumbling and scraping sounds as the machines work their way there. Cyrus looks at Lucy again. Her hair is partially covering her face, and she seems so at peace. Her bare shoulder is peeking out of the duvet. She has a new tattoo on her upper arm, a large, elaborate fleur-de-lis. Cyrus is surprised to see it.

Well, so much for the ballet career, he thinks. *What has she been up to these last months?* he wonders. He decides to let it go. She is like a cat returned home after some unknown adventure.

He thinks about Diana. He feels an obligation—one he does not know if he can fulfill—to do right by her. He wonders what she is doing. He wonders if she is sleeping peacefully. He doubts it. He wraps himself tighter in the duvet and closes his eyes, trying for a second round of sleep.

Chapter 38

MAY 3, 2006

Because of the Supreme Court decisions overturning the mandatory requirement to follow sentencing guidelines, Cyrus determines that as an alternative to Diana's appeal, they can file a writ of habeas corpus in the district court, the Western District of Wisconsin, that sentenced her. The petition asks the court to discard the sentence and set a new sentencing hearing or, in the alternative, vacate the entire judgment and grant Diana a new trial. Cyrus knows from law school that "habeas corpus" means "show me the body," but he can never remember the ins and outs of why that matters today or what it means for the procedural rule allowing the challenge that he is now bringing in front of the court. It doesn't really matter; the rule allows him to do it.

The Bureau of Prisons puts Diana on a bus up to Madison to appear in person at the argument on the petition to vacate the sentence. Because there are no federal prisons in the Madison Metro area, Diana is moved to the women's floor of the Dane County Jail, which is right in the middle of downtown Madison, not far from the Capitol. It is a jail that, for a small, mostly peaceful college town, has a reputation for being rough. It is overcrowded, and there is constant conflict between the weekend incarceration of college kids getting drunk and rowdy, and townies up to more serious crime.

After having been to the Lee Penitentiary, Cyrus is less nervous and feels like he knows the procedure. He's wrong. Upon arrival, he flashes his state bar card and driver's license to a guard at the door and says that he is there to meet with his client, who is being held for a hearing. The guard talks into his radio, and someone walks through a door to escort Cyrus to see Diana. Cyrus has a whole binder of materials with him. His outline for the hearing is prepared, and he has even anticipated the possibility that the judge will ask Diana to allocute, or express contrition for her crime in exchange for a more lenient sentence.

The guard informs him that there are no lawyer meeting rooms on the women's floor and that he will just have to meet with his client at a table they have set up in front of her cell. *Sounds weird,* Cyrus thinks, *but not much I can do about it.* They ride up the elevator and get off into a sort of lobby area where they are buzzed through two doors, and sure enough, there he is on the women's cell block. He follows the guard down a hall of cells, each with a bed, a toilet, and desk, and most with an inmate, usually lounging on the bed. Each inmate, without fail, perks up as soon as Cyrus walks past. It is an amazing ego boost. He has trouble not smiling to himself. A couple say hi as he walks past. One inmate even whistles. He tries to keep his eyes forward and head down. He realizes this is a captive audience starved for any distraction, especially a male who is not a guard, but still, the attention does put a little spring in his step.

About halfway down the hall there are a table and chairs set in front of a cell. He looks into the cell and sees Diana sitting on the single bed with her back straight and her hands in her lap. She smiles when she sees him and stands up, gracefully, without using her hands, turning the simplest gesture into a wonder of biomechanics. The guard unlocks the door, and she takes a seat at the table opposite him and secures a strand of hair behind her ear.

"How was your trip?"

"Oh, it was long and uncomfortable, but also such a nice distraction. Being in this position, you get such a different perspective on time. I have so much of it now, but it also just seems like it is slipping away."

Cyrus doesn't know what to say. He feels a tightness in his chest. The pressure of trying to help someone who needs help is pushing up from his stomach, threatening to overwhelm him. This isn't a breached contract and a company trying to minimize damages or some spilled chemicals that someone needs to pay to clean up. This is real life and the lost time of a person that he can't help but care about.

"Let's go through what we have discussed and what we will say tomorrow. I know we have gone through this, but I want to make sure that everything in my argument is accurate.

"First, what did you know about the Hounds of Hell motorcycle club's conspiracy to sell drugs?"

"I knew some of the guys and I was cleaning house for Donny. I knew they were getting meth from Mexico. I heard them talk about those details sometimes. I worked for them because they gave me meth sometimes. Okay, more than sometimes; that's how they paid me. Aside from cleaning, I answered the phone for Donny when he wasn't at the house."

She delivers the lines looking straight into his eyes. Cyrus wonders if this has gotten too automatic, too rehearsed.

"How much money did you make as a result of the Hounds of Hell's sale of methamphetamine?"

"I made nothing. When I was arrested, I had nothing in my bank account, and my only job was cleaning house for Donny."

"Diana, you've never really been straight with me about this. Who was making the decisions for the Hounds?"

Diana looks confused for a moment and is about to speak but then pauses. She looks down at her hands and then looks up at him, almost sadly.

"I knew that Donny and Walter were in the club and pretty high up. I knew some of the other guys and partied with them and stuff, but I don't really know their structure."

She is lying, Cyrus thinks. *It is, after all, one thing a meth addict is good at.* He instantly hates himself for thinking that.

"Diana, do you know who was leading the club and the conspiracy?"

Diana again looks down at the hands in her lap, "No," she says.

He lets it go. "Okay. Did you ever sell drugs?"

"No," she chuckles, "I was too busy doing them."

"Diana, at the time of your arrest, were you a methamphetamine addict?"

"Yes, I was. It's been a struggle in prison, but I'm totally clean now."

Cyrus gives her a little smile of encouragement and a nod.

"Diana, do you regret associating with the Hounds of Hell?"

"Of course," she says, "look at me. It ruined my life. I have lost my family. I became a drug addict. I'm in prison for essentially being a maid to one of these guys and hanging around to get free drugs. I'm the poster child for 'just say no.'"

They go on for an hour or so talking about the unfairness of her being tried along with the Hounds, as if she was part of the gang. They discuss the visual impact of Diana sitting in front of a table of guns, none of which were hers. They move on to how Diana is doing now and what she would do with her life if she got out of prison. They are both tired. The gravity of what will happen tomorrow is weighing on them. As much as Cyrus would like to keep talking, he can tell Diana wants to rest, and he needs to further prepare.

The question is what to do. They are sitting in front of a wide-open cell door with no guard in sight. Cyrus walks down the hall, past the gawking inmates. It feels strange to be given free rein. He knocks on a closed door. Eventually a guard answers. Cyrus tells her that they are done with their meeting. The guard escorts him back and he collects his things, and Diana says goodbye. There is an awkward pause, both wondering if they should shake hands or hug or what. Eventually Diana just twirls in place (like a dancer, reminding Cyrus briefly of Lucy), walks into the cell, and sits on her bed. The guard closes the door. As Cyrus turns to leave, he notices Diana reclining onto her back with her feet flat on the mattress and her knees bent, staring at the ceiling. He wonders where she is going in that mind of hers.

The guard walks him to the elevator, says goodbye, and walks through another door before Cyrus can ask for directions to get out. He gets into the elevator and presses 1, for the first floor. The elevator opens to a dark, dank room. Cyrus steps out. It feels like a basement. There is no lobby, just what looks like a chain-link fence and some people on the other side of it sitting on benches. It is dark. He takes a step forward and looks around, disoriented. They notice. It is the holding cell containing suspects waiting for processing. They smell this lost puppy thrown to the wolves. Several of them step forward and talk to him.

"You lost?"

One starts rattling the fence. Another spits at him and calls him a lawyer pig. Cyrus is reeling; he doesn't know what to do. Then, out of the darkness, a guard materializes from behind a door that Cyrus had not seen.

"Looks like you're in the wrong place, son." The guard presses the "up" button on the elevator. "The main lobby and exit are on three."

Chapter 39

MAY 10, 2006

Judge Cobb's offices are what Cyrus imagines a Four Seasons hotel room to be like. He feels soothed by the color scheme. Everything has a place. It smells nice. There is a dark wood desk with two straight-backed chairs upholstered in leather. The stained-wood floor is covered with Oriental rugs. There is an eight-person conference table with the same leather upholstered chairs as those in front of the desk. There are built-in bookcases on every wall with case reporters from Wisconsin, the Supreme Court, and the *Northwest Reporter*. There are also random books on subjects ranging from internal medicine to space exploration. On the walls, there are pictures of family and a few landscape paintings, mostly featuring Holstein cows. There is a hanging spider plant dangling in the corner. The office feels very much like a refuge, a personal space and escape from the public and often chaotic and certainly adversarial world that exists in the courtroom just beyond the French doors that are now closed. It is hushed inside the office, as if the vast collection of books absorbs the words spoken by anyone inside.

Judge Cobb is at the head of the table and Cyrus sits on one side, opposite Joe Nelson. Nelson's close-cropped hair betrays a remembrance of blond but is now mostly gray. He wears a well-worn blue suit that looks good, but not too good. He looks like someone who wears a suit every day, including this day, and wearing one now is not a big deal. He is overweight. He is deferential to the judge, but not overly so, not like a civil litigant pandering to the judge and agreeing with every point. Nelson does not feel privileged or nervous to be there. This is his job. This is where he belongs.

Cyrus, on the other hand, is nervous. He is trying to control his blinking. It is not going well.

Judge Cobb sets her hands palm-down on the conference table and says, "I like to invite lawyers, especially those I do not know, back into my chambers before their first appearance in my court. So, I thought for starters we would just talk informally about the case a little bit. Mr. Nelson, you did an excellent job prosecuting the case, and I think we can all agree the extent to which this motorcycle club was distributing very dangerous drugs into our own community was shocking, as was the mayhem and violence that the club was willing to wield to maintain its illegal business. I hope I am not speaking out of school here or putting words in your mouth Mr. Nelson, but I think we all always felt uncomfortable about how Ms. Davis fit into this conspiracy and the punishment, set forth by the guidelines I might add, that came down on her as a result of the conviction."

Nelson suddenly wakes from his relaxed daze and the grin on his face turns slightly sour. "Well, Your Honor, I am not sure I totally agree with that. You know, we apply the facts to the law as we find them, and there was Ms. Davis participating in this conspiracy, facilitating it even, and we both know that the cost that this group inflicted on the community was even greater than that presented at trial;

certainly there is no question that the convictions and sentences were fair as provided for in the Federal Code."

Judge Cobb smiles a tight smile. "Well, Mr. Nelson, I wasn't asking for your argument, which I assume I will hear in a few minutes, but was hoping to visit informally here." She stresses the word "informally."

Cyrus reads the room. It doesn't take much special skill to see he has an opportunity here. The judge's eyes move from Nelson to him.

"Well, Your Honor, first of all…" Cyrus's voice warbles a bit as he starts talking, and it surprises him. He thought he would be able to keep his nerves under control, or at least better conceal them. He even felt calm a moment ago listening to Nelson refuse to agree with the judge that Diana got a raw deal, but now this is getting real. "It is just a privilege to be here and to be able to argue in your court. It has been an incredible experience to dig into this case and see all the work that Mr. Nelson and his team put in to unravel this conspiracy, and it has also been really eye-opening to get to know Ms. Davis. I am hopeful that I can put my best foot forward and find justice for my client."

"Well said, Cyrus," says Judge Cobb, "I want to give you a piece of advice. And, for the record, I give this advice to all young lawyers appearing in my court for the first time. There will be a lot of people out there. Ms. Davis's family, I'm sure. Members of the media, interested lawyers, and other various legal buffs. My bailiff tells me that the gallery is filling up. I don't say that to make you nervous; I am sure you are prepared, and from your briefs I know you have some excellent arguments. But my advice is this: look like you know what you are doing out there. It will go a long way."

With that, the judge stands up, puts on her robe, and motions for the two lawyers to proceed to the courtroom. "I will see you out there momentarily."

The bailiff is right. The gallery is full. Cyrus walks out to see Diana turned in her chair at counsel's table, waving and blowing kisses to her daughter and baby granddaughter—*how can this woman be a grandma?* Cyrus thinks, *she is not yet forty years old*—and other members of her extended family. Her eyes are already flooded. Cyrus takes a seat next to her and asks how she is doing.

"Fine, how are you doing?" she asks.

Cyrus just nods.

Nelson unbuttons his coat and takes his time lowering himself into his chair in a manner that reflects the respect that he affords himself. Just as Nelson gets situated, the bailiff commands everyone to stand and Judge Cobb whisks into the courtroom, her robes flowing like those of a Halloween witch. She asks that everyone be seated, and the bailiff calls the case. The bailiff directs the lawyers to identify themselves and whom they represent. Mr. Nelson does first, and then Cyrus stands. The vibrato is back in his voice, he can feel a dryness at the back of his throat, and he can feel his eyes starting to blink. After choking out his and Diana's names, he sits down abruptly, emergently even, and fills a foam cup with water from a plastic pitcher placed next to the microphone on the table. He takes a sip and closes his eyes for maybe three seconds. It feels like a year.

"This is defendant's motion, so Mr. Jackson, please proceed."

"Thank you, Your Honor," Cyrus says, fumbling to not spill the cup of water held in his shaking hand. He stands and attempts to gracefully collect his binder and notepad before smoothly proceeding to the lectern in front of the high desk from which Judge Cobb looks down with a benevolent expression that can almost be interpreted as a smile. He does not quite succeed at getting there gracefully, but he gets there nonetheless.

The judge nods slightly at Cyrus as he reaches the lectern and places his materials in front of him. He can almost hear her telepathically say to him, "Look like you know what you are doing." Cyrus takes a deep breath and opens his binder that contains a typed outline, which he takes out and sets on top of his legal pad. He nods at the judge and begins.

"May it please the court, Diana Davis was convicted of a crime of which she was a tragic victim and sentenced to thirty-three years in prison. Justice requires a new trial where her guilt or innocence is considered separately from that of a motorcycle gang of which she was not a member and was, instead, as the evidence strongly suggests, their victim.

"Let me remind the court, although Judge Cobb, I know you need no reminding, but indulge me for context, of what this conspiracy, this case, was about. This case was about a motorcycle gang that carried out an operation for years, a decade maybe even, in which they imported factory-grade methamphetamine originating in Mexico, smuggled it into California, and shipped it across the country using businesses they operated to conceal their efforts. They then used their network to distribute methamphetamine throughout Wisconsin and the Midwest, maintaining their territory through violence and subjecting our communities to a scourge of drug addiction, violence, and despair unknown in our lifetimes. The evidence presented by the government, and Mr. Nelson here, demonstrated that the

Prairie du Chien chapter of the Hounds of Hell imported and distributed over $50 million of methamphetamine into southwestern Wisconsin over the course of five years. The evidence, presented by the government and Mr. Nelson here, showed that the Hounds profited greatly from this, and most importantly, preyed on and destroyed the lives of countless addicts whose futures were lost to the suffocating and ruinous addiction unique to this drug. But what is important to remember in considering whether this sentence and trial were fair is that Diana Davis was not a member of the Hounds.

"Instead, Diana Davis..." at this point Cyrus is rolling, the nervousness is gone, and he is speaking with his hands. He turns back toward his client and offers a sweeping gesture as if revealing a mystery guest that no one knew was coming, "...is one of their victims. One of the addicts that the Hounds preyed upon. They destroyed her life, they bankrupted her future, they took away her choices. Then what did the government do? Did it protect her and help her pull the pieces back together? Not quite. Sweeping her up in the vast net cast by their investigation, the government tried Diana along with her tormentors—the Hounds of Hell—as if she was part of the gang and not their servant, and sentenced her to thirty-three years in prison. This is the court's opportunity, presented by the holdings of *Blakely* and *Booker*, to look again at her sentence. I further urge the court, as it considers whether additional factors beyond the sentencing guidelines should have been considered in sentencing, to consider the new evidence presented in our appendix, not presented at trial, that illuminates the minimal, nominal connection Ms. Davis had to the conspiracy and whether the unfair prejudice of being tried alongside her alleged co-conspirators warrants a new trial here. Objectively, it is hard to imagine how one is not warranted.

"What the jury did not get to hear is that at the time of her arrest, Ms. Davis was a meth addict, and despite the conspiracy funneling $50 million into the coffers of the Hounds motorcycle club, Diana saw none of that money. When she was arrested, she had no assets and less than fifty dollars in her bank account and unpaid bills of every imaginable sort. She had been fired from her last job at a resale sporting goods store, and the only work she could find was to clean the house of her oppressor, one of the leaders of the Hounds, Donny Jones. He let her sleep in one of his various properties scattered throughout Crawford County and paid her what would not be considered a living wage anywhere in the United States—a hundred dollars per week. But he also gave her methamphetamine. This is the evidence the jury did not get to hear, but should hear to fairly determine whether Ms. Davis was truly a co-conspirator, or, more accurately, a victim of the conspiracy.

"The truth is that Ms. Davis in no way profited from the vast conspiracy perpetrated by the Hounds. In reality, Ms. Davis was imprisoned by their conspiracy long before she set foot in this courtroom for her trial. Her conviction and sentence are not only unjust, they are a failure of the criminal justice system to liberate a victim of crime. The Supreme Court's decisions and the new evidence of the lack of any benefit to Ms. Davis offers an opportunity to correct this injustice and give a victim of the conspiracy her life back. I respectfully request that this court vacate Ms. Davis's conviction and sentence and schedule a new trial. Thank you, Your Honor."

Cyrus turns to see Diana looking down at her hands. He sees the top of her head and the part in her dark hair. There are tears washing down her face.

It hardly matters what Nelson says. He argues about black letter law and the clear evidence of Diana's participation, but his heart seems not to be in it, and the judge is only just listening. She already knows that this is a wrong she must correct.

Everyone rises once the prosecutor is done speaking, and Judge Cobb says she will take the arguments under advisement. Nelson packs his briefcase and moves to leave as soon as the judge disappears back into her chambers.

He nods and says, "Nice job," tightly as he passes Cyrus. Nelson then pauses and leans in closer. He puts his hand on Cyrus's shoulder and whispers, "I know you think you are doing good here, kid, but these guys are dangerous. She is too. They killed people. We couldn't prove it, but CIs disappeared. This isn't the god's work you think it is."

Cyrus looks at Nelson and recoils. *This is what a true believer looks like,* he thinks. *Brainwashed by his own propaganda. He is trying to justify his cruel, vindictive tactics. Pathetic.*

The marshals sitting in the first row, who are there to escort Diana back to the county jail and ultimately onto a bus back to Virginia, allow her to lean over the bar and into the gallery to hug her family.

Chapter 40

JUNE 1, 2006

Cyrus spends the day writing and rewriting evasive discovery responses for a groundwater contamination case for an electronics company. The death stench of the defeat keeps Song—and any work for his clients—from Cyrus's side of the floor. (When Cyrus is finally fired, or strongly counseled to find another job, and he feels like that inevitability will soon occur, he imagines Song having an elaborate smudging ceremony, burning sage, or more likely a Cuban cigar, to rid the office of the horrible spirits of failure and defeat that Cyrus has let enter the hallowed Earnhardt halls.)

Cyrus struggles to even understand the discovery requests he is answering much less actually give a shit about the case, but he has to keep billing hours—especially because he had to drop his life savings on a down payment for a new condo to stave off Lucy's complaints about the fact that they still live in a one-bedroom apartment. His life is a daily battle of finding motivation to overcome boredom, occasionally tinged with bouts of anxiety.

But there is one beacon of light on the horizon. Not a day goes by in which Cyrus does not find himself thinking about Diana at some point. He cannot shake the memory of turning from the lectern to see the white of her scalp revealed by the part down the center of her black hair and her hands in her lap as the tears fell from her face. He cannot forget the feeling of being near that family as they touched each other and hoped for the first time in five years that she would be back in their fold, and maybe for real this time. He felt that he wanted to be closer to them. Of them.

It has been three weeks and no decision from Judge Cobb. He walks past his secretary's desk after every mail run, hoping, praying even, to see something from the court—but also dreading what that something could be.

He takes it slow walking home through the Third Ward. It is hard to even remember what winter was like, how the air stings your cheeks, how it is always dark. It is light well into the night now, and what was once white and gray is now a riot of green. Everyone is outside. The Ward is loud with voices and music, which changes from bar to bar. The thick air is filled with the conflicting smells of spring; life decaying to give life to something new. It occurs to him how much things constantly change.

Cyrus presses the elevator button. It is six thirty. He wonders if maybe he should take Lucy out—enjoy a night on the town and participate in the celebration of the new season raging outside. They could, they should, also celebrate the new condo.

Cyrus turns the key and presses the door. He finds a pile of garbage bags, some filled with garbage and others with clothes packed haphazardly for the coming move. The kitchen is a riot of pots and pans and crumbs and half-eaten bags of tortilla chips. There is a tipped-over open bag of dog food behind the couch from which Biggie is enjoying an appetizer course before Lucy rises to make a surf & turf, or whatever she has planned for the spoiled dog.

As for Lucy, she sits at the bar with her MacBook open, illuminating her face in an unnatural green light. Her lit features look slightly menacing. Her hands fly over the keys; she is engrossed in whatever she is doing. She wears a mischievous, wine-tinged grin—there is an open cabernet in front of her. Her grin disappears as she looks up and nods at Cyrus before her eyes turn back to the screen.

"What the fuck, Luce?"

Lucy again peers up over the screen to contend with the annoyance that has entered her atmosphere. "Cyrus, I am working on this presentation. Sorry I can't also be your personal maid and assistant."

Cyrus tries hard to stay calm. He doesn't want to fight. He doesn't want to smash another cabinet. He turns on his heel and walks back out the door. He walks down St. Paul Street and turns on Broadway, crossing under the interstate spur that separates the Ward from downtown.

By noon the next day, having slept on a couch in an empty partner's office, Cyrus realizes he has done nothing both with his life and nothing in particular that morning. This knowledge is based on the fact that he knows that the *Drudge Report* has not refreshed any stories in the last hour. The hunt for Bin Laden continues, there are no nukes in Iraq, and the wars go on and on. He is now a month out from his argument in front of Judge Cobb, and all he can think of is finding out the result. That, and the recurrent image in his mind of Diana curled up in her jail cell waiting. And her smile.

Cyrus is adrift as much as he has ever been in his life. He closed on the new condo a week ago. He has two weeks left on the lease on the old apartment and he is in a kind of limbo, slow-moving his stuff over to the new place. Lucy hired movers that were supposed to have moved the larger items earlier that day. But given the state of the apartment last night, he wonders whether that actually happened. He realizes that he and Lucy are now more roommates than anything else. They should be excited about this new place, but neither seems to be.

He toggles back from the internet to an incomplete set of discovery on his screen. He senses someone crossing the threshold of his doorway. He turns to see Grayson Asher's smirk.

"Hard at work I see. Want to grab a couple at Kenadees?"

Cyrus has no reason not to. It is either do that or go home to the unpacking, or packing, or whatever the fuck is going on. He is pretty sure Lucy wouldn't want him there. She would second-guess his every choice, from where to put the silverware to which part of which closet he gets. Better to just let her get settled and then find a way to fit himself into her space.

Kenadees is dead. The after-work crowd has left to treat their families to pizza on Friday night, and the college kids and twentysomethings are hours away from venturing out. There are several NBA games on the screens above the bar, and the Badgers are set to tip off against a very strong Michigan team at eight on ESPN. Cyrus indulges Grayson's attempts to engage him in a political debate about lowering taxes and whether human activities are really leading to climate change. Grayson's arguments get more pointed with each Captain and Coke. Cyrus's heart is not in it.

He leaves before midnight. He walks past a couple of homeless guys setting up tents under an on-ramp. The sky is clear with no moon, and even downtown he can make out the North Star and a ghostly Orion. He realizes that he does not have the keys to the new place—Lucy needed them for the movers. He pauses for a second, then turns right, instead of left, on St. Paul and starts walking back to the old apartment. He gets there to find it almost completely empty—the movers have come after all—except for a pile of his clothes in the middle of a large area rug patterned with stains that represent where furniture used to be and the detritus of life.

He texts Lucy. He paces around. The apartment seems huge, a huge cube with no furniture, and the more time he spends there, the dirtier it seems to him. There is dust everywhere and spider webs in every corner. He is wasting his time. It is Friday night and he would rather be drinking beer in front of the TV or reading or doing something other than imitating a caged tiger in this stupid loft. He takes off his button-down shirt. Underneath he has on just a V-neck T-shirt with a coffee stain running from the point of the V down toward his belly button.

The beer is wearing off, and he is antsy. He decides to try to get in a workout. He will do a set of ten push-ups followed by ten v-up sit-ups eight times, or less if he can't finish the push-ups. He gets through the second set and sweat squeezes out of his pores, expelling the impurities he spent the first few hours of the night ingesting. He starts to feel loose, and the third and fourth sets actually feel good. He is snapping to the top of his push-ups, his elbows locking, his core tight. He can feel his muscles stretched and taut from his shoulders to his shins.

Around set eight, fatigue sets in. He has trouble finishing the last push-up, and his v-up form is shit. His T-shirt is damp. He lies down on his back and stretches his arms across his chest one at a time feeling his shoulders crackle and pop. The physical diversion past, he starts to wonder where the fuck Lucy is again and why she can't ever, never, not even once, answer her phone when he calls.

He rolls to the middle of the floor and lies flat on his back with his head resting on the pile of his clothes that Lucy so unceremoniously left in a heap. *Am I going to sleep here tonight?* He tries closing his eyes, but he is pissed and really does not want to sleep on the fucking floor of an apartment when he owns a condo full of his furniture less than a mile away. He tries to calm himself. He thinks of the black line at the bottom of the pool gliding under his body. His breathing starts to slow and deepen. Then, he hears the door click.

Lucy peeks her head in. He sits up and Lucy looks surprised, at least he thinks she does, for an instant.

"Well, there you are. I was wondering," she says.

Darkening the door behind her is a huge man. He is well above six feet. He is bald, with a salt and pepper goatee. He is wearing a Harley-Davidson leather jacket over a button-down shirt with several buttons undone at the top. He has a bit of a gut, but big arms, huge really; the arms of a dedicated weightlifter.

"This is Scooter Larioux," Lucy says as the man takes a couple of steps into the empty apartment and Cyrus scrambles to his feet while trying to straighten his shirt. "This is who I have been spending all of my time working for on those PowerPoints."

Cyrus is embarrassed and hopes that he looks somewhat presentable. Here he is sleeping in an abandoned apartment in an undershirt like some homeless person, and now he has to meet this successful businessman for the first time. Cyrus is also groggy. He smiles awkwardly and shakes Scooter's hand.

"Um, nice to meet you, sorry I am kind of a wreck, I didn't have a key to the new place and..." Cyrus trails off. What else is there to say? He bought a condo that Lucy has already taken possession of, and he is a man without a place and without even keys to his house. He feels like a dog left out in the rain.

"Well, we are glad we found you," Lucy says in a sort of sunny way that reads particularly fake to Cyrus.

"I don't know why it was that hard, I left about six texts and a voicemail," says Cyrus.

Scooter is smiling broadly in the background, as though this is a normal way to meet the partner of his employee. Lucy's smile grows a little harder. Cyrus wonders how tightly her teeth are gnashed together as her lips pull back.

"Thankfully, Scooter agreed to help me find you. Wasn't that nice of him?"

"Um, yeah," says Cyrus. "Well, it was nice meeting you, sorry it was such a weird circumstance."

"Okay, yeah, nice to meet you, I hope I get to see you again," Scooter says as he moves toward the elevators and then turns back at the last second. "Hey, do you ever ride motorcycles?" he asks Cyrus.

"Yeah, well, I did, but I sold my bike a couple years ago."

"No big deal," says Scooter. "If you are up for it, I am riding up to my cabin in Elkhart Lake next weekend with a couple of buddies. Maybe you could join us. Just a guy's weekend; beer, fishing, a couple of cool bars up there. Just tell Lucy, and I will make the arrangements. I could hook you up with a good loaner."

Lucy is still smiling, but her jaw muscle is clenched.

"Yeah, sounds great," says Cyrus. "I'll see what work looks like, but I am definitely interested."

Lucy steps past Cyrus and gives Scooter a polite half hug, reaching up to put her hands on his shoulders and lifting one foot behind her in a sort of graceful, tennis-on-Sunday kind of gesture.

"Thank you for the help tonight," she says.

"No worries," says Scooter as he disappears into the elevator.

Lucy steps back into the apartment. Her smile is gone.

"What is your problem? You can't just be normal, there is always something. Why do you look like a homeless person sleeping in the middle of a dirty, empty apartment?"

Cyrus shakes his head. "I guess because I don't have the keys to the condo I just bought. Can I get those?" Lucy reaches into her purse and throws the keys across what now seems like a vast expanse of clothes and dust bunnies. Cyrus watches them skid into the corner.

"Did you drive, er...?" Cyrus asks as he puts his shirt back on and kicks around the pile of clothes on the floor.

"I did, but I am going to make sure I got everything in here and straighten up a bit. I'll see you back there."

Cyrus walks out and pushes the button to the elevator. *So, now I am walking home at two in the morning and she's mad at me, what the fuck?*

Chapter 41

JUNE 12, 2006

The early summer sun forces him awake. Lucy must be out on an early walk with Biggie. There is an island just off the shore of Lake Michigan constructed of tailings from a massive sewer project decades ago. The island has become a nature preserve with prairie grasses and countless birds. Lucy takes Biggie there often. She lets him off leash to chase geese with abandon. They both come back with a kind of damp lake smell, the dog completely exhausted.

He likes parts of her, maybe even loves. She is beautiful; that is a start. He likes a kind of wildness that she has. He sometimes catches a glimpse of it when she returns from her adventures with Biggie. But Cyrus knows that he and Lucy are on different paths, only occasionally intersecting. He's not sure they really know each other. He's not sure why they got back together only to find this distance again.

His concerns about his relationship fade as he stretches across the bed and looks out at the Hoan Bridge and its blue arch rising seemingly ridiculously and unnecessarily high above the confluence of the Milwaukee River and Lake Michigan. He can see the traffic moving over the bridge like toy cars passing in front of a painted blue background. He can see the lake too, just beyond the Summerfest grounds.

The condo smells new, and he has his bed to himself. He stretches and rolls around a bit more, lingering before facing the reality of getting ready for work.

He presses the play button on his clock radio, and he can hear the disc start spinning. The straining vocals and eccentric guitar of Built to Spill's "In the Morning" makes greeting the day better. There is something jangling and dissonant about the chords that, for him, encapsulates the way he feels in the morning and in particular this morning: incomplete, awkward, just trying to keep it together, but also happy to be alive. He dives under the covers for a few more minutes.

Fuck it, I'll be late, he thinks to himself. He skips the shower and pulls on khakis and a sweatshirt. He puts the rest of his work clothes in a backpack. He grabs his iPod, which has a mix including gangster rap and nineties indie classics. He heads out the door to DMX. He stops at Starbucks for a cappuccino with a triple shot. DMX is quickening his pace. He stays on Water Street heading north giving a wide birth to his office building. He keeps his head down in the lobby of the Milwaukee Athletic Club. He wants to avoid recognition by any lawyers meeting clients for an early breakfast or coffee. He almost feels like he is playing hooky working out in the morning. He could be at work cranking away at a brief, really getting after the day like the gunner everyone wants him to be, but today he doesn't care.

The locker room is virtually empty. It is eight thirty by the time he gets there. The early morning crowd has already left, and the early lunch crowd is hours away. The pool is empty too. He slowly eases himself into the water with his palms on the edge of the pool—feeling his lats and triceps work for the first time that day as they support his weight until his feet find the pool bottom. He starts out slowly and deliberately, keeping his rhythm smooth, rocking from side to side with each stroke. His flip-turns are on rhythm with his breathing, and his streamline is tight as he glides off the walls. His mind is quicker than usual to switch off and become nothing more than an observer to the physical process of his body pulling itself through the water. He picks up the pace on the second five hundred, peeking at the clock to get some sense of how long the first half of his thousand has taken him. He changes his kick from two beats to four and controls his breathing despite his body's demand for more oxygen.

He finishes feeling a little out of breath but still loose and happy to have chosen to start his day with exercise. He towels off next to the lunch tables as the attendants set out the buffet for the day. His attention drifts to the ridiculous Greek-island mural, and he can't help smiling thinking of the first time he swam here: Before Lucy. Before losing the Hebert trial. And before Diana.

He finds the steam room empty. He puts his towel on a bench and turns on the steam, letting his body adjust to the extreme heat. He feels the chlorine expelling through his pores, and he stands and puts his hands on the wall to stretch out his calves, then drops his head between his hands as far as he can to stretch his back and lats.

He is clean shaven, shiny, and new by the time he finds his way to his office. It is now almost ten. His secretary, Julie, comes in with the day's mail, and there it is sitting on the top of the pile. An envelope from the Western District of Wisconsin. It is thick, as if it contains several folded pages. Julie has already opened it neatly with a letter opener.

As soon as she leaves his office and closes the door behind her, Cyrus closes his eyes, takes a huge breath, and takes out the folded writings contained inside. He skims the first page. It is indeed Judge Cobb's decision. He skips to the end and he almost starts crying. It reads: "It is hereby ordered that the Petitioner's sentence and judgment of conviction is vacated. This matter is set for a scheduling conference on June 30, 2006, to set a new trial date." Holy shit! Diana gets a new trial!

The rest of the day is a complete blur. He tries to call Diana and gets her counselor, with whom he shares the news. The counselor promises to arrange a phone call for another day that week. He calls Quinlan and tells him about the result. Quinlan is completely shocked. He actually comes down to Cyrus's office to read the decision. Quinlan keeps saying over and over, "This is unbelievable." It's not exactly the reaction Cyrus expected; he thought there would be something of a more congratulatory tone. But he doesn't really care. He'll take it.

Chapter 42

JULY 29, 2006

They have agreed to meet in front of the 414 building just after six o'clock on Friday. Cyrus feels like a bit of a poser, having ridden the loaner bike he picked up from the dealership to work. He puts on the leather jacket that he purchased just for the occasion. On one of his office chairs sits a black helmet that looks far too big for his head.

He feels especially stupid firing up and riding the bike out of the parking garage. The thing is so loud. He hasn't ridden for a few years and is a little rusty, stalling out a few times in front of the exit gate while fumbling for his key card. He looks back nervously over his shoulder and can see a Jaguar and Mercedes impatiently waiting to get out of the parking structure and on to whatever weekend festivities the partners have planned. He hopes no one recognizes him. But given the gigantic helmet and the leather outfit, he doubts that is really an issue.

Cyrus waits for Scooter at the side of the building, on the corner of Milwaukee and Wisconsin. He is nervous, unfamiliar with the bike and not wanting to get honked at by the buses as they swing into the bus stop in front of the building. He hears Scooter before he sees him. Cyrus thought his rental was loud, but it sounds like a Vespa compared to the low-end growl that bellows forth from Scooter's ride. Scooter's bike is all matte black and burnished metal; nothing on the bike shines. It makes any shine or chrome seem trite, superfluous. This is a bike with a singular purpose, and whatever that purpose is, nothing will stand in its way. The handlebars are narrow, sleek, and all the wires and cables are hidden. The bike is nothing more than it is: an engine with a seat. It is also fast as hell.

They ride north along Lake Michigan until veering west onto Highway 57 toward the heart of the state. It is warm and humid. The previous night's storms have left a sheen on the roadway that reflects the softening sunlight. Actually, it isn't so much a sheen as a grime or film, like something that would coat the skin of a very sick man. Cyrus rides faster than he is comfortable doing, just to keep up with Scooter. Neither have windshields. Cyrus feels the pressure from the wind as it tries to rip him from the bike. He tries to push away the mental image of his body skipping down the shimmering road in his stiff new leather jacket. He instinctively closes his eyes at every bump and crack, preparing to take the ultimate journey from ride to road.

Scooter, on the other hand, is relaxed, languidly swerving past car after car as if his interaction with the traffic is a repeated musical pattern. He sits his bike with the nonchalance of someone who has ridden countless miles at speed. He does it without a helmet, just sunglasses, and at times he takes a hand off the handlebars and rests it on his thigh.

Cyrus wonders if Scooter is doing something aerodynamically to change the way the wind hits his body. Cyrus actively fights the wind. He cannot squeeze the grips any harder. His forearms are starting to cramp. Eventually, Cyrus gives up the chase and lets Scooter slide out of sight.

Cyrus slows to a more comfortable pace. He knows generally where they are going, and he is tired of contemplating death.

About a mile before the turnoff to Elkhart Lake, Cyrus catches up to Scooter. Scooter has slowed and is, amazingly, lighting a cigar while riding his bike at highway speeds despite not having a windshield. He takes his hands off his handlebars and ducks his head down into his leather jacket to light the cigar inside the tented shelter. Scooter holds the cigar in his teeth and flashes a rictus grin as Cyrus pulls up alongside. Scooter gives Cyrus a thumbs-up and raises an eyebrow to inquire as to whether everything is okay. Cyrus nods and returns Scooter's signal.

It is the golden hour as they ride down the main street of Elkhart Lake. Couples from Milwaukee and Chicago stroll down the sidewalks past the restaurants, shops, and bars. Between stop signs, Scooter pulls slightly ahead of Cyrus. All eyes are on Scooter, this giant man smoking a cigar astride a loud, stripped-down instrument of speed and violence. Everyone stares but no one reacts, lest they attract the attention of the primitive beast. Little do they know, this is a respected and successful businessman, up to visit his cabin with a few friends. Just like the rest of them.

Scooter's cabin is only a few miles beyond the last stop sign in Elkhart. There is a small grocery store that sells mostly organic food and meat on one side of the street. Beyond that, the road twists and rises as it navigates the drumlins, kettles, and moraines left by the last glacier, here at its former edge. The small-town streets and sidewalks give way to a mix of deciduous and coniferous forest divided only by entrances to long drives that end at houses on the lake. Despite being only an hour and a half from Milwaukee, it suddenly feels like Northern Wisconsin. Scooter's place is on a parcel of land that fans out from the lake to the road. There is a dip and then a rise in the road as it ascends one of the many moraines. They turn toward the lake at the crest of the moraine, the driveway diving and twisting toward the lake.

The house is a sprawling modern walkout ranch set on a flat area above the lake but below the road. There are parking spaces for four or five cars. The house is dark wood with decks and outdoor patios all around it. It has the prairie architecture feel of a Frank Lloyd Wright design with geometric windows inlaid with lead. It is tucked into the undulous landscape. The small window slits, visible from the driveway, suggest a den for its inhabitants to secret themselves away from the world in an almost subterranean space.

As they park the bikes, Cyrus can smell the woodsmoke. It is acrid, almost bracing to the nose, mixing with the thick evening air. He can make out a column of smoke coming from the back, or lake side, of the house. The sunset is just showing under the clouds, like a lifted dress revealing a shocking slip underneath.

There is a large, flat stone patio that sits above and maybe half a football field away from the lake. Leaves from a few scattered deciduous trees have dyed the flagstone patio orange and brown with leaf patterns, as if the whole thing were an art project completed by some first-grade savant. A light mist coming down from the low clouds disperses the patio lights and gives a glowing effect to the house lights circling the lake.

There are a group of dudes standing around a fire pit on the patio. *Looks like a brodeo*, thinks Cyrus. There is a massive metal grill built into a stone wall that protects the patio from the house and holds back the hill sloping toward the lake. The men form sort of a half circle around the grill. Some are smoking. They all have bottles of craft beer in their hands pulled from the icy interior of an antique Coleman cooler parked next to a metal table on which several racks of ribs sit speckled with rubs. There are also some open bags of chips and an array of lighters, cigarette packs, and even a marijuana pipe strewn about.

This is not exactly the type of gathering Cyrus was expecting from a successful serial entrepreneur, but Cyrus is down with it. He is introduced to Bo, a sarcastic motor-mouth and owner of the local Ford dealership. He is chain-smoking Marlboro Reds and holding court with a few of his mechanics and salesmen, spewing a variety of conspiracy theories, including the CIA's involvement in 9-11. He is entertaining, but a guy named Marc is the life of the party. He has a boom box set up on the metal table with a stack of old CDs. He is essentially DJing, alternating between Meat Loaf, Motely Crue, and A Tribe Called Quest. He uses the grill brush to karaoke every new song he plays. He is a big guy, wearing a button-down work shirt that he has sweated through, despite the chill of the night. He points to the sky, giving devil horns and rock locks, and swings his arms in a wild Chuck Berry-inspired air-guitar routine.

People shuffle in and out of the circular gathering on the patio. Scooter introduces Cyrus to the owner of a local bar, who shows up with his bartender and a huge bag of weed. They all drink too much and pack bowl after bowl. Marc carries on with the music, getting louder and louder.

At some point someone casts a fishing line out with a hunk of rib on a hook and walks the rod and reel back up to the patio, propping it between stones that line the patio.

Midway through the night, the rod comes to life. In a fit of excitement and surprise, they chase it down the hill toward the lake. Scooter dives and grabs the rod just before it drops off a retaining wall into the black water. He stands on the wall and holds the rod aloft, its tip bending down toward the water and the whir of the reel playing harmony with the guitar solo in "After Midnight." Scooter pulls and reels, yelling for Marc to go into the boathouse and get a net. Five minutes later, he is smiling in the moonlight holding a forty-inch Muskie as the men on the patio cheer.

Chapter 43

JULY 2, 2006

Cyrus sits at his desk staring at Westlaw pulled up on his screen. His face is pale and tinged greenish-blue by the electronic light of the screen. He is staring at the Federal Rules of Evidence, clicking through one rule after the other. He had an epiphany, or more like a wake-up call, coming back from Scooter's Elkhart place, feeling like crap with drinker's remorse and a little jealous of this dude who has built this whole successful life and basically just does whatever he wants. These feelings caused Cyrus to reflect on just what the fuck he is doing with his life, and as if some defense mechanism was triggered, Diana's face popped into his head—her slanted grin and the wise eyes. And then dread and realization smashed into his forehead. He is going to have to try this case. Someone's life is on the line. And the last case he helped try was an abject failure. Because of him. So, he sits, essentially memorizing the rules of evidence and wondering how the fuck he is going to do this.

Just then, Quinlan knocks on his open office door and leans against the doorframe. Cyrus looks up.

"I just got off the phone with Scooter Larioux. He is looking to make some deal with the Oneida, and we are working to try to put together a proposal to win his work away from the Trout firm. Not your concern, but he did mention that he has been spending some time with you. He was very complimentary, and he said that I should look after you."

Quinlan gives a kind of condescending chuckle, looking down at his hands. He then looks up at Cyrus, who sits there staring, trying to project the confidence litigators are expected to project.

"In all seriousness, Cyrus, I am very impressed that you are socializing with such a major potential client. I will definitely let management know. That is the type of thing we expect partners to do, and it is impressive that you are doing it as an associate." With that, Quinlan turns and leaves.

Whatever, thinks Cyrus. He starts searching Westlaw for cases discussing retrials of criminal matters. He types in a broad search using the keywords: evidence, retrial, and criminal. He expects to get a million hits, but it is a place to start and seems more productive than memorizing the Federal Rules of Evidence. His first hit is an appellate decision regarding the release of a prisoner pending retrial.

Holy Shit! It hadn't even occurred to him. He could ask the court to release Diana pending the new trial. Shit. He could even ask the prosecutor to just cut a plea deal saying that she has served enough time. He starts racing through the cases, writing down cites, and cutting and pasting quotes. By 5:00, he has drafted a motion for the court to release Diana. He sends it to the night secretaries to proofread and format.

CYRUS FILES THE MOTION FIRST THING THE NEXT MORN-ing through the court's electronic filing system. He files it as an expedited motion, giving the other side only five days to respond. About an hour after the filing goes through, the phone rings. The display on his office phone shows that it is the United States Attorney's office calling. Cyrus's heart starts beating a little faster, and he dreads what is coming. He picks up the phone. "Cyrus Jackson," he answers. There is a bit of a pause.

"Cyrus, this is Joe Nelson, I am calling about the motion you just filed."

"Okay," says Cyrus. There is another pause as if Nelson was expecting more of an explanation.

"Listen, Cyrus, I know you are green, and you don't really do this kind of work, but in our world, we don't just drop these types of bombshells on each other. Frankly, it's a candyass kind of way to practice law."

Cyrus can feel his throat tightening up as he digests Nelson's words and tone.

"Is it as candyass as getting a thirty-three-year conviction for a meth addict who happens to be essentially a slave for a motorcycle gang? Joe, why the hell do you even care? She's done five years, isn't that enough? And, by the way, Joe, if the point of this call is to amicably ask me to withdraw the motion, your delivery needs some work, and the answer is no."

"Listen Cyrus, there is a lot you don't know about the Hounds. This is not a good group of people."

"I believe it, Joe," Cyrus says, "but that doesn't justify keeping a grandmother in prison whose greatest crime is knowing the gang was distributing meth and doing their bidding so she would get some. Let's be honest with each other Joe, the only reason you prosecuted her was because she wouldn't testify. Why? Because she was scared shitless she would fucking get killed. And now you are basically telling me she was right to be scared. You don't really give a shit. Your lazy brand of justice is to pick low-hanging fruit—victims like Diana—and then try to get them to flip so you can build your case or else inflict upon them the wrath and might of the federal government. Shit, Joe. You never even figured out who was in charge of this organization. You prosecuted a bunch of bit players. Nice job."

Nelson sighs. "Well, Cyrus, you're right about one thing. We never found out who was running this. We didn't count on the Hounds to help, but we thought maybe Diana would. We could have helped her. She refused to say anything. If she was such a victim in all of this, as you say, you would think she would want a chance to turn her life around. And to keep it from happening again. She has a duty to help out and get whoever ran this off the street.

"And I can still make a deal Cyrus. I still want to get whoever was in charge. If she gives me a name and agrees to testify, this is all over for her. We can protect her, she can trust my word on that."

"God Joe, why in the world would she trust you? I'm sure the trust has just been welling up inside of her while she sat underground for the last five years."

"Fine, Cyrus," Joe says, exasperated, "you are clearly brainwashed by your client. You are a little punk who has no clue what he is doing." With that he slams down the phone.

Cyrus screams "Fuck you!" into his phone, even though no one is on the other end.

Chapter 44

JULY 7, 2006

Scooter invited Lucy and Cyrus to come out to a party and stay over at his friends Misty and Spencer's house, just south of Prairie du Chien. Scooter actually made the invitation through Lucy, who continues to work on some PowerPoint presentation that Scooter apparently plans to take on tour around the country, giving it to various business organizations, proselytizing about taking risks in entrepreneurship and equating that to glory on the football field and how that has all paid off for him. (And it can for you too!) Cyrus is a little skeptical that anyone would want to hear that shit, let alone pay to hear it, but he realizes how little he knows of the business world. The more he learns about it, the more he thinks it is all just about bullshitters bullshitting.

The party at Misty and Spencer's is supposed to start around seven. Spencer is big into home brewing, and they apparently have an amazing house above the Mississippi. Every year, they have this blowout party with kegs and kegs of Spencer's homemade beer and people show up and crash on their property. At least, that is what Lucy told Cyrus.

Cyrus hopes he and Lucy can use the trip to reconnect. They stopped speaking to each other about a week ago, since Cyrus went to Elkhart with Scooter, and Cyrus isn't sure why. This is the way it is with Lucy sometimes. Cyrus commits some slight. Sometimes he doesn't even realize it. Lucy doesn't fight with him or confront him about it. She just punishes him. Usually that takes the form of her simply not talking to him at all. It is icy and awkward. The only way out of it is for Cyrus to start a fight. But even then, Cyrus has to push and push to get any kind of reaction, and by the time he gets one, the two are at war, saying things that are impossible to take back.

Cyrus decides to rent a big touring bike and make a day out of it. He gets up early and drives to Milwaukee Harley-Davidson, on the south side of the city, and picks up a maroon Harley-Davidson Ultra Classic. He is nervous getting on the giant bike and worries about the thing tipping. He probably wouldn't be able to get it back up. But on the drive back to the condo, he is surprised at how nimbly the bike handles. It is so stable, he feels he could comfortably take his hands off the handlebars and, light a cigar, for instance. He rumbles up in front of the condo and parks on the street in a parking spot reserved for visitors. Lucy is still in the shower, and Cyrus packs the saddlebags with a tent, sleeping bags, and a change of clothes. He is sipping a cup of coffee when Lucy gets out of the shower. Her hair is wrapped in a towel, with another towel barely covering her torso.

This is why I put up with it all, Cyrus thinks.

"Hey, we're ready to go whenever you are."

She says, "Yeah, Cyrus, I'm moving as fast as I can for your little excursion." She makes a point of noisily banging about in the bathroom as she finishes getting ready. Finally, she emerges in tight jeans and a thin Rolling Stones T-shirt. She still looks annoyed. But she looks good.

"Are you ready for an adventure!?" Cyrus asks trying to inflect some excitement into his voice.

"I guess," she says, deflating the sentiment like an old balloon.

As they head toward the door, Cyrus grabs Lucy's white leather coat from the hanger, and she gives him a confused and still annoyed look. They walk down the main staircase, which is encased in glass, giving them the illusion of descending into the bright blue lake. Lucy follows Cyrus out the door. He thinks she must be wondering why they aren't going to the parking garage, but she stays silent, keeping a few steps behind. The huge motorcycle is parked in front, just outside the front door, its saddlebags filled with their camping gear and two helmets hanging from the handlebars. Cyrus puts one of the helmets on and hands the other to Lucy as he straddles the bike. She has her hand on her hip and her eyes seem to be in a constant state of eye-rolling, as if she is in a semi-conscious state of REM sleep.

"You have to be kidding me," she says, but she ultimately puts on the helmet and gets on the bike behind him.

Cyrus can tell she is avoiding pressing her body against his. She grips the side rails of the seat and holds herself upright. But as they roll through the city, hitting pothole after pothole, she lurches into him from time to time. Once they get onto the interstate, the rattle of the engine smooths out into rhythmic background noise and the soft suspension of the bike smooths out the road. Cyrus can feel Lucy's tension ease, and she presses into him and relaxes. It feels nice.

Before Prairie du Chien, just after they cross the Wisconsin River, they turn off the highway and enter Wyalusing State Park, stopping at a little booth with a traffic gate. Lucy sits up and scooches herself away from Cyrus on the seat, separating their bodies as if the last two and a half hours of physical contact was a mistake she now regrets. Cyrus purchases a day pass. It is not yet noon. Cyrus pulls a water bottle out of one of the saddlebags, and Lucy stretches her hands above her head.

"The second leg of our adventure starts now! Are you ready?" Cyrus asks.

Lucy's eyes narrow and then sarcastically widen as she gives a little forced smile while shaking her head from side to side.

They follow a trail that starts on a boardwalk crossing over the marsh that the Wisconsin River floods every spring with melting snow and rainwater. It has been a wet summer, and the swell of the river is immense. The boardwalk is still flooded in some places. The wet conditions have bred a voracious and prolific generation of mosquitos that have been effective at keeping tourists away. Cyrus and Lucy seem to be the only ones there. They cross the marsh, and the trail begins to ascend the steep bluffs that guard the two rivers as they join.

Cyrus pauses at a placard that describes what they are about to see on the trail. It is a sacred Native American site. They should look for marked burial mounds along the way and will find hollowed-out storage chambers and even caves, where early inhabitants ate, slept, and worshipped. The placard says there is no consensus when the people who inhabited this area built these sites or even who they were. They likely predated the Ho-Chunk, Sioux, Fox, and other tribes that the French fur traders first encountered when they got to the area over three hundred years ago.

As the trail gets higher, it becomes walled on one side by exposed limestone as if it were carved out of the hill. There are trilobite fossils in the limestone and there are cubby-like shelves, some burrowing ten feet into the hillside.

"This place is amazing," Cyrus says, his hand grazing the limestone as they walk.

Lucy says nothing.

As Cyrus gazes into a cubby cut deep into the limestone wall by some ancient inhabitant, Lucy lights a cigarette. She takes a deep drag and exhales loudly.

Eventually, the trail ascends to the top of the bluff, which could be described as a mesa. It is almost flat, covered in tall grass and scattered deciduous trees, with steep sides dropping to the river valley below. The view that has been teasing itself as the trail wound up the hillside is now fully revealed. Below them is the confluence of the Wisconsin and Mississippi Rivers. Now, in this wet summer, the view is spectacular. It is like what Cyrus imagines the Amazon looks like. Everything is green, and you can see the greenish-blue Wisconsin waters mix with the already brown Mississippi. There are backwaters and tributaries divided by marsh plants and stands of trees. The riot of green and blue fills the valley below, extending to the rocky bluffs on the Iowa side of the river valley. Cyrus sighs, awestruck by the view.

Lucy looks out over the expanse and, without looking at Cyrus, says, "I can't do this anymore."

Chapter 45

JULY 7, 2006

The house is on top of a bluff. The driveway is a steep incline of washed-out road base and dirt. Cyrus strains to keep the bike upright and maintain his nerve to keep the throttle twisted, spinning the rear tire, and pushing the mass of metal up the unforgiving slope. He grits his teeth and fights the handlebars. The bike leans from side to side. At the top of the hill, the driveway flattens into a large cement slab with a detached three-car garage perpendicular to a mammoth log cabin. Opposite the garage is a restored barn and a riding corral with a wide-open gate, where about ten vehicles, including bikes, trucks, and cars, are already parked. Cyrus crests the hill and almost tips the bike one more time. He jerks forward and awkwardly stops, giving Lucy the opportunity to dismount, take off her helmet, and shake her hair out. Cyrus pulls the bike into the corral and manages to park next to some other motorcycles, most of which look cobbled together, customized, fast, and mean. Like Scooter's bike.

Cyrus wonders why the fuck he is here. He can hear voices outside, probably at the back of the house. Lucy is nowhere in sight. Already vanished. It is just beyond him why she would agree to go to this party and then break up with him on the way there. It occurs to him to just get back on the bike and leave.

Then, out of the front door and down large steps of hewn logs comes Scooter, waving to Cyrus.

"Cyrus, I am glad you came," Scooter half-yells across the driveway. He is wearing cutoff khaki shorts, a faded red polo shirt open at the neck, and retro Air Jordans, the original red and black ones. He holds out his hand as he approaches. "This will be a blast, you'll see. Let me introduce you to some people."

Scooter takes Cyrus through the front door and into a large front room with high ceilings and a central fireplace that is open to a kitchen on one side and a family room on the other. The walls are lined with built-in bookcases and custom cabinets. Despite the heat of the day, there is a large fire burning in the fireplace. French doors from the kitchen open to a large deck that runs the length of the back of the house. The doors are wide open, as is every other window and door in the house. The view is spectacular: the deck sits above the tops of oak and maple trees that descend a steep slope and then end at a cliff that drops, what looks like five hundred feet, into the Mississippi below, which is spread out in all its glory.

Cyrus follows Scooter to the end of the deck that forms a sort of hexagonal sitting area with a fire pit in the middle of wooden benches. Around the fire pit are small kegs hooked up to a mass of tubing and a tank of some sort of gas. There are taps drilled directly into the deck railing and a picnic table with about a hundred steins there for the taking. Scooter introduces Cyrus to a guy who, like Scooter, looks to be in his midforties, with long hair thinning on top and a trimmed beard. He has on a Hawaiian shirt with the top two buttons unbuttoned and faded cargo shorts that go past his knees.

"Cyrus, this is Spencer. He built this place with his bare hands, and he made all this glorious beer for us to enjoy."

Cyrus shakes Spencer's hand. He has the broad, hardened hands of someone who works with his hands, but from the look in Spencer's eye, Cyrus can tell that Spencer works with his hands because he can, not because he must.

"Pleased to meet you and thanks for having us…me," says Cyrus. "This place is incredible."

"Aww, thanks, man," says Spencer, handing Cyrus a stein. "Do you like IPA?"

At that moment, Cyrus decides he is going to enjoy himself. Fuck it. Why ruin the opportunity to enjoy an amazing setting, some nice people, and some homemade beer? Who knows, maybe Lucy is just pissed off about something and they can figure it out.

The IPA is everything an IPA should be. It is crisp, fruity, and hoppy, with a nice dense head. Cyrus is enjoying the beer and the sun, which is warming the party and sparkling on the river below. He talks swimming with Spencer, who apparently hung out with some of the divers on the UW swim team when he was in college and wound up going to a lot of meets and getting into the sport of swimming in the process. Spencer swims at the high school in Prairie a couple of times a week and has even swum down the Mississippi from Prairie to Ferryville.

Spencer's wife, Misty, comes out with a bowl of thick tortilla chips and homemade salsa that marries mangos and ghost peppers into a sweet and spicy tang. Misty has crimped blond hair and dark eyeliner that makes her bright blue eyes pop. She is wearing a floral, Hawaiian-themed dress with embroidery around a low-cut neckline. There is a pocket in the front of the dress from which she pulls out a large pipe carved from pipestone in the shape of an eagle head. She winks at Cyrus and hands him the pipe and a lighter. He shrugs and sparks it up. That too tastes fruity, fresh, and homegrown. Spencer confirms that it is.

CYRUS DOESN'T KNOW HOW THE BASKETBALL TOURNAMENT started or when so many people got to the party. But a dozen of the guys have moved to the front of the house, bringing one of the kegs with them. They have paired off, playing two-on-two on the concrete driveway in front of the garage, which has a regulation hoop mounted above the garage door. The winning pair holds court. Cyrus also doesn't know how he got paired with Spencer, but they are a good pair. Spencer is taller than he holds himself, with a bit of a natural slouch. Cyrus guesses he is six foot three and a touch over two hundred pounds. What he lacks in speed, he makes up for in strength and smarts. His big hands and long arms grab rebounds and distribute the ball to a cutting and shooting Cyrus, who has found that magical twilight when the beer and weed mix in an alchemic miracle to enhance his athletic performance. He can see the holes in the defense and knows where Spencer will pass the ball before he does. Cyrus catches passes and rises up to hit shot after shot from every angle. He can't remember ever playing so well. He does not feel tired. Cyrus and Spencer hold court for four or five games. And their opponents aren't bad. There are some youngsters, mostly Scooter's relatives, who recently played high school basketball. Some of the older guys are solid too, likely still playing pickup somewhere, setting hard screens and making steady bank shots.

In between games, the players drink IPA and some smoke cigarettes and bullshit each other about missed shots and past glories. Cyrus has sweated through his shirt, but he still feels good. He wants to keep playing. He grabs the ball and starts making jumpers, progressing around an imagined three-point line.

Scooter comes across the slab from the front door and says, "We got next."

Behind him is one of his cousins, Cubby Bear, who Cyrus finds out is a junior at Minnesota and is on the basketball team there, although Cubby doesn't get much playing time. Cubby is six foot ten but very skinny and wears a shit-eating grin. He looks a little stoned, but also like he fully expects to dominate.

Cubby checks the ball to Cyrus and Scooter matches up with Spencer. The two old friends hand fight and shove for position under the basket. Scooter is pressing his back and sticking out his butt into Spencer, creating space. Spencer braces his forearm across Scooter's back. Scooter holds one hand in the air to receive the pass. Cubby passes the ball over Cyrus's outstretched hands to Scooter, who catches it above his head and pivots to his right. Spencer follows Scooter's shifting weight while shuffling his feet, Scooter pivots back to his left and rises before Spencer can recover. Scooter sinks the jump-shot off the backboard.

"One-nil," he says.

Cubby tries to bounce the next pass in to Scooter, but Spencer's long arm reaches and bats the ball away. Cyrus grabs it. Cubby stabs at the ball for the steal. Cyrus dribbles behind his back and moves to the side. He crisply bounce-passes to Spencer, who touches the ball and immediately bounces it to the space where he knows Cyrus will move next, more quickly than Cubby can get there. Cyrus finds his spot—just inside the (imaginary) free throw line. In one motion, he receives the pass and raises his hands as if he is going to shoot. Cubby, scrambling to recover, is off balance and leaves his feet, desperately trying to block the shot that never comes. Cyrus takes two dribbles while moving to his right as Cubby flies out of the play. Cyrus sinks a wide-open jumper.

It continues that way for some points. Cyrus is still hot, and Spencer is seeing everything before Scooter and Cubby do. Cyrus thinks they might run the table and close out the game eleven-one. But Scooter and Cubby have not given up.

Cubby checks the ball and backs up, giving Cyrus space but staying in front of him with his long arms stretched out to the sides, cutting off Cyrus's passing angles. Cyrus manages to lob the ball to Spencer, who then dribbles to the corner, pulling Scooter with him and clearing out the middle. Cyrus feints as if he is running to the left corner of the imaginary free throw lane. Cubby slides laterally to stay in front of Cyrus and be in position to block his shot. Cyrus then cuts hard, right down the middle of the lane, before Cubby can change directions. Spencer side-arms a bounce pass to about ten feet in front of the basket. It is perfectly timed. Meeting the ball, Cyrus dribbles once and jumps as high as he can toward the rim.

Just as Cyrus stretches out his hand for the finger roll, he feels an immense force slam into his head. His whole body tips out of plane and he free-falls toward the ground. He manages to get his feet roughly under his body. His right foot lands first, stopping his fall and rolling. He feels an electric jolt slam up his leg to his hip and he crumples to the ground. His nose is gushing blood and his right ankle doesn't feel right—as if it has a weird vibration. He stays down for a few seconds, stunned, not knowing what just happened.

"Sorry," says Scooter, with a half-convincing wince. "That was a little aggressive, but we couldn't just let you win that easy." He chuckles.

That's when the laughing fit starts. Cyrus can't stop. He can feel the pain, but it is a distant pain, a numb pain in his ankle, and all he can do is laugh, somewhat crazily. Everyone is looking. His laugh is maniacal and becoming almost like a sob. He is seeing stars.

"Well, I think my run was about over anyway," he manages between giggles as he sits on a picnic bench just off the slab and takes a deep drink from a fresh beer. He loosens the laces on his right high-top and stretches the leg out. The ankle is already swelling. Spencer comes over and pats him on his back.

"It was a nice run. Scooter hates to lose, sorry about that. I may have something to help with the pain, though, follow me…here, let me help you."

Cyrus has his arm around Spencer's neck as they hobble toward the stairs. Cyrus hops up one stair at a time, not putting any weight on his right leg, not trusting it now. They get into the house, with its grand entrance and golden flash of wood. They can hear the women on the deck. Bob Marley is bouncing through the speakers, boosting the party and getting revelers to their feet. At the top of the stairs, Spencer directs Cyrus toward a side door that opens to carpeted stairs going down into a large basement with a pool table, leather couch, and a big-screen TV. Cyrus can smell the chlorine of a hot tub somewhere nearby.

Spencer takes Cyrus down a hall to a closed door at the back of the house. Inside is what looks like a recording studio, with a big control board and a hopeless number of knobs and dials and buttons and two large leather office chairs on rollers. Spencer plants Cyrus in one and opens a large built-in cabinet under a window, through which Cyrus can just make out the orange sky, the setting sun already behind the Iowa bluffs. Spencer pulls out a large bong, a bag of dense bright green and purple marijuana buds, and a bag of dried mushrooms. He opens a drawer within the cabinet and takes out a couple of pill bottles and sets them out on the desk. He breaks up one of the buds and packs it with his thumb into the bowl of the bong.

"Here, take a hit of this and sit tight, I'll be back in a second."

Spencer exits the room on a mission and Cyrus sparks the bong inhaling deeply, feeling the sting in his lungs as his head starts to drift. He feels a lightness spread to his extremities. Before he can decide whether to take another hit, Spencer opens the door with a beer stein in hand, a washcloth, a gel pack, a huge bag of ice, an ace bandage, and a plastic boot for Cyrus's leg.

"Young Cyrus, we are going to treat this conservatively. First, we will try traditional medicines, and if that does not do the job, we have to move on to the medical industrial stuff that we must resort to in desperate times."

Spencer hands Cyrus the stein of beer and kneels down by Cyrus's right foot. Spencer pulls a small stool from under the mixing board and sets it in front of Cyrus. Squatting next to the stool, Spencer carefully starts taking off Cyrus's shoe. The pain is like a lightning storm. As Spencer starts rolling down his sock, Cyrus thinks he does not want to look.

"Well, it is super swollen," says Spencer, "but it doesn't look out of joint or displaced."

Spencer gently wraps the gel pack around the ankle and foot and props it up on the stool. He carefully wraps the ace bandage around it. He then fits the boot over the ace bandage and loosely connects the Velcro straps. Once Cyrus has the boot comfortably resting on the stool, Spencer drapes the bag of ice over it.

"Is that comfortable?" asks Spencer.

Cyrus lets out a little laugh and says, "Yeah, it feels fine."

"Okay," says Spencer, "should we go down the traditional path first?"

"Um, I guess," says Cyrus. Spencer takes the bag of mushrooms and pulls out several individual pieces, spreading them in a row in front of the mixing board on the desk.

"We're in this together, teammate," he says as he takes two and puts them in his mouth, chewing hard at the half-desiccated, stringy woody fungi. He takes a big gulp of beer and shakes his head back and forth, washing them down. "Grew these myself. I'm pretty sure they will kill the pain, or at the very least, you won't remember it tomorrow." He starts laughing.

Cyrus follows his lead and chews two of the mushrooms, washing them down with the IPA. Spencer tinkers with the knobs on the control board. They sit and listen to a bootleg of a Dead show from the early '80s. The sound system is incredible. Spencer occasionally leaves the room to attend to his guests, returning with fresh beers and appetizers. Cyrus feels more than comfortable.

Halfway through the first set, Cyrus asks, "So, what is this room for?" The mushrooms are just starting to kick in, and Cyrus detects a little echo in his own voice. He is starting to notice the changes in light all around him, and as the day turns to night, the air itself seems almost visible.

"This," says Spencer, "is an illegal radio station that broadcasts twenty-four hours a day. It's a little hobby of mine. Misty and I come down here sometimes and DJ and have Grateful Dead night or Bob night, stuff like that, and sometimes we talk to our friends out there across the expanse and people call in and it is really just a blast. But the FCC frowns on this shit, so if you tell anybody about this, I will have Scooter finish you." He waits a beat and then hits Cyrus in the shoulder. "Just kidding. But seriously, don't tell anyone. The FCC are fucking Nazis, and they will fine the shit out of us if they find out what we are doing."

The rest of the night is like a dark web of textures, layers, and sounds. Cyrus limps here and there in the boot that Spencer has secured over his ankle. Cyrus bums a cigarette from some girl, and it tastes rich, herbal, and somewhat floral. He wishes he had a pack. He can see the animals moving below on the plateau.

He catches a glimpse of Lucy on the far end of the deck, surrounded by people, mostly guys, her white teeth flashing in the moonlight. He instantly and palpably misses her. He feels she is pulling something out of him, away from him. He thinks they could have had a family; that maybe they were meant to be together after all. He goes toward her, limping awkwardly through the crowd of revelers. Unable to make small talk, he feels like he is at a Viking battle party, and he is the only non-savage there. He cannot stand these people. They smell and they are loud. Everything is moving and menacing, flowing with a dark energy. He tries to tell himself that he is on mushrooms, it is not real. He clumsily weaves his way through the revelers until she is in front of him. Her dress is moving in the night breeze and she looks so lovely. But as she sees him her face reveals a kind of distaste that borders on horror. It is a look that Cyrus is not prepared for.

All he can manage to say is, "Are we really done?"

Lucy stands there with her hands out like it is the stupidest question ever. The boards supporting the railing are bending behind her, swaying with the wind, and the clouds, infused with moonlight, are swirling above. They form faces, flashing their teeth at him. He retreats. He needs to close his eyes.

He hobbles up the split-log stairs, pressing hard into the railing and hopping on his left leg. He founders and flounders around upstairs. He finds a dark room at the end of the hall with a table and some high-back chairs; some kind of office or something. He curls up in the corner as far from the door as possible. He forbids himself from staring at the wood paneling. The knots in the wood turn into demons and move and work together to menace him. He closes his eyes.

He again questions why Lucy brought him to this place. *What was the point?* But he can't seem to steer his thoughts in a singular direction. He gives up and watches as the blood pumps rhythmically through the small blood vessels in his eyelids. He starts to relax, and eventually he feels at ease. The images of the day flash on repeat in his mind's eye like some 1990s music video montage. He smiles, thinking of his streak on the basketball court. He thinks about the people who were here before him, maybe thousands of years ago, carving recesses into the limestone walls that line the paths they and the people before them cut into these bluffs. He thinks of the sacredness of this place as his mind gradually allows him to sleep.

He wakes in the middle of the night. It must be two or three in the morning. He can hear echoes, the dregs of the party, the last people standing, still carrying on below, reveling toward the dawn. He hears them chanting, "Ferris! Ferris!" At some point he hears a loud boom, like a cannon, and then a splash in the mighty river hundreds of feet below.

The mushrooms have worn off; at least he thinks they have. His ankle is throbbing, and he is slightly nauseous. He needs to pee. He peels himself up, balancing his weight with his hand pressed hard into the wood paneling. He stumbles into the hall. *One of the doors must be to a bathroom.* He guesses it would be the one at the end of the hall. Limping, he moves as quietly as he can in the boot and turns the knob and presses against the door.

As soon as he does there is movement inside. It is a long room, like some kind of closet, with clothes hanging on both sides and a leather upholstered bench in the middle. It is also a pathway to other rooms, maybe a bathroom, maybe a bedroom. He thinks he sees a flash of Lucy's dress.

He thinks he hears Scooter say, "Not a bathroom," and laugh.

He turns and tries another door, finding a bathroom. He stands and pees for a long time. He looks at his ragged self in the mirror. There is blood on the collar of his shirt. His hair looks like he has slept in the dirt; it is matted and dusty. He shakes off the negative thoughts and the bad echoes from the trip and finds his way back to the office to find more sleep.

He wakes again in the corner of the room, half under a large conference table surrounded by big chairs.

There is light coming in from the windows. It is finally morning. It is early. The house is silent. He pulls his phone out of his pocket. It is 5:17 in the morning.

His ankle feels so swollen it occurs to him that it might burst. The skin is stretched. The ankle itself vibrates with a stinging pain, as if a dozen bees are stinging him over and over. He pulls himself up and stretches his upper body, which is also sore from the exertions of yesterday. He runs his hands over his face. There is still blood crusted below his nose, which is sore, but perhaps not destroyed. He stretches his hands up, pressing his palms toward the sky, and looks around the room for the first time in the light.

Hanging on the wood-paneled wall is a framed motor-cycle jacket with a patch sewn on it. The patch has cartoon-ish a dog face in the center. *Fuck!* The top of the patch reads, "Hounds of Hell." He needs to leave.

He thinks for a minute, maybe a minute, probably a minute, about whether he needs to find Lucy and take her home. She brought him here, after all. She was his girlfriend yesterday, after all. But that's all gone now. She came here for her own reasons. She broke up with him. She may be more attached to these people than she ever was to him. She likely is. She is the reason he is here, not the other way around.

He does an inventory. He has everything—wallet, phone, keys. He limps and lumbers around a house he doesn't know with a destroyed ankle and with the need to maintain absolute silence.

He looks at the sky with thanks as he stumbles out the front door and crosses the driveway/basketball court to the horse corral and finds his rented Harley-Davidson Ultra. He almost laughs aloud when he thinks about how differently he saw the bike yesterday morning when he surprised Lucy.

He thinks he should be okay riding with the boot. If it was his left foot, he would not be able to shift gears, but he thinks he is fine to push the brake.

He starts the bike and it is loud, thundering down into the valley, destroying the placid morning. He knows he doesn't have much time. The metallic clicks and clunks echo against the trees as he finds first gear and eases the throttle against the clutch, negotiating the big bike out of the corral.

Down the steep drive is a whole other fucking matter. He can't put a foot down, but he has to be fast. He fishtails the whole way down, squeezing the handbrake here and there and standing on the foot pedal, pressing his throbbing appendage into the brake the whole way down. He makes it to the bottom and lets out a whoop. Finding smooth road, he races to Highway 12 and back across the state.

Chapter 46

AUGUST 10, 2006

Diana steps down the steep narrow steps into the hot morning sun. The tarmac in front of the bus station is shimmering in the morning light. The oil and gas and spilled coffee make rainbows on the surface of puddles from last night's storm. Cyrus stands on the sidewalk, between the bus station and the street, holding two coffees. He has on a button-down shirt and some wrinkled khakis. His hair is messed up and he is smiling, but his eyes look squinty and tired, and he is trying not to smile too hard.

"Welcome to Milwaukee," he says, handing her a Starbucks cup. "I hope you like latte."

"Thank you," Diana says. She looks like she has woken from a dream. Her black hair is tangled and frizzy. She wears Lee jeans that look to be from the 1980s. The waist is folded over and held to her by a narrow belt. She has on a white cotton button-down shirt with the sleeves rolled up and Nike tennis shoes, the old kind with almost no sole.

They cross the street to his car. Cyrus clears the papers and empty Starbucks cups piled up on the passenger seat. Diana gets in and Cyrus starts the engine and blasts the air conditioning. They both just sit for a second.

"How was your trip?" Cyrus asks, "How long was it, anyway?"

"I think they said it was twenty-four hours or something, but I lost track. It was actually wonderful. I just sat and looked out the window at the green countryside passing. It seems like so long since I have been able to sit in peace, without a guard sitting next to me or being chained to the seat, and look at the countryside and the houses and farms and cows and lakes and towns and cities. I have missed so much." Her voice catches.

Cyrus has no idea what to say to this. "I got you a room at the Milwaukee Athletic Club. It is a little old, but the rooms are big, and it is only a few blocks from my office. Do you want me to take you there? Er, I guess, what do you want to do today?" He had planned to just drop her off and go back to work and start preparing for the trial, but he realizes, and he should have thought of this before, that this is really her first day of freedom in more than five years.

"Could we just go for a drive? I know that sounds weird, considering I just got off a bus, but I kind of want to be outside and moving as much as I can."

"Um, sure."

Cyrus pulls out of the parking lot and starts driving north on Highway 43. He thinks of Elkhart Lake and the little restaurants, shops, and bars he saw as he rolled through town with Scooter while trying not to die on a motorcycle. *Maybe they should go there and walk around.* Diana is staring out the window.

"What is it like, being free now, or at least being out?" The question sounds stupid to Cyrus as soon as it comes out, and Diana is slow to answer, making him think it is probably the dumbest question ever.

"I haven't talked to my daughter yet. I don't know what to say. I don't know if I should get her hopes up, or mine. I don't know whether I'm going to be free or not. I don't know what to do. I feel like a bobber floating down a stream," she says.

Cyrus wishes he could comfort her, offer some assurance that she won't wind up in prison. But he is scared of that very thing too. They sit in silence and watch the farmland drift by.

"It's weird, the things you think about in prison." She says it as if the thought had just occurred to her.

"I bet," Cyrus says, trying hard to empathize.

"I realized in prison that I gave up control over my life a long time ago. I wasn't in control before I got arrested with those guys."

She pauses, and Cyrus doesn't know what to say.

"Have you ever been addicted to anything, Cyrus?"

"I smoke cigarettes…on and off."

"Well, before we got arrested, I would wake up and do drugs and do whatever those guys told me to do to get drugs. I really didn't make any decisions about my day. There was nothing to decide.

"And then you wind up in prison and you tend to think you have even less control. That's the first part of prison; you sit around and mope about how you have lost all control. The guards tell you when to wake up, what to do, when to eat, when to shower, where to stand. While I was in there I started thinking about when was the last time I actually had control. Was it when I chose to try meth for the first time? But did I really even have control then? Was it when I got pregnant? Were there any other choices I could have made? Ultimately, I think this: I don't think there are any choices. There is just a path we are on."

As they cross into Sheboygan County there is a sign for the county fair. Cyrus tries to process what she has said. He's not sure she's wrong. He sometimes feels the same way.

"Hey, want to go to the fair today?" Cyrus asks.

Diana shakes off her reverie and laughs. "That sounds amazing," she says.

They spend the day walking through fragrant barns, looking at well-groomed sheep and enormous pigs with seeming acres of pink flesh. They eat hot beef sandwiches and go on the Tilt-a-Whirl. They watch a corn-shucking contest and listen to a local cover band. Mostly, they laugh and smile.

THE DAY AFTER THE FAIR, CYRUS WAITS FOR DIANA IN the Earnhardt reception area. The trial starts in a month.

Diana timidly steps beyond the polished brass elevator door. She peers into the wood-paneled reception area with its untouched furniture. Cyrus leads her back to a corner conference room that overlooks the emerald lake, the Summerfest grounds, and the island where Lucy walks Biggie, or at least used to. Cyrus is moving quickly. He seems stressed.

There are bagels, yogurt parfait, coffee, and juice lined up on a back bar. Along the middle of the long conference table are neatly labeled bankers' boxes containing the transcript and exhibits from her trial.

"How was the Milwaukee Athletic Club?" he asks.

She smiles a little and shakes her head. "I can't tell you what it's like to sleep in a big hotel bed in a big hotel room after years in a tiny cell underground. Seeing the sun stream in through the windows…it was hard to get up this morning. Reliving this and worrying about going back to prison is about the last thing I want to do."

"I know. But we have to do it to have any shot. Have some breakfast and coffee. We have a lot of work to do."

They spend the morning going through the transcript. Every now and then, Cyrus reads a question and answer with emphasis and turns to her and demands, "Is that true?" Diana mostly shrugs and smiles apologetically.

"I really didn't know much about any of that," is her common refrain.

At the end of the day, Cyrus asks whether she needs anything. Diana mentions that she wishes she had some other clothes and wonders if she will need new ones for trial.

"Oh my god!" Cyrus says, embarrassed not to have thought of that or noticed that she was wearing the same clothes as yesterday. She must have somehow washed and ironed them. Even the jeans have a crease in them.

"I am so sorry," he says, "where do you want to go, where do you shop?"

They drive west of the city to a mall with a big Macy's. Cyrus hands her his credit card. "Here, get whatever you need, or want. Get whatever. But you should probably get a suit for trial. I am going to wait in the car and make some phone calls."

Cyrus sits in the car and tries to call some people at the firm. It is just after five. He really doesn't have any calls to make. He has nothing going on. The only work he has is this trial. And it is pro bono. And he is overwhelmed. How is this going to be different from last time? How will he get the jury on his side? How is he going to be ready to try this case in a month?

He takes out a pad of paper and writes a list of motions in limine. Number one, No Gun Evidence. Number two, No References to a Motorcycle Gang. And on and on. He feels like he is spinning his wheels. He feels like he is losing it.

He is staring at the yellow legal pad of paper, trying to think of what else needs to be done, when Diana raps on the passenger window. He is startled and turns to face whatever new threat awaits him. There she is, in a white dress with a large purple floral print, holding down the front of her skirt in the breeze. She has a big smile on her face. She pushes a strand of black shiny hair behind her ear. He unlocks the car door and she gets in. For a moment, he forgets it all.

"Follow me, I have something to show you."

It is Friday at five o'clock. They have spent the whole week rehashing the first trial, considering whether there are any witnesses that they could call in Diana's defense, and calling some of the women that used to hang out with the Hounds to see if they will testify. Few of them even answer their calls. The ones who do are moms now, far removed from the storm of meth that spun a fog around years of their life they would now like back. They don't want to be involved.

Cyrus and Diana take the elevator down to the lobby and walk along Wisconsin Avenue, crossing the street and walking past the entrance to the Pfister. There is a velvet rope there and a group of mostly men, camped outside, hoping for a chance to get autographs from the visiting team players staying at the hotel. Cyrus and Diana walk past them and turn right on Mason Street, walking toward the lake.

Even a block off Wisconsin Avenue, the feel of the city is different—more neighborhoody than urban. The trees lining both sides of the street are deep green now in late summer. They turn left to go north on Cass Street. It is an almost forgotten oasis of old Cream City brick buildings, with a school at one end and the ancient, castle-looking Plaza Hotel and apartments at the other.

Cyrus stops in front of a Cream City brick apartment building. They pass through a thick, old, black wooden door, its paint shiny and cracked. Inside is a small entryway, with mailboxes for the two dozen or so residents of the building. Cyrus reaches in his pocket and fumbles with a key. They walk up a wooden staircase; the treads are bowed in the middle from years of use. On the third floor they exit the stairs. Cyrus opens a door at the end of the hall. Inside is a one-bedroom apartment with a small kitchen that has a bay window overlooking Cass Street and its trees. There is a little couch and a TV on a stand.

"I got you a little bit of furniture, but I figured you might want to pick up some things that you actually like."

Diana shakes her head slowly and smiles a little. "You didn't have to do this. I don't know what to say."

"I couldn't leave you in that old hotel. This is just month-to-month, and I figure you would want your own space. I even got you an ironing board and an iron."

She walks to him, puts her arms around his neck, and kisses him on the lips. "I'm sure I'm not supposed to do that, but it has been a long time since someone has supported me like you have, and to be honest, a long time since I have done that." She lets out a little laugh and then kisses him again. "Thank you."

He squeezes her tight. He pushes the thoughts that he is crossing a dangerous line out of his head.

"Let's go get something to eat," he says.

They walk down Cass; the crickets' music is reaching a fever pitch. There is a small café, The Lakeside Café, on the corner of Cass and Mason. They ask for a table for two and are seated on the wide sidewalk at a wrought-iron table on which sits a candle inside red glass.

Cyrus orders a bottle of white wine and some scallops as appetizers. The scallops are seared perfectly with a golden-brown crust on both sides. They are tender in the middle, not unlike a perfect fire-roasted marshmallow.

They talk about places they have not been but want to go and why. They forget about the case and what brought them there. Couples stroll by. The light fades, and for a time the whole street turns pink. Cyrus takes off his sport coat and gives it to Diana as the wind turns and the humid August air is displaced by the chilled lake breeze. They wait for a slice of flourless chocolate cake and coffee.

HE TELLS HIMSELF HE NEVER INTENDED THIS AS HE LIES next to her on a mattress on the floor of her new apartment after they have made love for the first time, but the truth is he did, he has; he hoped for this from the first time he saw her in that antiseptic conference room underground. He knows it is wrong and he could be disbarred and lose his job, but he honestly doesn't care. The thing about her, well besides her beauty, is she is the most at-peace person he has ever met. She has been through hell, no doubt. He saw it; he saw the pain and he saw her break down that first time they met. But despite all of that, she isn't broken, she still has this mischievous glint in her eyes. She has a way of winking at the world as if she is in on something. She has this peaceful way about her, and it rubs off on him.

As they drift off to sleep, he says quietly, "Diana, we have to think of something to give the prosecutors to end this. I don't want to risk losing this trial. I don't want to risk losing you. Just try to think of something you saw or heard. Who was really in charge of the Hounds? It couldn't have just been Donny, Walter, and Dickie. Was there a guy named Spencer that was involved with them when you were around?"

She kisses him without opening her eyes and rolls over, pressing her back against him. "Goodnight," she says.

Chapter 47

SEPTEMBER 10, 2006

I t is evening. The sun is a perfect orange ball suspended over the Iowa bluffs. The light makes the muddy water look gold. There are river birds all around. Herons, flying low over the water or standing still in the shallow backwaters waiting to spear a fish. Eagles are perched high in dead trees. Seagulls shriek at each other, moving restlessly in the hot, humid, still air.

Scooter looks over the controls of the converted tugboat. He strokes the wood steering wheel, admiring the craftsmanship. Everything is done in nickel and polished cherry. There are displays for radar and speed and engine speed. The dual throttle is imposing.

From a distance, the boat looks like other tugboats working the Mississippi pushing the long, low barges mostly south, using the current to maximize efficiency. The tugboats push everything from iron ore to soybeans down the slope of the continent. But the details of this particular tugboat, the trim, the polished cherry, the living quarters, make it a distant cousin to those everyday workhorses.

And another difference—there is Lucy, on the clean wood deck at the bow of the boat, stretched out on a lounge chair, her long legs deep brown, her stomach toned and taut. The speaker next to her chair is barking out the Black-Eyed Peas. She takes out a dark bottle of tanning oil and starts rubbing it on her stomach, arms, and legs. This is not like those other tugboats.

Scooter sets the boat on autopilot. The navigation system is state-of-the-art and allows him to program a destination and simply let the boat do its thing. Such systems were developed for easy, reliable, and low maintenance transportation down the river, allowing pilots to push barges twenty-four hours a day without worrying about crashing into a sand bar or another boat. Scooter has waited over a year for this beauty and wishes he had more time to break it in, but that luxury did not present itself. He wears a baseball cap, a tank top, and cutoff shorts along with leather Reef flip-flops. As he walks down the steps from the control room, he can hear Lucy complaining about the heat, humidity, and bugs.

"Why did we start this vacation on the Mississippi, babe? I thought you said we would go to the Caribbean."

Scooter shakes his head. "Patience, Lucy. Relax and just enjoy the cruise. We will get to paradise soon enough."

He looks at her on the lounge chair, adjusting her top strategically to avoid tan lines. Biggie is splayed out on the deck, gazing adoringly at her and the chop salad she has brought for dinner. Scooter smiles to himself, thinking that Biggie may have some sightseeing of his own to do when they get to Memphis.

Scooter opens one of the French doors into the sleeping quarters, which looks like a nice hotel room but with a 360-degree view of the river. There are windows on every wall, with lace curtains tied to the sides to let light in. There is a sitting area at the edge of the bed with a leather sofa and two overstuffed chairs.

Scooter moves the coffee table in front of the sofa to the side and slides a Navajo rug out of the way. In the floor is a metal plate with a combination lock. He types in a combination and a handle pops out of the plate. He twists the handle. The plate is a door that swings open to reveal steep steps leading to a below-deck compartment that is adjacent to the engine room, but sealed off from it. The compartment is about eight by eight and has a large metal box in the middle of the space.

Scooter enters another combination into a keypad and opens the metal box. Inside are row after row of hundred-dollar bills, three actual bars of gold, several passports with pictures of both him and Lucy, two nine-millimeter handguns with extra clips full of bullets, and one long assault-style rifle. He reaches in and pulls out a satellite phone and dials.

"Cyrus, it's Scooter Larioux calling, sorry to disturb you on Sunday night. I wanted to let you know that I retained your partner Quinlan yesterday to represent me in some business deals. I'm selling some of my properties in Wisconsin. So, I guess that basically makes me your client too, right?" There is silence on the other end as Cyrus's brain swims with the information and what it means to the case he intends to present tomorrow, or any deal they hope to cut with Nelson.

"Listen, Cyrus, you're a nice kid with a heck of a jumper." Scooter laughs. "Don't do anything stupid, this can all work out. Anyway, say hi to Diana." Scooter hangs up, turns off the phone and drops it back inside, and closes and locks the box. He smiles as he ascends the steps, looking at Lucy and listening to the cries of a couple of whooping cranes flying low over the river.

Printed in Great Britain
by Amazon